I0526201

Scent of Bergamot

Historical Women's Fiction

By

Ms. Višnja Rašić

First published 2021

Creator: Visnja Rasic
Title: Scent of Bergamot
ISBN: 978-0-6451843-0-3
Target Audience: Mature Adult (Adult themes)
Subject Mature: Relationships – family, friendships and sexual.
Historical. Mystery/Secret.

Editors: Julia Gibbs (UK) Visnja Rasic (Aust.)

I have always been a voracious reader, perhaps in part, this stemmed from starting school in Australia unable to speak, read or write English. While the other children were learning to read, I was learning to ask where the toilet was located.

At home, I was reading in Croatian before I was reading in English. Some might think this was a disadvantage, and perhaps, in the beginning it was. I struggled with spelling and grammar, constantly two-steps behind my fellow students.

Perhaps that's why I focused on maths; 1+1 always =2.

But, as I got older,
I found not only my voice but the logic of grammar.
And I didn't find it through hours of endless study of verbs and adverbs, I found it through the stories told to me
by my parents and my nanna.

My parents encouraged my imagination, and my nanna filled my head with endless tales of magical places and wonderous mythology – not the stuff everyone else was learning and reading, mine where Slavic Gods and ancient, almost lost tales of myth and magic.

Mum and dad told tales of the ancient Greeks and Romans, of Gods and Demons & of the Brothers Grim, while also filling voids with Latin phrases and French proverbs – I was blessed and for most of my childhood I didn't even know it.

So, this is a thank you to my parents and my nanna.

Thank you, dad for the stories of St. Ilija
riding his chariot through the thunder clouds.

Thank you, mum for magical tales of the Bavarian Black Forrest.

Thank you, nanna for the often-frightening stories of Jezi Babas
and other scary monsters, of our Slavic mythology.

Thank you for the seed of imagination, for the hunger and drive to
indulge that seed and for the haven which protected me when the days
were darker than nanna's evil spirit stories.

CHAPTER 1

Ghosts of Bergamot and Rosin

The day they buried Mother, a thick grey Brittany sky crackled with electricity and the air smelled of burning leaves and tasted of rain. My clump of dirt hit the carved French oak coffin with a hollow thud.

That was two weeks ago.

Last week I was disposing of the well-intentioned frozen quiches and casseroles as snow flurries danced past my Paris apartment window.

And this morning – this morning I'm slumped in one of Gran's kitchen chairs, picking at my memories and my cuticles... in Melbourne.

Nothing fit. Not Mother's death, not my detachment, and certainly not the bullshit with Gran's passport.

Pushing out my chair, I winced as a phantom squawk shuddered down the hall the nanosecond I scraped Gran's precious flagstones. "Didn't wake her," I whispered. I have no idea why I whispered. If Gran hadn't heard the chair scrape, she was hardly likely to hear me talking to myself.

Walking to the kitchen window I could see the first signs of daybreak. The 'just before dawn' grey now saw the first amber and crimson wisps emboss the odd cloud, a promise of light and warmth. Aside from a crow's caw, everything outside remained library quiet.

Inside, the only sound was Gran's massive kitchen clock with its sunflower face and hands the shape of stalks. Ugly thing. It didn't even tick-tock, just a steady tock-tock-tock as the second-hand stalk moved time along.

Beneath it, on the kitchen bench, the crusty remnants of last night's pizza taunted me to clean up. I was good at ignoring housework. One of the few things I'd inherited from Mother. I picked off a sliver of burnt anchovy, as 'birthplace – Moscow' drifted into my head. That's what the email from the passport lady said. I rolled my eyes. "Pfft. Don't think so."

I nudged the pizza box a little further out of view and reached for the Royal Doulton ceramic tea container. Gran's tea ritual. "Marica," she'd huff, "Good tea warrants correct preparation." Gran only drank good tea.

I listened for the water to reach a simmer, bubbles no larger than champagne, before pouring just enough water to cover the tea leaves. After three minutes precisely, more hot water could be added before straining. Certain I was breaking some rule of etiquette, I grabbed a mug and put two teaspoons of sugar in. Before the tea – sacrilege! Just as I'd done a hundred times, I followed Gran's tea ceremony protocol, sans sugar, and began my three-minute countdown.

Even as the sun did its best to remain snuggled under its cloudy duvet, the smell of Summer roses seeped through the open window, bringing back images of my Dida Nik in the garden. Croatian for granddad, Dida Nik was dad's father. Calling him Dida rather than Pop or something equally Anglo made him happy. I didn't mind. It offset Mother's and Gran's side with their French heritage and pompousness. Not that Dida Nik didn't like the French, after all, he married his *bride de français,* Nana Marguerite. Despite Mother's death just weeks ago, it was Dida Nik who I missed.

While waiting for the minutes to elapse, it occurred to me I should check out the attic. Having convinced Gran to have the attic converted into my art studio, it seemed a good idea.

Three minutes later the smell of bergamot overwhelmed the kitchen. I adored the fragrance. It was the smell of afternoon tea with scones and jam and Sunday brunch with crispy bacon and crumpets. It was runny honey over hot porridge flavoured with cinnamon in the Winter and lemon slice tea parties in the Summer.

I strained the tea into my mug, added milk and headed to the attic as I recalled the song Dida Nik used to sing to me as a child. "*Mari-ca, Mari-ca my pretty little Tsari-ca...*" Sung with a Croatian accent, it rhymes.

Come to think of it, why was my Croatian grandfather singing about a Russian princess?

I stopped half-way up the hall. It had never occurred to me until that moment. It was just a silly little song that made me giggle when he sang it. Maybe there was something to Gran's mother's birth certificate error? "Gran would go wild if it was true!"

Upstairs, it took my eyes a few minutes to adjust, but even in the half-light I could see I was surrounded by cloth-covered furniture and precariously stacked boxes. At my feet, dust swaddled more boxes and several stacks of books, mounted pyramid-like.

"This'll take for-*e-v-e-r* to clean out."

I put my cup on what seemed a solid surface. As soon as I moved the first box a faint smell of rosin mixed with mould lifted with the dust. The scent tickled my nostrils and settled on my tongue. In the corner sat Dida Nik's dark-blue, velvet violin case. With a few well-chosen steps and a lunge, I was soon brushing away a decade of dust before I clicked the brass latches.

Even before I'd opened the case my senses were engulfed by it. Rosin. Strong. Pungent. Trapped in the violin case for so long, the moment I set it free, an ignition of memories erupted. Dida Nik's rosin-stained, sticky fingers running after me with his hands in front, growling like some sort of monster, and me, happy, screaming and giggling, running down the hallway, slamming doors and hiding behind the big sofa-chair. Well, it seemed big at the time. I widened my eyes to stop the tears.

Lying on a bed of royal blue silk was his violin. I closed the case.

With my eyes now adjusted, I saw hanging from a hook on the ceiling his infamous ukulele. He loved that thing. His words, even his husky grizzled voice replayed in my memories. "While violins often cry, ukuleles always laugh."

I shook my head, returning my focus to the boxes. Things had been moved since I'd been up here last, a decade and a lifetime ago. Before 'Uncle' Maurice became stepdad number three. There was too much junk to really plan anything, and I should have gone back downstairs but something... guilt? Or, remorse maybe? Something wanted me to find a link between the mother I had lost and the mother I'd always longed for, and maybe there was something in one of these boxes.

Birthplace Moscow popped back into my head. Gran loathed Stalin's Russia, wearing her French heritage like a combat metal, and God help anyone stupid enough to question its authenticity. She'd die at the prospect of a Russian link. *But*, a smirk wriggled over my face, *if her birth certificate was right*? The idea of Gran's potential mysterious past somehow made Mother more present. I did miss Mother. Yes, no, I did – I did love her. I just hadn't liked her for most of my life.

Many of the perilously stacked boxes were atop cloth-covered this-and-that's. I chose the three least likely to cause an avalanche, and sat myself, cross-legged, on Gran's dusty attic floor, rummaging for treasure.

The combination of a lack of natural light and my dislike of wearing watches meant I had no idea of how much time had elapsed until I heard "Marica?" Followed by some mumbling and then footsteps.

She must have seen the attic ladder.

"Marica?"

Damn!

"What on ear-r-r-th are you doing up there!" Gran's voice could slice old leather at times, its power foreign to her aging body – fragile, except for her crystal blue, mesmerizing eyes. Gran insisted their colour was cornflower blue.

"For heaven's sake, must you force me to scream until I am hoarse!"

I imagined her standing at the attic opening. Those damned eyes! I hadn't inherited them. Her eyes, I mean. Mine were moss green at best. Green hazel with golden flecks was more accurate.

"Marica!" My tornado Gran with the heart of a suffragette and the manners of Queen Victoria. Sometimes she'd allow me to ignore her. Clearly, this wasn't one of those times.

"Yes?"

"What are you doing up there?"

"We talked about this in Paris and then again on the plane, remember? Making the attic into a studio?"

Armed with fluent French, English, and Croatian, an almost useless arts degree majoring in Medieval Art and Renaissance Poetry, and a natural talent with a brush, I was entrusting my future to providence.

I didn't need to see Gran's face to know her eyebrows had formed a V in the creases of her forehead while her hands sat defiantly on her hips, her favoured 'I'm not kidding' stance.

"And you plan to achieve this exactly how, all alone in the attic?"

Yelling at each other through floorboards wasn't working. "Be down in a min!"

Footsteps, steady, firm, moving away. Even now, Gran could muster the march of an army officer, each clip-clop echoing on the floorboards and through the house. The sound reminded me of those black-and-white wartime reels, with regiments of soldiers, each country's army having a slightly different stride. Russian soldiers always seemed to have the most impressive one.

To hell with it, I'm just going to ask her.

I dusted off my legs and butt, knowing I should head back down before Tornado Gran returned. But just as I looked past the attic opening, beneath the small window partially blocked by a tumble of boxes, one crumpled, tattered box poked out further than the rest, with what appeared to be a postcard or photo protruding from it. Something was written on it in black marker-pen, in French and in Gran's distinctive penmanship.

The box wasn't big. Five minutes tops to go through it. Squirming between furniture and balancing better than a ballerina, I started to nudge the box out of its Jenga-tower position. As the rest of the boxes trembled, I enticed it down, first resting it on my head – *crap, now my hair will smell of mothballs and heaven-only-knows-what* – then balancing it on one shoulder and onto the hidden desk, perhaps a table.

'*Non triés mais être sauvé*' (unsorted but to be saved).

I never fully understood why Gran spoke, and wrote, French in preference to English. Before the funeral, she'd never been to France. Perhaps she imagined it made her more aristocratic. She'd always thought herself better than her circumstances.

Inside, the newly freed shaft of light from the attic window shimmered over mounds of photos. Most were loose; some seemed to be grouped in little stacks.

My greedy fingers dived into my new treasure trove. Clusters of photos, crinkled, time capsules. Small lots secured with ribbon or rubber bands. Dida Nik in full song with one arm wrapped around my Pop Colin, Mother's dad, the other swinging an over-sized schooner of beer; Dad dressed in a red T-shirt and black jeans, leaning against his first car, the infamous purple Monaro. Mother in a bikini, another playing tennis, and one I never expected: Mother pregnant with me. I touched the image. The number of times Mother moaned at having had me, *if it wasn't for getting pregnant with you I'd have been...* and she'd add one of a dozen exotic and envied lifestyles, none of which had the word 'mother' in them.

Almost at the bottom and half stuck to the box side, I saw a fragile, old, sepia photo, of a skinny little girl, her slender hand resting on a chair, in a sailor-style dress, with magnetic yet vacant eyes and no smile, just looking into the distance.

A tingle shivered through me. "Gran-Gran." I was sure it was my great grandma. Both my great-grandma and Gran were named Ana, so Great-Grandma was Gran-Gran, and my Gran was just Gran. But my excitement lasted less than ten seconds. This little girl's hair was light, and Gran-Gran's hair was dark chestnut.

I turned the photograph over. There was what remained of a faint message in Cyrillic – my family didn't write in Cyrillic. The only person who *might* be able to read it would be Dida Nik, or maybe someone Russian.

Couldn't possibly be. Gran hated communists, and communists wrote in Cyrillic. As communists were Russian, and no communist could be trusted – Gran's words, not mine – Gran hated all Russians.

Who was this girl? Now, as I sat half-hunched over the box in the half-light, the inconsistency on Gran's birth certificate pressed at my thoughts.

Someone was hiding something; something about the loathsome Russians; some*one* with a soldier's stride perhaps. Why did Gran hate Russians? Because they were once communists, or did she hate communists because of former Communist Russia?

"M-aa-rr-ii-cc-aa!"

Oh God. "Yes?"

"I swear, child, if you do not come down this minute!"

I scrambled to my feet, shoved the box half under a piece of over-

7

hanging cloth and almost tripped over the mini-mountain stack of books near the entrance of the attic. Second from the top was an old hard cover of *Pride and Prejudice.* I stashed the photo into the back pages and, completely forgetting about my mug of tea, scuttled down the attic ladder, the book safely tucked into my armpit.

"Sorry."

Watching my legs appear first, Gran demanded, "what were you doing up there?"

"I, I found this book and..." *And I'm twenty-four, Gran, not sixteen,* is what I wanted to say. *Twenty-four and a woman full-grown.*

Gran snatched the book from my hand and flicked through the first few pages. I couldn't put my finger on it, but I just knew I should keep the discovery of that photo to myself.

She snapped it shut, freeing years of dust as though liberating family ghosts. "Your grandfather bought this for your mother," she said, her voice and tone softening.

"Lunch is ready."

CHAPTER 2

Lie No.1

As we ate lunch Gran talked about the builders who were due to meet us in a few hours. Before we left Paris, Gran contacted a friend of hers to help us secure workers for the attic conversion.

"I suppose you managed to clean up somewhat while you were up there?"

I sipped my drink.

"With all the time you spent in that attic this morning."

My silence told her I'd done nothing remotely close to cleaning up.

"I see, well, then, I am quite sure these builder-type people are familiar with filth and mess."

Gran's friend, Edek, had arranged for someone called Tom to drop by.

I'd been excited about the attic conversion, up until a few minutes ago. Now my mind was more focused on the photo and Gran's birth certificate. I nodded with fake interest as Gran waffled on about the renovations.

I couldn't hold it any longer.

"I've been meaning to ask you, why did your birth certificate show Gran-Gran's place of birth as Russia and not France?"

Gran stopped talking. She stopped chewing. I swear she stopped time. I don't think I even blinked. I'd never experienced deafening silence but understood it now.

Gran smiled, breaking the trance, cut a piece of ham, pricked it with her silver fork and brought the pinkish cube to her mouth, before saying, "Where did you get a silly idea like that?"

"From the lady at the passport application office."

"Hum?"

I smirked at my Gran's attempts at hedging. "You remember, I called the Australian authorities and started your application over the phone, to speed up the process. That lady, the one you sent the document copies to, she told me."

Gran kept her eyes on her motionless black coffee as she said, "Told you what, dear?"

"When I called her, she said we would speed things up if I gave her your details over the phone. Then all she needed was the certified copy of your birth certificate to complete the rush passport application."

I waited a second. Nothing. *Mental note; don't play poker with Gran.*

"Then she contacted me saying she would have to redo the application because of my error about Gran-Gran's birthplace."

Gran looked up from her coffee. "And what did you say?"

"I didn't, it all happened over email. I was mostly at the hospital. I sent her an email back asking her to please do what she could as quickly as possible."

Gran stared hard at me. "So, what makes you think your great-grandmother was not born in France?"

"Because it was in the email, from the passport lady. Gran-Gran's place of birth was marked as Moscow, Russia."

Gran didn't flinch.

"Seems so odd. Why would Moscow be on Gran-Gran's birth certificate, Moscow of all places?"

"Marica, please, you know—"

"No really, Moscow, of all places?"

Gran sighed. "You are making this out to be very cloak-and-dagger, Marica, but honestly, there's no big mystery."

"Then why didn't I know about it?"

"Because it was such a long time ago and means nothing." Gran huffed as she played with the food on her plate. "Honestly, I'd forgotten all about it."

The way she was tormenting her ham told me there was something in this. "I still don't get it; how did Moscow get on the birth certificate?"

"Really, Marica?"

"Yes, re-all-y!"

Gran rolled her eyes. "Well, if you must know, then I –"

"Yes, I really must know."

"Fine, perhaps if you let me speak?"

She waited for a second too long.

I tilted my head, and she gave in. "It was safer at the time."

"What? What does that mean?"

"Oh, for heaven's sake! Let me think." Gran slowly and delicately placed her knife and fork in their proper table etiquette place.

"Now all of this, of course, was before my time, but I recall your great-grandmother talking about this once or twice. You see, she was born in a world on the brink of chaos. The Germans were close to declaring war against the French and, at the time, the Russians had not yet entered the war. So, her parents paid to have their documents forged, showing them born in Russia, but having emigrated to France."

Gran was lying, and worse still it wasn't even a good lie. If she'd had time to prepare, she'd surely have come up with something more plausible. She'd re-written WWI history. Something told me the girl in the photo played a part in Gran's lie, which made the photo gain significance and confirmed I should keep quiet.

11

Gran took a sip of lemonade.

After too many years having to pretend to be fond of people I loathed, having to lie for Mother and disguise my disgust of her many admirers, I'd learned to play the deception game as well as anyone.

For a moment I sat quietly, allowing Gran to think I was believed her crappy explanation.

To the left of the kitchen was the formal dining room, and from it there was an even better view of the garden than from our little breakfast table. I could just see the old oak dining table without turning my head, and instantly I imagined Gran and Nana sitting at the table holding court. Even though Dida and Nana were Dad's parents, they'd often spent time at Gran's, Dida in the garden and Nana and Gran in the dining room. There they'd sit, two modern-day duchesses, perfectly postured, watching Dida in the garden.

Delicate clinks of hallmarked silver teaspoons against fine china, while the divine, citrus fragrance of bergamot from the Earl Grey tea leaves swathed the room. The only thing missing; each holding a parasol while a struggling artist immortalised them on canvas. It's where I first, unknowingly, saw Gran playing 'The duchess' – just as she was with me now.

I added half a teaspoon of sugar to my cup, stirred and tapped the side twice and then looked up as I fake smiled. "Oh?" I said, "Wow, that's really interesting."

Gran, who hadn't taken her eyes off me until I spoke, seemed satisfied. A flat lip smile followed by a sip of her lemonade while she continued to study me, apparently confident that was the end of the conversation.

But neither my maths nor my memory of history was so poor. Gran-Gran was born in 1904 and WWI didn't begin for another decade.

The Cyrillic message *must* have been in Russian. A link to Communist Russia existed in my family tree. And the inscription on the picture of the little girl with the vacant eyes seemed to be the key.

"Seems a shame I didn't know, as it delayed the application several days."

Gran let out her infamous exhale. "Marica, I was in such a state at the time. I'd completely forgotten about; it simply didn't enter my mind."

She sighed. "I wish I had thought of it, I truly do. As you say, I would have been on that flight earlier, if only I'd recalled, but I didn't. I was frightened for your mother and you, and I worried about the plane trip. I hardly had a single clear thought."

Bullshit. Gran's mind was as sharp as her kitchen knives.

"And I will always hold regret for not having thought of it."

"It couldn't be helped." It was my turn to lie.

CHAPTER 3

Pop and Tom

An hour or so later, Tom the builder arrived. Stomping to free the caked mud from his boots and patting the obstinate dust from his overalls, Tom cleaned his hands with a cloth he conjured from one of his many pockets before offering a firm but friendly handshake.

"Afternoon, I'm Tom, you must be Miss..."

"Hi, Tom, I'm Marica, come through."

With some effort, Gran joined us in the attic. Mind you, my half-drunk mug of tea didn't escape her notice. I shrugged, hoping she'd not look down too closely as my secret box was hardly well hidden. Thankfully, Tom had her attention now.

As Gran talked, I could see her judging Tom with the same half-cocked left brow lift Mother had inherited. The very same one I'd also inherited when some guy tried a crappy one-liner, or worse, professed his love and devotion after knowing me for a hot second.

Gran's head tilted as Tom spoke, but she wasn't paying much attention to his words. She was stalking his mannerisms, hunting for clues to his character.

Gran was tall for a woman, taller than I, even after age had diminished both stature and strength, and she was imposing. Tom, though slightly shorter, seemed to hold his own even as Gran made no secret of her judgemental nature. I could almost hear her thoughts, *Scruffy pants, didn't even bother to clean off the dirt from his overalls; minus one point. Carefully trimmed beard and tidy haircut, not prone to comb-overs; plus one point. Neat legible handwriting; plus one point.*

When Gran did speak, Tom listened, making notes and rough sketches with an occasional "Ah-ha" or "Yes, sure," interruption.

When Gran was done, Tom walked around the attic, took measurements, even crouching down where the roofline fell to meet the ceiling.

"OK," he said. Clearly Tom belonged to the 'man of few words' crew. "We can do this." He gritted his teeth and I felt a *BUT* coming.

"But it—"

There! Now let's see how much this BUT costs me.

"—won't work, not the way you want it to. We'll need to create more light. I suggest opening up the attic window to make a larger dormer-style window." A friendly smile before he added, "Maybe with a window-seat and either shelves or cupboards beneath it."

Tom left Gran and me to talk while he stomped the wooden floorboards. "I like his idea," I said.

"Indeed," she added. "Perhaps if we put two windows, one on the other end too," she said, pointing to the opposite side of the room, "It would add light and air circulation."

I nodded as Gran shouted, "Excuse me, Thomas." *So, Gran! He introduces himself as TOM and she addresses him as THOMAS.*

"I have another suggestion," he said.

"Yes?" asked Gran.

"These old floorboards, they are made of oak, old, seasoned oak." Tom knelt, pulled something similar to a knife from his tool-belt, scraped free the dust between the boards and forced the tool between two of the boards before smiling. "Just as I thought, twice as thick as

15

today's boards. Boy, they knew quality back in the day, and no damage at all."

Tom smiled. "I'd like to cut out the oak where we will put the window and shelves, replace it with pine and use the oak to inlay a workbench or table?"

Tom must have guessed what Gran's thoughts were. "Before I went into building full-time, I did my apprenticeship as a cabinet maker." He grinned. "Not much business in fine furniture unless you can afford the time to develop a reputation.

"Here." Standing between Gran and me, he shared photos of some of his pieces stored on his phone.

Gran smiled at me and then looking at Tom, offered her hand. "Done! Get us two quotes, one for the work and one for the furniture."

An hour later, Tom and his toolkit left.

As afternoon turned to evening, Gran remembered the book I'd brought down with me from the attic. "What are you going to do with that book?" she asked.

"Oh, I don't know, read it?"

"Marica, it's been up in the attic for more than three decades, perhaps it would be wiser to put it somewhere safe. It would be a shame to damage a memory given from Pop Colin to your mother."

Pop Colin moved to Melbourne to visit his kid-brother. He was a talented artist and wanted to spend time in Australia painting the unique fauna of this country. Then WWII hit. He couldn't stop his younger brother from enlisting. The day Pop Colin got his letter, the one all families of enlisted soldiers fear, changed his life. In 1942, he enlisted. Pop's brother never returned.

After the war Pop was a broken man until he met Gran, instantly falling victim to her eyes. Gran was already well over thirty when they met in the early 1960s, and him a full decade older than she.

On the 6th of December 1970, Mother was born. Gran desperately wanted a daughter, but only a daughter. I never asked why they waited so long to have Mother but suspected it had something to do with Pop Colin's condition after returning from the war. "It's what wars do to people," Gran once explained. "The only winners are the weapon's manufacturers."

Gran helped with the emotional, nothing helped with the physical. Well, almost nothing. Dida Nik's home brew kept Pop Colin alive beyond anything the doctors expected. *Doctors! What do they know, look how they let Mother die!* Only one photo exists of my Pop and me, before my christening. I call it my little treasure.

That evening, while I was stirring the coq au vin, Gran's age struck me. To me she seemed ageless; except she wasn't. I brushed aside the realities of mortality. She remained formidable.

After dinner, Gran, still suffering from jetlag, went to bed early, giving me my first opportunity. I Googled Russian to English and set about translating the inscription on the back of the photo. It took a bit of effort, but I finally got what seemed a close translation.

With eyes almost identical to her sister, our little blossom is becoming more pretty with each day though we must watch her because we fear she bruises too easily. Dated, April 1914.

I stared at the girl, perhaps ten or twelve. She had a pretty face, oval with high cheekbones and long cherry-blond hair. She looked so sad, so very sad, as though no one else was in her life. But if I'd translated correctly, she had a sister so she couldn't have been alone. Besides, someone paid for the photographer, an expensive luxury way-back-when. Someone loved her, someone with the financial means to pay for family portraits and pretty sailor suit dresses. I wanted to know who this child was. Gran never mentioned any relatives. A friend? What Russian family would they have known so well as to keep a photo of a pretty girl, born just after the turn of the century? And Russian? No, no, something wasn't adding up here.

17

"Edek!" I squealed softly. Gran's friend, or neighbour, or more likely 'gentleman admirer' Edek. I got online and Googled Edek. *Damn!* It was a Polish name. I slumped defeated. "Polish is not Russian."

1914. School friends? Still, the Russian inscription made no sense. I mentally kept Edek alive as a possible suspect in this developing mystery. But for now, the girl in the photo bested me.

What I'd hoped would be answers only presented more questions. If the girl was French, which would make sense if she was a school friend of Gran-Gran's, then why write in Russian? If my family was part Russian, then why didn't anyone speak Russian and why did everyone in the family detest Russia? And why the lies?

CHAPTER 4

Love Always, Dad

Frustration caused me to toss in bed for most of the night, my mind switching between Mother and the girl in the photo. I opened Mother's copy of *Pride and Prejudice*, thinking perhaps I'd read myself to sleep. I hadn't noticed the dedication the first time.

To my princess on her 16th birthday, may you find your Mr. Darcy. Love always, Dad.

Sometimes, little things like this made me realise all I never had. Maurice was the closest thing to a father figure after Dida died.

Mother. She finally got lucky with her fourth husband, Maurice.

"At least I won't have to be introduced to any more *uncles*." As soon as I said it, I felt guilt, the kind that makes you revert to a stupid giggle to defuse the burning sensation behind your ears.

Maurice. His face at Mother's funeral. The loss and helplessness. If I'd tried harder, or if Mother had, things might have been different.

Mother's hospital ward. The light sand-coloured laminate floor stained with a thousand footprints, the pale grey-green walls devoid of texture, and the sterile smell, as I sat slumped in one of the functional, emotionless chairs. The only real colour, or life, was the vase of purple irises Maurice brought in, and the beeps on the monitor beside Mother.

All I knew, *I must call Gran*, she needed to be here.

I watched. Nurses in their sensible shoes rushing to, somewhere; toward another pre-dead body, most likely. Doctors in their white, lab-coat uniforms, holding stethoscopes or files or people's lives. Their darting; in and out; seemed almost comical. Orderlies, pushing trolleys with food or catheters; how disgusting, food and human waste mixed together as though no distinction existed.

I watched. Mother's hand in his, as Maurice argued with the doctor. "*Quel* complications?"

She looked so pale, so weak. Her eyes, her beautiful eyes, when she found strength enough to open them, had lost all their luminescence. It hurt to watch her try to breathe. At that moment, I loved her. Despite wishing I felt nothing, I loved her.

I listened. Maurice's Gaelic temper never more evident. Still convinced that by shouting French obscenities at the doctor he'd somehow outmanoeuvre death.

I recognised their *nothing we can do* style. I understood that look doctors get when they wish there was another way to give bad news.

The doctor walked toward me. "Mademoiselle Marcia?" he asked.

I rose from my seat. Correcting him, "*Non, mon nom est* Marica, pronoucé MA-RI-CA." I have no idea why the pronunciation of my name mattered so much at that minute; it just did.

"Oh, pardon, Mademoiselle Mari-ca?"

I smiled. That awkward smile: when you wish you could re-ingest your words.

The doctor explained everything not happening. Mother *was not* responding to treatment. Because her body *was not* reacting as expected and they *were not* confident of the remaining options having any positive effect.

Maurice pulled me away from the doctor before saying in English,

"Marica, these doctors may know medicine, but they do not know your mother."

While I respected his determination to outwit the Grim Reaper, one of us needed to be sensible. As death seemed to be a bigger part of my life than I wished, I'd become somewhat desensitised to its haunting.

I stood silently as the doctor offered his hand. As Maurice refused it. The doctor's wrist became slightly limp, before he retracted his hand and quickly hiding the offending gesture in his white-coat pocket.

I was an audience member, watching a scene from a play; not really a part of it, unable to alter what was happening. The characters carried on with their performance. Mother, attended by two nurses, having breathing apparatus attached to her as life became measured by the consistency of an endless *beep, beep, beep, beep*...

I stared as the doctor lowered his head and walked away. As Maurice turned away, swiping with his shirt sleeve an obstinate tear longing for freedom from glassy eyes.

I realised I needed to do something active, something to become part of the play. "I must call Gran."

That call. The one with so few words, the one when Mother was still breathing, and us, waiting for her to die.

2.00am Melbourne time. There'd be little doubt in Gran's mind.

When Mother first fell ill, I hadn't worried too much. Yes, she had pneumonia, but people don't die from pneumonia, not in France at least. It wasn't as though she had typhoid fever and lived in the jungles of New Guinea. So, when I first told Gran, neither she nor I fretted too much. But the pneumonia seemed to get worse, until we were forced to move her into hospital care.

2.00am Melbourne.

I heard the international phone connection; blurp blurp, blurp blurp. It seemed to ring on and on, until Gran's voice broke it with a questioning tremble. "Hello?"

"Gran, it's me," was all I needed to say before I heard the hollow sigh on the other side of the phone, and the world. I imagined Gran collapsing into the chair by the phone, as I wiped the first of what must have been one hundred, thousand, tears.

Neither of us wasted time with pleasantries.

"What have the doctors said?"

"It's not good; it's really not, I...I think you should—"

"Yes, yes, I think so too. Marica, darling, can you arrange this for me?"

Instinctively I nodded, as though on Skype, before correcting myself. "Yes, I'll..." I forced the tremor of hopelessness back into hiding. "I'll book the ticket today."

"Oh, but Marica," I felt her hesitation, "I think my passport has long-since expired! I didn't think I would need it again, not for..." Gran's words stumbled; she couldn't say it.

Me neither. "No, no, of course not. Don't worry, I'll sort it all out, do you know where your old passport is?" I asked.

Silence.

"What about your birth certificate? Do you have that?"

Gran's voice steadied, "Yes, yes, Dear, I have that."

"Good! I'll contact the Australian Passport Office tomorrow your time, or today, in a few hours, oh, you know what I mean."

I took a deep breath. "You go to the post office and start the application process; can you do that?"

"Yes, Dear." A silence echoed over the receiver before Gran whispered, "But, Marica, have you any idea...?"

I clamped down tears and fears and tried to sound calm. "They're not sure, anything from a matter of days to weeks perhaps. Gran, please, we both need you."

The tears won as they flooded my face and my voice. They must have been infectious because I heard them on Gran's side of the phone too.

* * *

An isolated tear ran down my cheek and landed just below Pop Colin's inscription. I *was* upset, but I also felt frustration and yes, rage.

Another tear traced the path of the previous one until it got to my chin, and stubbornly refused to drop. I smudged it, along with my resentment. Angry at Mother for dying, and at her not being the mother I wanted. Frustration that Mother was only ever a mother and never a mum, like she should have been. Bitter at Dida Nik and Nana and even Dad for abandoning me, and irritated at Gran, although I didn't quite know why.

My grandfather's inscription to my mother felt like a dagger, cutting into wounds of no real memories: no father to kiss my cheek on my sixteenth or eighteenth or twenty-first birthdays; no driving lessons or attending my graduations. No father-daughter talks or awkward caught-with-first-boyfriend nights.

To my princess on her 16th birthday, may you find your Mr. Darcy. Love always, Dad.

It was no secret Gran was not happy when Mother ran off with *that tradesman*, as Gran referred to Dad, forcing the delicate fabric between Gran and Mother to fray a little more. Because of this, and despite Gran's fondness for my Nana and Dida, I never felt comfortable discussing Dad with Gran. And after Nana and Dida died, Dad died all over again for me.

Fate gave me a mother unlike others. It stole from me moments fathers and daughters are supposed to share. Now fate had led me to a box, and a photo, while denying me answers. I snapped the book shut and lay in silence, angry with no one and everyone.

23

CHAPTER 5

A Lost Life in Journals

With Tom and his team occupied with measurements and Gran re-occupied with *literally* watching the dust drift down from the attic and through the rest of the house, I decided this might be an ideal time to get myself a new phone.

Evidently, signing up a twenty-four-year-old with no employment history, onto a plan is not an issue when you have a house in your name, Nana and Dida's house.

Naturally, I got the shmickiest phone available, not an iPhone. *Sorry, Apple, I'm just not that into you.*

With my new phone charging and Gran muttering *something*, I headed up the attic ladder. I stuck my head through the opening to check on the progress and gasped – parts of the attic floor resembled a checkerboard, and not in a good way!

I scampered up the ladder. I initially sighted one of Tom's employee's, probably not much younger than me working away near the attic window, though his age was a little difficult to assess given the dust clinging to his face and hair.

Then I looked down. "Good grief! All this." I pointed to the darker seasoned floorboards and the new honey gold ones. "You *are* going to hide this?" My words echoed Mother. Heat coloured my cheeks and I wished I could rewind time.

Tom chuckled. "Yes, Miss." Tom didn't bother to explain further. "If you give me fifteen minutes, I'll have a close estimate."

His confidence impressed me, removing floorboards before final figures were quoted and agreed. "OK," I replied, "It's almost lunchtime. Why don't you join us, and we can discuss the details over a meal?"

Tom laughed and then shook his head in mock disapproval. "I don't think I'm dressed for the occasion."

Tom did a guy-style curtsy, mocking his boots and overalls. This time I laughed. "Perhaps we should meet in the garden after lunch?"

With a nod, Tom said, "Might be better."

I turned to head downstairs when Tom said, "Miss?"

"Hum?" I turned.

"I almost forgot Andy, that's my apprentice, Andy." Tom pointed to the young man covered in dust, now busily removing old nails from seasoned wood.

"Andy found something under the floorboards; journals, two of them."

Tom turned to Andy, "Right, two?"

Dusty Andy replied, "Yeah, two."

"Journals?" The floorboards faded into disinterest. "What kind of journals?"

"Don't know? Looks to be in foreign, Russian maybe. Wife's part Russian, can't read it myself, but it looks like it, kind of."

Fuck! Russian again. My ears started to tingle hot. I held a hiccup and forced it back down my throat. In my head, I could hear ghosts of secrets past whispering *something evil this way comes.*

"Though, the last few pages seem to be French. My high-school French isn't great—"

I scrunched my nose. *Going through our things, who do they think they are?*

"—and the handwriting makes it harder but I'm sure some of it's French, the rest, well as I say, could be Russian."

Then I heard it. Russian!

Ignoring their overstepping, I focused on three words. Even as I heard every word, I barely comprehended them.

I understood Journals. Russian. French.

The little girl with the vacant eyes! I thought. *They must be hers!*

Frozen in a kind of suspended animation, I didn't notice Andy standing beside me until he nudged a tin box at me, old and covered in dust and patina, battered on several sides with what remained of some sort of sticker on it.

"Here, that's where I found them," he said, pointing to a cleared spot under the current small attic window.

"Under the floorboards."

Perhaps the idea of a Russian link should not have been so emotionally and physically moving, but it was. It was a link to the photo and, and maybe a link to Gran not being truthful about Gran-Gran's birth certificate. I trembled with a kind of frightened excitement. My seemingly wasted years studying medieval art and renaissance poetry might, at last, have found a purpose. My mind skipped straight to the novel *Doctor Zhivago* and then to the movie. In an instant, I was envisioning Omar Sharif and fabricating my magical world. Romantic notions swirled into visions recreating a time when fine elegant young ladies were accompanied to dances or recitals by handsome soldiers or noblemen with titles of Baron, Earl or Duke before their names and numbers like III or IV after.

When the Summer days were filled with arranging flowers or painting seascapes, and Winter festivities meant travelling to Moscow or St. Petersburg, as the jingle of sleighbells and laughing rose-cheeked children announced the arrival of baroque carved sleighs pulled by silver-gilded reins on heavy-hoofed horses. When low-light days were completed with hot chocolate, roasting chestnuts, open fires, and gift-giving, punctuated occasionally with game-playing and snow-crystal gazing.

And even though I knew the era was far from romantic for anyone below the status of the clergy, my imagination dismissed the realities of the Revolution and WWI, and only focused on elegant women dressed in extraordinary ball gowns, wrapped in the finest of furs when furs were the fashion, not a faux pas.

But beyond the fantasies of adolescent romantic notions, which, it would seem, never left my psyche, there was this odd nagging feeling I knew nothing of those who came before me, emphasised more so by Gran-Gran's birth certificate inconsistency. These strange journals somehow both highlighted this and offered me a possibility to answer so many questions I didn't know existed. Perhaps a hidden family secret, maybe a lost school friend of Gran-Gran's and a possible insight into a culture and a time I didn't even know I wanted to learn about. All this might be in those journals and the frail little picture with the faded loving message.

The third, and the silliest thought; I wanted more. I wanted there to be more. More than a father I didn't know and faux-uncles I'd rather not have known and a mother I loved but only because I felt a daughter was obligated to love her mother. I wanted more of anything, and these silly, probably pointless and likely boring journals, these little books I'd not even opened yet, represented all this in one heart-stopping breath. All this flooded my thoughts in what I'm sure was only seconds in the way dreams are short but seem not to be, before the sound of a kind of shuffle, followed by a soft clearing-throat grunt, brought me back. With Andy still holding the box, I flipped the lid free to reveal two dark crimson journals.

Andy said, "I, I wasn't sure if I should open it but I..."

Tom stepped up. "He'd opened the box before I saw it."

Tom rubbed the back of his neck. "We probably should have left it alone, kind of got our curiosity and I told him he should've left it alone..." he said, seeming concerned trust had been broken, but my smile settled any possible tension.

I should have been annoyed, Gran would have been all over it, accusing them of violating her privacy, but something came over me, not fear or shock, but more excitement. Andy must have sensed it, so he put down the box and took out the journals. I reached out for them, each not much bigger than the palm of a person's hand and perhaps a centimetre thick. One thousand thoughts clouded every reason I possessed and swished about in twirling colours on a paint palette, but this time nothing mixed right. I couldn't make sense of a single one of them.

Tom interrupted my motionless state. "Do you know what they are? They look old."

"Yes, sorry, yes they do look old but no, I've no idea what they are or where they've come from. And, Tom, it's Marica, not Miss."

Tom grinned. "To be honest I couldn't remember how to pronounce it correctly and," Tom chuckled before adding, "And I thought that Gran of yours might slap me if I got it wrong."

"It's M-A-R-I-C-A, the C sound is pronounced like the 'c' in essence or sentence. My father named me; it's a Croatian girl's name, like the English Marissa."

"Kind of sounds Russian, that's why I thought the journals might be Russian because when you introduced yourself to me, the way you said your name, I thought you might be Russian."

"Yes..." Dida Nik's song filtered through my head. "Yes," I said again, "I guess it does sound Russian?" Like Dida's song, I'd given my name no real thought. My French heritage was always the emphasis in my home, even with Dida Nik's influence. It had always just been my name, my Croatian girl's name.

"Perhaps they belong to a previous owner?" suggested Tom. "The journals, if they aren't yours, I mean?"

"Perhaps," I replied, knowing I was lying. This house was built at the beginning of the Great Depression by ggYves, my French great-grandfather and Gran-Gran, and while plenty had stayed in the house, no one other than my family had ever lived here.

I flipped the first few pages. Cyrillic. I flipped through the second journal until I got to the few entries in French and started reading the lines. These must have been the most recent. Even with perfect French, I couldn't make out much of it. Between the handwriting and a tendency to write Frenglais – a mix of French and English – I struggled to make sense of even one sentence. But the dates were clear, all after WWI, and the handwriting, though consistent as coming from the same hand, was much steadier as the date moved further from the end of the Great War. A quick skim further and I sensed with a bit of study of the handwriting I would quickly enough translate French entries. But I had no idea what the Russian entries said. I was determined to find out.

"Marica!" Gran was shouting for me. It must have been lunchtime.

"Be right down, I just need to clean up," I replied.

Just before I headed back down, I said, "Tom, if you and your men find anything else, please don't mention it to Gran."

I returned the journals to their metal coffin which, on closer inspection, showed it to be an old cigar box, and snuck down the ladder. Checking that Gran wouldn't see me, I hurriedly hid the box under my bed. With no time to look over my new treasure, I washed my face and hands and joined Gran in the kitchen. As we ate lunch, I let her know that we'd meet the builders outside in the garden in an hour or so, to discuss their suggestions and the estimates.

Not suspecting a thing, Gran only added, "Then we must make some lemonade."

Always the proper hostess, I thought.

Helping Gran with the lemonade on the terrace, I had my first real look at the garden since returning, or at least what could be seen. *Gardens are like people: nourish them, and they will flourish, abandon them, and they will do the same to you.* Dida Nik's words replayed in my head.

So much of it was overgrown, which saddened me. It was as though Dida Nik had died again. I closed my eyes. The sun's light was so strong that my eyelids felt transparent. My skin tingled from its rays. I felt my nostrils flare as I drew in the aroma. With my eyes closed and the fragrant scent pricking at my memory, in my head, I saw the garden as it had been. I thought back to when my Dida Nik planted them, a mix of Madame Isaac Pereires – *French, of course* – and Double Delights. Fragrant sentinels in big terracotta pots dividing the garden from the house. It was almost as though Dida was there with me. A fragile grin formed. "After all this time, I remember their names," I mumbled. I was only a kid then. Mother had finished with husband number two and I'd felt safe.

"Marica?"

"Hum?" Gran's voice frightened Dida's ghost away. I opened my eyes and turned to see Gran lifting the lemonade tray toward me.

That evening after Gran was safely in her room, I closed the door to my bedroom, retrieved the two journals and, as though they were two volumes of a novel, I flicked the first few pages of each. Unable to read any of Vol one, I did what everyone tends to do: turned to the last page of Vol two, as though by reading the last page of a novel I'd know if it was worth reading the first. It was in English.

1st Jan 1933

This will be my last entry.

You have been a dependable confidante and reliable companion for so many years and through more lives, than I sometimes care to remember; yet it is time, Dearest Journal, for us to part.

When I began this journey with you, I was so young and naïve. I knew nothing of love and hate or even of life and death, yet it seems we both have lingered too long in death. I feel it is time to let life breathe in complete freedom.

I do not know if I shall ever visit you again, yet I know I cannot bring myself to read you ever more. The pain of those first entries, memories, where I was able to feel happiness without fear, I think perhaps they hurt the most. Is it not true that the death of innocence is the very worst kind of death?

Good-night, sweet friend, some secrets are perhaps too much, even for time.

CHAPTER 6

Turning Squiggles into Sounds and Words

The next twenty-four hours, I could think of little else but the journals.

Paris! That day Gran suggested we find Gran-Gran's old apartment block, before Gran-Gran and my great-grandfather Yves – ggYves – moved to Melbourne. I knew something was amiss with Gran's story. I tried to remember our conversation.

* * *

We were both up early. We'd not talked about Mother or Maurice or anything much, allowing Paris to consume us. Gran passed me a piece of crunchy French bread and I attempted to broach the subject of Mother.

"How do you feel about Mother's grave being in Brittany?" I asked.

She shrugged. We had our coffees on the balcony. It was cold and still with fluffy white clouds bruised with indigo and ash grey, and only the occasional sliver of duck-egg blue sky peeking through.

"Your Mother and I were lost to each other long ago," she said. "When your father died, much of what remained between us died also." She sighed. "And then when she took you away..." Gran's words drifted on a non-existent breeze. It took me a moment before it hit me; Mother had no reason to drag me off to France. I was almost fully-grown and had a stable life with Gran. Could it have been Mother demanded I live with her not for my sake but because of some hidden resentment toward Gran? I was too afraid to ask, not because it would upset Gran but because it would show Mother to be even more heartless than I believed.

Then, without blinking an eye, Gran changed the subject. "Do you know where this place is?" She held a scrap of paper with '29 Avenue Rapp' on it.

"Not exactly but I can find it. Why?"

"It's where your Gran-Gran lived before she moved to Australia." She paused.

What was she thinking about, why didn't I ask her?

"I've always wanted to see it."

Looking it up on the net, I was amazed to find it was a famous building:

"29 Avenue Rapp is Jules Lavirotte's masterpiece. Whether or not you love it or find it shocking, it's hard not to stop and stare at this outstanding building. Lavirotte designed this wildly decorated façade in 1901 for his friend Alexandre Bigot. A frequent collaborator, Bigot was a talented ceramist and he gave Lavirotte complete freedom with the design for this building. Bigot created the ceramic details himself, working closely with Lavirotte to execute his outrageous and lavish designs, along with the sculptor Jean-Baptiste Larrivé."

A quick train ride later and there it was, in all its Art Nouveau splendour, the most incredibly ornate wooden door with cut glass inserts that I'd ever seen, no, not just seen, ever imagined. A stone's throw from the Eiffel Tower, it stood apart from every other building with its barouche- style decorative features. I couldn't help but wonder why Gran-Gran and ggYves would leave such a place for Australia.

"Do you know which apartment was theirs?" I asked.

Looking up, Gran pointed. "One of those on the top. I'm not certain which one, although I believe it was large and had a view of the Eiffel Tower."

Something close to a brain-freeze overtook me as I tried to absorb what Gran was claiming. This was not an area for the poor, not now and not in the 1920s, and the top floor—? Looking directly into her eyes, I said, "Are you telling me that ggYves was that rich?"

The look on Gran's face as she scrunched it! With a flush of disappointment, she said, "Why do you assume the money came from your great-grandfather's side of the family?"

"Well, did it?" My voice carried too easily in the morning stillness. As cold as it was, I felt a ribbon of sweat trickle down my back. Gran just stared at me; that stare, her stare, the one that could melt ice and scorch paper.

"Are you saying Gran-Gran had serious money?"

"I'm not saying your great-grandfather didn't have money, he was very good at what he did. But Gran-Gran inherited the home from her parents and..."

Gran squinted a little before adding, "I think Gran-Gran said something about working for a rich household and the apartment was some sort of bonus."

This sounded both way too little information and way too difficult to believe.

"That's some bonus!" I demanded.

And yet, I didn't push. Why didn't I push?

"So how did it become Gran-Gran's home?" I asked.

No way is an entire apartment given as a work bonus, not now, not then, not ever! Yet another thing which made no sense.

All Gran did was shrug it off. "I don't recall the details."

Lie!

Gran seemed more interested in the location, saying, "I had no idea the apartment was located so close to the tower. I don't know Paris so when Gran-Gran mentioned it I didn't listen all that much."

It's located in one of the very best parts of Paris, with the Eiffel Tower so close you can almost touch it. Why didn't I say that at the time?

I only managed, "So, I don't understand, why would they have left, for Australia, I mean?"

"Your ggYves moved to Australia for work."

Must have been some job offer.

"They sold it, after they moved to Melbourne; I think your Gran-Gran once said it was later converted into two apartments."

"It must have been large?" I questioned.

"Aha, three or four bedrooms and a formal sitting room, balconies on both sides. That's how they could afford such a good life in Melbourne, it was before the Great Depression and your Gran-Gran knew her real estate."

Then Gran shut me down. "I'm happy now, to have seen it."

That afternoon a still cold rested over Paris. Pure white clouds promising snow hung above us, cold and silent, the air around and between us. I wanted to know more but Gran either didn't know or didn't care to elaborate.

It was that afternoon that we decided to return to Melbourne. Maurice was much more helpful than I expected, saying he would arrange for all my personal belongings to be sent to me, and he even took care of finding someone to rent my Paris apartment for the remainder of the lease. A week later, we were in a taxi to Charles de Gaulle Airport, and a week after that, I was deconstructing every one of Gran's words.

* * *

The journals were haunting me. The most telling for me were the little sketches. The ones in the beginning, often taking up entire pages, were bright, in vibrant watercolours that somehow had withstood the trauma of their journey. But, as I flicked through, the drawings and sketches became darker images, in ink or pencil with sharp harsh edges and toward the end of the journal, were little more than hollow, shamed caricatures, completely soulless.

I could feel regret and loss in the blankness of the black and white pages. It almost oozed despair. And it was those drawings, from the brightness of hopeful youth to the dimness of a kind of death, which convinced me I must find a way to breathe life back into these squiggles and sketches, from brilliance to bleakness; I just couldn't allow them to fade.

But I remained cautious. I didn't want strangers to know the journals' secrets before me. To be honest, part of me feared the journals held secrets I might not want to know.

Eventually, I unboxed Pandora and formed a plan. The first part was to distract Gran. She'd made a point of rarely discussing any family history before 1956. Whenever she'd fail to convince anyone of one of her famed facts, she would simply say, "Was that before 1956?" And the odd thing was, no one discussed it further. It was as though 1956 held some mythical power over us.

But I digress. Gran would not be willing to discuss the journals. If anything, she'd likely try to destroy them. It seemed clear that Gran was either hiding or omitting something about her past and given

36

Gran's dislike of all things associated with the former USSR, I felt it best to keep my secrets, for now. I don't how I knew this, I just did.

So, I needed to get out of the house and find a place without interrogation. Gran had a way of making me feel twelve. Hell, she had a way of making almost everyone feel twelve. And I desired neither her irritation nor cross-examination. What I needed was space. Simple! I'd lie about taking some refresher art classes while the attic was under renovation.

Given I'd already lived on my own in France, the logical step would have been to find my own place, or better yet, moving into Dida and Nana's old place. However, the inner twelve-year-old me needed her. Growing up, I'd missed something most take for granted – stability. I knew what stability was. I'd felt glimpses when I was younger, but never did I feel completely safe. Between an inconsistent mother and too many father figures, I was denied a child's security. But now, at twenty-four, I thought perhaps I could find it with Gran, without the fear of forced disconnection.

Even so, I felt guilt seep into my veins. To avoid Gran's wrath, I would have to lie to her, for lying to Gran. I decided to invent attending refresher community art classes. But if I was going to fib, I might as well be 'hung for a sheep as a lamb' and make it a believable lie, after all, if one is to lie, it's an insult to the other party's intellect if the lie is full of gaping holes.

I fabricated a student-artist-group. This would give me several months free from questions. Now I just needed to sort out how to translate the journals. It occurred to me that Croatian was pretty much 100% phonetic, and I thought perhaps other Slav languages might also be. If only I could learn Russian letters, I'd be able to translate with some degree of accuracy.

So, when Tom returned with the final plans approved, I put my own plans into motion. I coordinated with Tom and his team to work on the attic primarily when I was not at my faux-artist group. This way Gran and I would have little time to discuss anything other than the attic.

The next day, armed with my laptop and the journals, I headed off, hoping Michel, who I'd met before moving to France, still ran his café in Hardware Lane. Michel, lanky and Bohemian- looking and utterly delectable, was originally from Lyon but moved to Melbourne after meeting an Australian woman who was holidaying in France. They fell in love and he decided Australia was to become his new home. He made a damn fine coffee, an excellent pastry and among the best hot chocolates outside of Paris – the kind with *actual* melted chocolate.

After seating myself out the front, I watched to see if Michel was still running the business. Though he didn't recognise me at first, soon we were sharing hugs along with warm greetings in French. The last time I'd seen Michel, I was still a kid and I thought him sex-on-a-stick. I was a shy child who giggled every time he smiled at me – and my only experience with men was Uncle Steve.

But now, damn, Michel looked even hotter than I remembered! I was tempted to try my flirty eyes but for three things. I was kind of crap at 'flirty-eyes' anyway, and, if the friend-rule didn't stop me, the shiny gold band on his finger was a bolted gate. I'd tried the friends with benefits and even the married men with benefits after my emancipation from Mother. Both were disasters. Teen-girl mag's and Insta-influencers have a lot to answer for.

In the time it took for my double-shot large skinny latte to arrive, my laptop was up and loaded. By my second double espresso, I'd concluded translation was not going to be a simple task. By the time I was scooping the chocolate sprinkles off my hot chocolate, I'd further concluded it was almost impossible. Each Slavic language had variations on indentations with which to create a letter-specific sound, such as š =sh sound in Croatian while, ë = yo in Russian.

I tried Google translate online, but I didn't have Russian letter symbols on my keyboard. Sure, I could find most of them under 'symbols' but how long would it take to translate just one line? So that was a fail.

Michel wandered over. With his sexy French accent dripping over me like melted chocolate, he asked, "So heavy in thought?"

I blinked away his deliciousness, loudly cleared my throat –, *hum, yeah that was super sexy* –, and said, "I'm trying to translate some Russian poems."

Michel shrugged his shoulders. "Maybe try putting an ad for a translator on the internet?"

Brilliant! The ad didn't take long to write up. I gulped down a way too big last mouthful of hot chocolate as I hit 'post' on my advert. Shutting my laptop, I waved goodbye to Michel.

The next few days were spent checking emails and sending SMS messages in between meeting with Tom and reporting to Gran. After two days I had three potential candidates lined up. I decided to meet each of them at another café, I didn't want strangers knowing where I hang out, just in case.

There was a café on Collins Street, set high about the footpath, with big glass windows looking onto the street. At the right table, in the middle of Winter, when the trees were bare, you could see a smidge of the Yarra River. While Michel's place was my favourite haunt, this place was easy to find and gave me an excellent view of passing traffic.

I seated myself at a good-sized table and ordered my first latte from a tall young waiter with almost hypnotic grey eyes, bushed eyebrows and a beatnik-like mop of hair. I had to look away, because I could feel myself staring, yet I so desperately wanted to paint those eyes. I'd never seen eyes with that unique blend of blue-green-grey.

I sipped my latte and people watched. A couple darted through sludgy traffic. The woman, pencil-thin skirt, and killer heels; skipped over the tramlines with the dexterity of a gazelle. A man dressed in chef's whites was carrying a red plastic tray down toward the Yarra. Huddles of people walked past the café; one group hailed a taxi. I felt like I could have been in a scene from some 'set-in-New-York' 20 or 30-something telemovie.

My first potential translator arrived just as a tram clinked at an obstinate car in its way. I knew I shouldn't judge by appearance but?

The gentleman's name was Igor. Middle-aged but with his too-tight jeans, his 1980's style bomber acid-wash jacket and boy-band stubble, which was more grey than black, he was clearly struggling with his real age. Either that or I'd caught him on the way to a mid-afternoon fancy-dress party.

Seriously though. By the way, can someone please tell these old men that gold teeth are kind-of OK for eighteen-year-old wannabe gangsta-rappers, not podgy middle-aged men. It's not OK for gangsta-rappers either but looking stupid is OK when you're eighteen or nineteen, even twenty-nine, but forty-eight or nine, not so much.

"You never told me you were so beautiful," he said, giving a full view of his gold tooth. Yuck!

"Do you have a boyfriend?" he asked. I guess my face must have said it for me because he then added, "I bet you have lots of boyfriends!"

There were four chairs at this table. I expected him to sit opposite, but instead, he sat on the chair next to me and I wished I'd put my bag on it instead of on the floor.

He moved his chair closer to me. I tried to move away but the leg of the table prevented it.

"I see you're not married," he said as he looked down at my hand. "Or engaged."

His eyes moved from my hand and up to meet my eyes, lingering a little too long at my chest, and I wished I'd worn something less revealing, like a burqa. When his eyes finally met mine, he added, "No rings."

I wanted to say *you're creeping me out*, but settled for, "So tell me about your experience in translating. Are you Russian?"

The more his mouth moved the less comfortable I felt. Something about him echoed memories of Uncle Steve. Oh God, Uncle Steve. I shuddered at the thought of him. I tried to keep those memories hidden deep in the blackness of forgotten pain.

I was not quite three when Dad died. Mother wasted no time in remarrying after his death. I liked to suppose she felt I needed a father figure. She was quite young when she married Dad and likely more in love with the idea of love than loving Dad. Besides, she was never particularly sentimental. It's no secret that she didn't shed a tear for Dad. Not one.

Uncle Mike was the first. Thankfully, he didn't insist on me calling him Dad.

Uncle Mike was particularly good-looking. I think he was once in a band or managed a band, or something. Anyway, Uncle Mike enjoyed a drink and once drunk, drinking turned to gambling; on anything. Even though the marriage only lasted three years, it resulted in two evictions, one repossessed car and numerous weekends without electricity.

I was ten when Mother introduced me to Uncle Steve. Though he was better at providing than Uncle Mike, Uncle Steve's faults were much more repulsive. His unkempt appearance, though hinting at a handsome youth, mirrored his true personality. To call him filthy is an insult to the simply unclean. His griminess was more than tomato sauce-stained flannel shirts or an unshaven face. His dirt included lewd comments, sometimes aimed at strangers and other times at Mother. He had money, but he was miserly. Gran once called him "Fat-Scrooge." And his smell. Stale cigarettes and beer lingered around him like an apparition, made that much worse by the addition of a bath in whatever-is-on-special cheap cologne. Perhaps that's why I don't drink beer and dislike men soaked in cologne. I once asked Gran how my vain, superficial mother would marry such a pig. He had money and, it would seem, presented very well, until after the wedding day. For Mother, money trumped everything.

Uncle Steve's present to me for my twelfth birthday was being ambushed in the laundry and him groping my still undeveloped breasts through my sundress with one hand, while holding me down with the mass of his body and his free hand. His knee, splitting my legs apart, as he pushed the same knee higher and higher until it was pressing and rubbing me so hard, it hurt. Each time I tried to wriggle free he seemed to get a better grip on my breast, now completely exposed while his knee kept rubbing and rubbing, harder each time I moved.

I saw him grin as I winced in pain.

Terrified, I begged, "Please, please don't..."

This seemed to make him more aroused as though my fear was part of the pleasure. I went to scream but was shut down by his mouth cupping mine, the sticky paste of his nicotine-infused saliva making me dry-retch. His tongue was now free to attack my mouth as his free hand moved down from my breast. That was my first kiss, my very first kiss. Nothing can change or remove the memory, or the taste.

I didn't know much about sex, but I knew what was happening. He was going to rape me, and I couldn't stop him. I said a silent prayer, begging God to let me die as his body pressed even harder against mine, as what remained of my modesty was destroyed, the only semblance of clothing now scrunched around my waist. His fat, sausage-like grubby fingers touching my naked stomach as he whispered, "There's nothing more beautiful than soft smooth skin."

Bile rose in my throat as I felt my knees weaken almost to the point of fainting, praying for unconsciousness, or death. I found the courage to look down and saw it. Another first. The first erect penis I saw was his.

I clenched my stomach muscles and tried to squeeze my legs together as he began to force it into me. Fear and panic overtook me. Just as my eyes rolled back, an incessantly ringing doorbell became my hero, forcing him to release me for fear of being discovered, though not before he threatened me with Mother's life.

"Trust me, you're just like your mother, you'll love it," he whispered, adding if I didn't *keep our little secret,* my Mother would not be safe.

Secret be damned! I thought as I ran out the laundry door, freeing a long Winter jacket from the laundry-door hook, covering my body and shame as I headed straight to Gran's. I told her everything. Of course, he denied every word, but Mother was not fooled by his protests. Neither were the police, even if it would take another victim to stop him.

For all her faults, Mother did not for a moment disbelieve me. Yet part of me still wonders if her anger at Uncle Steve was for my sake or hers. Was she being protective at last or an angered jealous wife?

Gran insisted we move in with her but Mother detested Gran being right. Instead, we moved in with Nana and Dida. I started high school living at Dida's and hoped Mother would not find another uncle too quickly.

I'd managed to avoid that memory for half my life, but now, this creepy Igor guy brought it all back. I just wanted him gone, him and his tight jeans and lecherous, gold-toothed-grin.

"OK, thanks, I have a few other people to speak to, so I'll get back to you."

I swear the surprise on his face... gold, pure gold, unlike his gold teeth, which were likely only caps. Once I was sure he'd left, I first blocked his number and then deleted it.

43

The second person didn't even bother turning up. After latte number two, and four unanswered text messages, I figured they weren't coming.

The third candidate, a woman, arrived as agreed and as she sat with me and Waiter-grey-eyes brought her flat white, I hoped I'd found my collaborator.

Though her accent was strong, I quickly fell into understanding her. She had formal qualifications and a good history as a translator, and we were around the same age. This was looking promising.

I was almost ready to show her my treasure when she said, "Now, vit da peyment, you vil payy me every time in cesh, yes?"

"Yes, that's fine, so what's your rate?" I asked, hoping, given she wanted payment in cash, she'd say $15 per hour but prepared to pay up to $20 per hour if necessary.

"You see," she started, "As teacherr I get $60 forr von hour but if forr u dis I do, I vill looking to starrrt forr half dis, but forr cesh, yes; you underrstending?"

Sadly, I did understand.

She smiled a very satisfied smile, which made what I was about to say very uncomfortable. My heart sank. I could not afford $30 per hour. I really couldn't afford even $20.

"I was thinking closer to $15 or $20 per hour?" I said, a little embarrassed at offering so little.

She shook her head so firmly that I felt my face flush. "Dis is rrridiculousss!"

She stood up and began blasting me with hand motions as her tongue spat poison.

"Vot do you tinking? Do you tinking because I am Russsian I am forr peying notting?"

I didn't have time to reply, she was already collecting her bag, as she hissed, "I verking not forr notting!" turning even before I could reply.

I was beginning to feel despondent by the time my third coffee came when Waiter-grey-eyes spoke in an equally strong Slavic accent punctured with poor English grammar. "You lookingg to writingg forr RRusssian, yes?"

I almost fumbled my coffee over my laptop as I mumbled, "Uh, uh, um yes?"

Deep-set grey eyes, the colour of the sea just before a thunderstorm, rimmed with a dark black blue looked at me through almost jet-black bushy brows. He smiled an open mouth smile. Damn. Perfect teeth too!

He leaned a little closer. I caught a tickle of a familiar scent from him and wondered if their chef was baking cookies or something.

"Must firrrst you buy forrrr Russian typing." He pointed to my keyboard, as his accent emphasised the "R" in every word.

He'd obviously been following my unsuccessful attempt to find a translator and was suggesting I turn to Google Translate; but as he rightly pointed out, I needed a Russian keyboard.

"Yes, thank you, but I have too much to translate, it would take too long." I stopped. I'd no idea why I was explaining myself to Waiter-grey-eyes and I was in no mood for suggestions I'd already come up with myself.

"Hum. Den I tink u must forr finding new perrson? But, Miss, nott lyke dis!" He pointed into the street, suggesting I was collecting street urchins. Based on my success rate thus far, he was right, however, his observations were little help.

"Well, I'm not sure how to find someone who can speak, read and write Russian, it's not like people carry signs."

"If you lyke, I ken?"

"Sorry? Can? Can what?"

"I ken be rreadding dis forr Russsian forr you?"

Completely forgetting I wanted to keep my journals a secret (and

45

yes, they were now mine), I simultaneously thrust the first page of journal one, and said, "Is this Russian?"

Waiter-grey-eyes mouthed some words, looked at me, and mouthed some more before leaning down to ask, "Miss, who is wrriting forr dis?"

Without answering his question, I asked, "Can you read it?"

Damn, what's that scent?

Waiter-grey-eyes leaned down. "Yes, surrre, of courrse, but..."

A sharp voice interrupted us with a shout. "Victor! Table five's order is ready!"

Victor-Grey-eyes shoved the journal back at me, rushing the words. "Sorrrry, must my job be do-ving," did a 1-80 pivot and headed for two awaiting plates.

Thoughts rushed through my head. It was Russian! He could read it! Then I felt a pang of jealousy. The first person to read the journals' first line since someone hid them in our attic's floorboards, wasn't me? I knew I wouldn't be the first, obviously, but now it hit me. I don't exactly know why it mattered, it just did.

It says somewhere in the Bible that five generations can pay for each sin. I was beginning to wonder what sin Gran-Gran, or indeed her parents, had committed to warrant that my every small pleasure was fated to come with a measure of pain or disappointment.

Then I thought of Gran-Gran's apartment in Paris and I felt sure some mischief played a part in obtaining such an extravagant lifestyle. An unplanned snort freed itself as I considered my great-grandparents might have been forced to leave France after being involved in some less than honest real estate matters. What was it Gran said? *Gran-Gran was good at real estate* or something like that. How funny would it be to discover my very Victorian-mannered Gran was the offspring of nefarious dealings and fraudsters!

My laptop battery was low. I quickly jotted down a note with my number, asking Victor to call me, and handed it to him with a smile as I paid for my coffees. It wasn't until I was on my way home that it occurred to me the phone number could have been misinterpreted. Oh hell, how bad could it be, he was cute!

So now I was waiting for a call from a man who I'd met for a matter of minutes. A man whose struggle with English would be so much more highlighted over the phone, and I really knew nothing about. As my imagination flourished even through reasoning, my phone rang. Sure enough, it was Victor.

"Miss, is frrom coffee-house, you rrrememberrr?"

"Yes, yes of course, thank you for calling." I tried to sound as much school librarian as I knew how.

"Sorrrry, Miss, if you..." Victor Grey-eyes stuttered the last few words, forcing me to ask him to repeat himself.

"But, vat is it you vant-ing Miss?"

That, I understood. Victor Grey-eyes thought I might be looking for a hook-up. He was likely familiar with women giving him phone numbers. I mean, OK, yes, he was quite attractive, *but* I was interested in his translation skills. Besides, he was too skinny. Yes, definitely too skinny. Kind of scrawny, come to think of it, and...and; I was in no doubt I was protesting too much.

With as prim and proper English as I could muster, and ensuring I enunciated every syllable, I said, "I was hoping you could please translate what you read in the journal?"

The relieved sigh that came from the other end of the phone was so palpable that it offended me a little. Sure, I was never going to be the next supermodel but still. A girl has her pride.

My self-indulgence into vanity was interrupted with, "I try rememberrr forrr you, but lookking only vone minute."

"That's fine, but please tell me what you remember," I insisted.

15th July 1914

The world has changed today... for today I can no longer love my granny as I did yesterday.

"It vas dating July da 15th and person is saying dat day ken not loving da grand modder today lyke before. Dat is all I rememberrr. Miss, dis is very said, yes? Not to love yourr grand modder?"

Truthfully, it didn't strike me as such a big deal, a young girl angry at her grandmother, which I understood. But the date, the date was what struck me. WWI started at the end of July. 1914; Good God, that was just weeks before WWI started.

Now I wanted to know more, who was the authoress? A Russian soldier's secret lover? A Cossack, a member of the White Russian army? Maybe on the other side? Like a member of the Bolsheviks. Wait, wait! A young woman's journal in love with a soldier in the Russian army, perhaps planning to elope and her granny stopped her.

Hold on! The girl in the photo, it was taken April 1914 and she had a sister; what if the sister was older and *she* was the author of the journals? Now that was interesting. And it made sense. Though it didn't explain how they got into Gran's attic.

I mumbled, "Wouldn't it be great if this was the diary of a great love. Perhaps?" My imagination was running away. "And now?"

"Miss?" the voice from my mobile interrupted me.

"Yes." Groping to form a lucid sentence I said, "Sorry, yes, thank you."

"Miss, vat is writing dis?" I understood him to be asking who the author was but was unwilling to admit I had no idea. Instead, I put a proposition to him.

"Please, call me Marica," I said, waiting for a reply. None came.

"Would you be willing to translate the first page for me?"

Victor Grey-eyes remained silent, which unnerved me. "I cannot pay you much?"

"Miss Marica."

I was relieved he broke his silence. Stagnant silence made me uneasy.

"I vill forrr you dis read and you vill for helping me vit Englishh maybe?"

It seemed a fair compromise. Naturally, I agreed and arranged to meet in two days, one hour before his shift at the café. But I now had the first lines of my journal and I could check if Victor Grey-eyes had translated those lines. By asking Goggle to translate into Russian it became easy enough to confirm.

When I typed:

The world has changed today... for today I can no longer love my Granny as I did yesterday

I got pretty much the same Russian letter configuration as was in the journal. The variance didn't concern or surprise me. Computer-generated translations often lost something in translation. What I wanted, and what I got, was the start of a puzzle and someone to help me unravel it.

CHAPTER 7

Bleach

A pungent smell launched itself at me.

I rubbed my eyes and scrunched my nose and then pulled the cover over my head. It was too damned early to care what the hell that was.

There! There it was again. Even with the covers pulled over my head, it crept in. I half stumbled out of bed and opened the bedroom door. "Phew." What was that?

My conscious state and my nostrils joined forces. It was coming from downstairs, a combination of bleach and eucalyptus oil.

It was too dammed early. "What the hell is she doing up at this time of the morning?" A normal person would've shrugged it off and gone back to bed, but I hated the smell.

Disinfectant. Gran, eighty-plus and she was up with the kookaburras, cleaning the kitchen. I slumped back on the bed. I knew why she was up so early. Dear sweet old thing. She must have remembered.

Disinfectant. The smell of hospital wards. Each whiff drew me back to them, and their hypocrisy. Places appearing hygienic, though they were incubators of death.

Disinfectant. It clung to my lungs. It never failed to make me dry retch. And a few drops of eucalyptus oil wasn't enough to mask the memory.

Hospitals. As a teenager I watched both Dida Nik and Nana await death in hospital wards. Ten years later it was Mother's turn, and no fake nurse's smile or doctor's clipboard could ever convince me otherwise. People go there to die.

Clunk – Slurp – Clunk. Gran had moved on to the kitchen floor. Her flagstones made a different sound to floorboards being washed. There, another attack of foul disinfectant.

Doctors – Illness – Death. Gran's insistence on sanitizing the entire house drew me back to Mother's hospital bed, to hear the doctor say, "*Il y a eu des complications et l'infection est...*"

I registered, *Complications and infections.* Translation. *Death.*

Only one thing had mattered: getting Gran to France as quickly as possible. Perhaps if her birth certificate hadn't delayed her passport application, she would've made it a few days earlier. At least Gran managed to make it in time for the funeral, even if she hadn't been able to hear her daughter's voice one last time.

Mother's funeral had been a quiet affair. So few mourners.

She still hadn't spoken about it. Gran, I mean. Was it because it hurt too much, or not enough? I sometimes wondered if Mother was long dead to Gran, and if the priest and the undertaker simply made it official. They'd barely known each other.

Downstairs I could now hear Gran was clunking her stainless-steel pots. She must have finished with the floor.

Did I wonder if Gran thought of Mother? Today would have been Mother's birthday. Neither of us spoke of it. The cleaning needed to be done.

Mother. Well, she did get lucky with Maurice at least.

CHAPTER 8

Time

Tom and his team kept me busy for most of the day. Something I was grateful for because I just wanted it to be tomorrow.

The next morning Gran asked, "What did you have planned for today?"

"Hum?"

"Your plans, Dear?"

"Oh, umm, one of the other students from my class is struggling with understanding the assignment; he's Russian, I think..."

Oops! I should not have said that.

Before another word was uttered, her eyes, her beautiful, wild, crazy, cornflower-blue eyes, turned to ice. "I will never understand why you must befriend every stray, Marica, I truly will not."

Raised Catholic, I had to agree with Holden Caulfield. *Catholics are always trying to find out if you're Catholic,* but I'll amend that statement, *Gran* was always trying to find out if someone was Russian. "It's just that—

-And you should know that you cannot trust a Russian."

"Why?"

She moved her porcelain teacup from her lips just far enough to ask in a monotone, "Why what, Dear?"

"Why must I know better than anyone that Russians are not to be trusted?"

Gran pursed her lips as her hand seemed to move in slow motion, clicking her teacup to its perfectly matched saucer, patting each corner of her mouth with her perfectly ironed, perfectly starched white linen serviette before offering me her perfectly practised sarcastic smile.

"Marica, why must you antagonise me? You are aware of the atrocities of the Russian revolution, of the Bolsheviks, Lenin and especially Stalin." She wiped the slightest imperfect crease from her mother's embroidered tablecloth. "Do I really need to say more?"

I wanted to say, *actually yes, you really do.*

"But, Gran, is that the fault of the people? Are all Russians to blame for the atrocities of their leaders? If we blame every Russian citizen for the actions of heads of state, then surely the same rule must be applied to all nations. What about Germans, Turks, the French?" *Damn, never, n-e-v-e-r mention France before thinking it through!*

Gran rose from her seat like some sort of mythological creature. "So, I take it today's plans include tormenting me?" she hissed as she walked away, leaving me feeling like an 18th-century serf.

Thankfully, the alarm on my phone freed me from Gran. As I grabbed my bag, it occurred to me that my grandmother had again outsmarted me – and not answered my question. The woman was as much a femme fatale as Mother, though Gran used her gifts much more subtly. I admired their special skills and wondered why it was that I should not have garnered these genetic traits. Was it not enough their eyes missed my generation?

I was unsure of how she held this power over me. I could not shake fourteen-year-old Marica free when I was with Gran. Perhaps it was that frozen time theory. When you leave a place and years later you return and expect everything to look and act the same way, like with Gran's garden. Maybe it suspends more than memories. Maybe it suspends us to an age, or a hierarchy, or something.

CHAPTER 9

Page One of...

Walking into the café I found Victor Grey-eyes waiting for me at the same table I was seated at a few days earlier. Facing the door, Victor half waved, and half smiled. Both actions showed his nerves. I smiled and waved back.

Approaching, I wasn't sure if I should shake his hand, hug him or kiss both cheeks. If I leaned forward and he drew back, it would be a disaster! I settled for the two-handed handshake with the second hand clasped over both.

Shake over, I started removing my coat as Victor said, "I ordorr da coffee for you, is OK?"

"Yes, thank you."

I retrieved journal one, flipped to page one, and said, "Victor, if you-"

"Miss Marica, I must be tellingg my nayme is not Victorr."

This threw me. His boss called him Victor and I'm certain he responded.

"But I?"

The-Waiter-Formally-Known-As-Victor, raised one hand while shaking his head. "Is bosss. He not lyke to say my nayme so he call me everry nayme. Sometimes Victorr, sometimes Alexei."

I found this dumbfounding and terribly inappropriate. "You know he cannot do that? He can't ridicule your name or your nationality. Just because you are from Russia does not give him-"

"Not from RRRussia, is just speaking RRRussaiian."

Ok? I give up, who the fuckadoodle are you?

The-Waiter-Formally-Known-As-Victor's employer's screechy voice broke our conversation. "Oy, Boris, come get your girlfriend's coffee!"

Girlfriend. Girlfriend, what the?

My no-name, no-nationality, new kind-of-non-friend promptly collected my coffee without as much as a sullen smile. If it had been me, his boss, Mr. Paisley Shirt, would be wearing my coffee by now.

"So, what is your name?"

Setting a new record in fast speech he said, "Rrrreal name is Ilija – is lyke Englishh Elijah but vit "EE' like forr Igloo, and the "J" is saying like "Y, and, and, no "H" at back; you underrrstending?"

He didn't give me time to understand. Hell, there isn't a person on this planet that could take that in with one breath. He'd obviously re-hearsed this performance. "So, you say, EE-L-I-Y-A, see?"

Ilija, The-Waiter-Formally-Known-As-Victor, was becoming more interesting. The name Ilija was sometimes found in Russian and Slo-vak families but was also a Croatian boy's name. So, was he Slovak? He already said he wasn't Russian. Many Slovaks knew Russian; it seemed the most logical.

"I know of the name Ilija, but why doesn't your boss just call you Ilija?"

"He say it too hard to rememberrr." Ilija paused briefly to scope out his boss's location. "He is verrry little man vit verry little lyfe. I feel sorry, you know? Vat is to do? Forr lyfe to living lyke him? Sad yes?" Ilija had class, more class than me.

"So where are you from and how is it you can read Russian?" I rushed the words at him. Our hour was being eaten up and I'd learned nothing.

"I vas borrn in Croatia, you know it?" he asked.

I nodded yes. Time enough to tell him my story later. Right now, I wanted his.

"So, ven verry little, my fadder, is engineerrr, he get job, firrst in Austria for tree years, den he go to Russia for vorking for building da bridge, family too. Vas in Russia from seven to eleven years old. Den ve coming back to Croatia forr rest of schooling but I vanting to learrning English betta. I ken speak Russian, Croatian and some Gerrman but Englishhh is not good. Grammar. So, getting vone year studying also in Australia and getting dis job."

Ilija threw his hands up in the air. "Dis is all!"

It was more than enough. I smirked a little. I almost couldn't wait to tell Gran my new friend was not Russian at all, but a well-educated multi-lingual Catholic European. I didn't need to ask his religion. Almost without exception, all Croatians were Catholic; it's just how it was.

Feeling I needed to share, I said, "My father was Croatian."

Ilija's eyes widened. "You speak?"

"*Da.*"

Ilija's face lit up. "You know I vas tinking vit nayme lyke Marica, yes maybee, but den I tinking maybbee not, you know?"

I thought it best for both our sakes to speak Croatian. Aside from the improved communication, his boss would not understand what we were talking about.

"Of course," I said in Croatian. "I once met a girl called Ivanka and her family were English but simply liked the name."

Ilija didn't ask me anything about my father, which pleasantly surprised me. He seemed to comprehend the story wasn't open for discussion. I returned Ilija's attention to the journal, and continuing in Croatian, I asked him if he could translate the entire first page for me.

Ilija read in Russian, translated in Croatian and I wrote in English. Thinking on it, I could not imagine a better physical personification of the world.

15th July 1914

The world has changed today, for today I can no longer love my granny as I did yesterday.

Papa insists there is nothing to fear for Serbia is far from Russia but none of us believe him. And it is not just Papa. The paper says the assassination of Archduke Franz Ferdinand means the world is at war, a great world war. How can any war be called great? Papa spent much of the day in his office and when he did come out his forced smile hid nothing.

I interrupted him. He must have misread. "Ilija, stop for a moment. Are you sure of the date? Archduke Franz Ferdinand's assassination happened at the end of July 1914."

Before I successfully searched the WWI start date on Google, Ilija knew the answer. "You're forgetting the Gregorian and Julian Calendars. Russia was still using the old system then."

I stopped searching. He was right. Their July 15th is our July 28th. I pointed to the remainder of the page, prompting Ilija to continue.

There must be a God, Mamma tells us to pray every night and Monsieur Gilliard is always reading from the Bible, but I fear that if God exists, He has abandoned the world.

And Mamma, I have never seen her brilliant blue eyes look so sullen. Dear Mamma, how can she ever be happy again? Perhaps this is why she is more determined than anyone to hate the country which gave her life.

I know I shouldn't say this, but I hate both the Germans and the Serbs. I hate them for making Mamma cry and for making Papa so cross.

I know it is improper for a well-bred young lady to discuss such matters, so I share my thoughts only with you Madame Diary.

Ilija put down the journal, and I, my pen, and for a short time we just looked at each other.

"Hey, Vladimir!" His employer's nightingale-not voice broke our trance.

Ilija looked up to see his boss tap-tap-tapping his watch even though Ilija still had seven minutes remaining before his shift was due to start. Ilija rolled his eyes, rose from his seat and leaned down, allowing me to pick up that familiar scent again. I still couldn't place the aroma. Thankfully, I managed to stop myself from actually sniffing the air around him.

He said in Croatian, "I think you have stumbled on something quite incredible here. This seems to be a family of wealth and position and looks to have a first-hand account of one of the most horrific eras of modern history."

"Tick-tock, Nikolai," bellowed his boss, but this time Ilija found his voice. "I vill be coming five minutes forr ven my shift beginning!"

"Marica." Ilija bent down, his ear now close enough that I could almost feel the moisture in his breath. He drew the air around my ear, which made it tingle, the feeling running down my backbone. I pulled back just a little.

"Marica," he repeated, *Oh God, what's happening to me*? "I know we struck an agreement, my translation for your tuition, but I would like to renegotiate."

"Renegotiate?" I asked, "To what?"

"Whether or not you help me with my English is not nearly as important to me as knowing what happens next in here." Ilija tapped on the journal. "I'll manage to learn English either way. Why do you think I work here? Sure, I need the money but also because I can listen to English spoken by natives."

Ilija, who'd magically transformed from skinny and lanky to slim and sexy, cocked his head. "But these journals of yours, well they are kind of awesome and I want to help if I can."

Ilija took one step away from the table. "I'd like to fall down this rabbit-hole with you if you don't mind?"

Oh you mean? Right.

I cleared my throat as though I had something to say but settled on a nod and a big gulp of water.

Ilija retrieved his apron from the backpack on the seat next to me, swung the backpack over his shoulder, grabbed my empty cup and disappeared into the back room of the café. I remained seated. I wasn't quite sure what to do. I felt as though our conversation was only half completed. I re-read my translated notes.

Ilija was right. This was a well-off family, aristocratic perhaps, soldiers at the very least. The reference to talks of war and Germany and the comment: *"Monsieur Gilliard is always reading from the Bible."*

A family friend? 'Monsieur' clearly showed the gentleman to be French and the French, much like Croats, are almost all Catholic and Russian Orthodox. The Julian calendar date confirmed this family was Orthodox and the gentleman was *'always'* reading, so this Frenchman must have been a family friend, or a regular visitor.

Ilija returned from the back with another coffee, apron firmly sitting on his hips and his wavy black hair tucked behind his ears. "I thought you might be ready for another. And this gives me a chance to talk to you. When can we meet again?"

"Tomorrow?" I suggested as this fitted in with my faux art-group.

"Tomorrow morning. I have an English class in the afternoon."

"Perfect!" *Jesus, Marica, just drink your God damned coffee and get a grip.*

CHAPTER 10

Gigglers

Ilija's boss was staring again. "I'll come back in a few minutes and we'll confirm details."

I watched Ilija move around his area, taking orders and wiping down tables. Every so often we'd share a glance. I couldn't stop staring as he dropped off orders and smiled at patrons. Something about him drew me in. Then he moved from a young couple with a toddler to a table of three giggling teen girls, and I realised I wasn't the only one watching him.

Few things can stop three teenage girls and their texting-fest. A shoe sale, a manicure, some Tik-Tok gone viral, and a hot guy.

Ilija leaned down. The gigglers put their phones down, their chests out and their flirt smiles on. My ego poked at my unreasonable sense of betrayal. He was only doing his job, and the two of us were little more than acquaintances.

There was a time I'd have bedded him because I could. But I'd out-grown that. Yet for the first time in several years, Ilija's grey eyes had me wondering what it would feel like to surrender myself rather than have them surrender to me.

As Ilija walked away, one of the giggler's snapped him from behind.

I imagined the photo on Insta, minutes later, with a caption, 'hot waiter guy's butt' or something equally predictable. One of the gigglers glared at me, or should I say, over me, gave me a curt smile, rolled her eyes, and turned to whisper to her little swarm.

I glared back. There they were in all their barely out of high-school glory. Daisy-Dukes, tops held together with dental-floss, make-up straight from the *Kardashian School of Not-so-natural Beauty.* And me. V-neck cotton top, three-quarter jeans, flat Summer sandals and my hair pulled back in a ponytail. My make-up routine consisted of SP30 sunblock, some foundation, barely-there mascara and lip-gloss, most of which was now stained on the edge of my coffee cup. Still, even without all their weaponry, I'd had my share of male attention. Not to Mother's level, thank God. The thought made the hairs on my arms prickle. Yet after my emancipation, and escape to Paris, there'd been more than a few men in my life.

I felt the heat in my ears as I recalled my first year in Paris. I'd like to think I was more Audrey Hepburn's Holly Golightly, but I think in truth I was channelling a twenty-something version of Samantha from *Sex and the City.*

I flittered through a smorgasbord of men, most of whom I'm struggling to recall. Then one weekend I watched a *Sex and the City* marathon and realised Samantha wasn't so impervious to insecurity. The final straw was when I decided to read *Breakfast at Tiffany's* rather than simply watch the movie over and over and discovered Ms. Holly wasn't going along so lightly. She was a victim, used and manipulated; and I was finished with nothingness-sex. I REALLY dislike the song 'Moon River' now.

Still, Frenchmen are so different to Australian men. Secretly, I hoped Slavic men were more like Frenchmen.

The gigglers reminded me of a swarm of bees on a David Attenborough wildlife special. They kept snapping pics of Ilija and he kept returning smiles, and I couldn't help but think I wanted a super-sized can of insect spray to magically materialize. I resolved not to do my best to avoid this café. Ilija approached me as soon as his boss was called to the kitchen to referee a dispute between the chef and sous-chef. "So, tomorrow morning then?" he asked.

"Where?"

"How about your place?"

"Your place might be better." I was in no mood to have the gigglers overhear I lived with my gran.

Ilija looked to see the coast was still clear before suggesting my place again. I jumped back with his place and instantly saw a blush over his cheeks. "My place isn't all that great," he said.

I wanted to know why his home was not ideal, but as I had reasons for not bringing him to my place, I was hardly able to question him. Instead, I suggested Michel's little café in Hardware Lane. He knew the one. 9.30am. We'd have at least three hours, and Michel would have no issue with using his power for my laptop so I could type Ilija's translations directly onto the screen.

The gigglers were staring at us. One had her camera pointed at him. "Do you know them?"

"Who?" He half-turned, giving the gigglers a better profile angle. "Nah," he said, with his gaze still on them. One mouthed and used her hands to ask him to lift his t-shirt. While he taunted them with fake shirt-lifting, I considered how I preferred Serena to Samantha in *Bewitched*. Serena would just make them disappear or change them into something useful – like a toilet plunger. He smiled as they clicked any-way. I'm not sure my flat clenched mouth expressed my *I don't care*, all that successfully.

"I've never seen them before. Girls come in all the time."

"I bet they do, and do all of them ask to see your abs?"

Ilija chuckled. He leaned down and purred into my ear. "If I smile back, I get bigger tips." *Fuck.* I tried to compose myself. "Besides," he added, "I'm becoming partial to green eyes."

Tingles pricked my neck and I felt my face heat up. I leaned further into him, as much for the gigglers as me. "So, tomorrow then." Ilija nodded as he grabbed my cup.

Just then the café echoed with, "Dimitri!"

Shrugging, as though he'd read my mind, and, still in Croatian, Ilija said, "As I said, he's a little man with little to amuse him."

As my new, hot-as-holy-crap-non-Russian-kind-of-crush disappeared into the back room I collected my things and disappeared into the clear Melbourne afternoon.

CHAPTER 11
Café Michel

Michel's café turned out to be ideal. Aside from the fantastic coffee, the location, with its narrow-cobbled stone alleyway, its mix of late 19th and early 20th-century red-brick and cream- plastered terrace buildings and its wrought-iron lampposts, it could not have been a better backdrop to read journals from the same period. Add to that Michel's French accent and award-winning crêpes and you have urban Melbourne escapism at its best. The bonus was its protection from the weather. Narrow streets offer little direct sunlight in the heat of Summer and outside heaters are more than ample to brighten bleak rainy Winter days.

As the sky closed in with clouds, while the hidden sun forced streaks of gold through the cracks, my thoughts drifted back to Mother and Gran and me, and those last weeks in Paris.

Paris, the place where, for a while, even the loss of Dida and Nana seemed to diminish.

* * *

Even though my apartment in Paris was a one-bedroom, after the funeral I wanted Gran to stay with me. My couch was big and comfy enough to support two or three weeks of my weight on it.

Gran, who'd never been to France before, quickly recognised what drew me to, and kept me in Paris. And even though our reason for being together was sad, I longed to show her all the sights, and not just the tourist stuff, but the quiet little streets and the hidden places that only the locals knew. There was the Art Deco store with cranberry-coloured glass perfume bottles and King George V silver. Or the little restaurant I frequented, walking distance to the Moulin Rouge. From the outside, during the day, it was nothing more than an open window to the public, selling an assortment of specialties. But to the knowledgeable few, at night it turned into the best place in town to get foie gras prepared with softened baked apple slivers, white bean puree and divine sweet wine. An indulgence for all the senses in a room crammed full, with only twelve odd people seated and served by a happy husband waiter and an even happier wife chef. It was a place where you were treated as family. You weren't expected to eat quickly, and I don't think there was on offer a single bottle of wine under fifty Euros, yet it was always worth every mouthful, every sip, and every Euro.

Even though it was late January, it felt more like Autumn than Winter, though nothing could disguise the bleakness. Lifelessness surrounded us. From barren trees to dull streetlights, to the pursed-lipped pouts of the others brave enough to challenge Winter. There's no protection in the chill Winter. Although I was normally fond of colder weather, I longed for sunny days again.

After almost two weeks and several calls from Maurice to check on us, Gran hinted she should return home. I was reluctant to see her go. Gran was all that remained of any semblance of a family. Gran must have felt my loneliness too. "Marica," she asked one morning as we munched on fresh pastries on my balcony as the fog lifted over the rooftops. "Have you given thought to what you will do next?"

I hadn't. I didn't want to. I wanted the world to stand still just for a while.

"Easter falls at the end of March this year," she said.

"Dear, we must talk about what to do now that-"

"-Mother's dead?"

Gran didn't answer.

"Do you mean now that I'm all alone?"

"Not so much alone as, perhaps, lonely?"

Gran knew I loved Easter. During lunch, she brought up Easters spent with Nana Marguerite and Dida Nik, and I must admit the memories were a pleasant reprieve from several months in death's shadow.

"Do you remember, Marica, before your Dida Nik passed away, how it was at Easter time?"

Gran was hatching something.

"I don't know where the two of you found the motivation, every Good Friday, to rise before 5am just to go fishing!"

Gran had me.

I was now invested in the memory so much that I shouted, "Well, it was such fun!"

With the memory of Dida rubbing his whiskers I said, "The day always began before daylight had kissed the sky." The day before, Dida prepared fishing rods and worms. Good Friday was a family fishing day. Each year Dida found a new place, I'm sure of it, and we'd spend the day fishing, and he and Nana would tell me stories about Dad. I'm sure that's why I wanted to learn to fish, to be close to Dad, or like Dad, or know Dad, or something.

"Without fail we got home before lunch, do you remember?"

Gran seemed almost as invested in my memories as I was.

"I don't recall a time when I didn't know how to scale and clean a fish! Still, delicious as Nana's fish was, we had to FAST! There were so many things we couldn't eat and all the while the delicious mouth-watering aroma of roasting pork tempted me."

"That's right!" interrupted Gran. "Your Dida kept to fasting on Good Friday, didn't he?"

"Yes, we all did. Well not Mother, but Nana, Dida and me. No meat, no dairy only vegetables and fish.

"After lunch, I'd go out to play. Returning inside just at the very moment when Nana's roast pork came out of the oven, cooling for Easter Sunday breakfast and lunch. *Torture!*" The pork needed to cool down before being put in the fridge. No! Even the sizzling fat and juices from the pan, all saved, for another day – not that day – *More torture!*"

Gran laughed.

She suggested we go for a walk around the parkland surrounding the Sacré Coeur and as we walked Gran admired the lovely gardens, which, even in the Winter, looked stunning. Gran made comments and I nodded with several "Uhum" and "yes, lovely." But my mind was still back in Melbourne, Australia before Mother, Nana and Dida all died. The only time in my life I could recall having what was even close to a family home.

* * *

Good Friday, late afternoon, TV time. Not for Nana, it was full-production biscuit baking time. She was like a robot. We never had less than a dozen types of biscuits, all made from scratch and all melt-in-your-mouth deliciousness. Was not the smell of yummy roast pork enough? Clearly not.

Me, muddling through the remainder of the day, listening to my stomach rumble and churn, wondering if God really would punish me if I stole one, a single a biscuit, one, sweet-smelling cinnamon and ginger biscuit treat; just one. But Nana went from friend to security guard, sealing and locking away all the biscuits, and cakes.

* * *

Gran touched my arm as she pointed to the steps up to the Sacré Coeur. She wanted to climb to the top, but they were steep. Instead, we found a seat at the café opposite with a good view of the two-level ornate carousel. With the fog lifted, the clear day encouraged more people than usual to tempt Winter's bleakness, with the laughter of happy children playing, warming like Spring. Even sounds in the Winter were different; perhaps it was the lack of leaves. Voices echoed and twirled around buildings, clattering together to form a sort of invisible force.

Gran, keen as mustard to have the opportunity to speak French to French people, marched into the café to order our drinks as I drifted back to memories of Easter's Past. Recalling how Nana's house smelt more and more delicious. I was sure I could see swirls of caramel over Nana's house and I did not doubt how real gingerbread houses smelt.

"Well, I must say, it's such a treat to hear perfect French," said Gran as she shuffled into the seat beside me.

I just grinned.

"What is it?"

"I was just remembering how I'd come into your room at first light on Easter Sunday morning shouting, 'It's Easter, Gran. It's Easter Sunday!'"

Gran chuckled. "What are you talking about? You never just came into my room, you roared in. And you squirmed and wriggled for the rest of the morning, making a complete nuisance of yourself until we finally made our way to Nana's."

"Those few Easters, I was happy, safe. Shame it was only for a few years."

Gran was determined to make it to the top of the Sacré Coeur steps, but I insisted we use the glass tram. Moments later we were inside the beautiful dome just as one of the numerous daily Masses was finishing. I whispered to Gran to wait as we were about to be given a real treat.

Gran pointed as a group of nuns appeared from a side door, "What happens here?"

"Shh, just listen."

I honestly believe no place could you feel closer to God than when those nuns started to sing. Their voices were so enchanting and dreamlike, and the acoustics of the dome carried their music to every podium and every wooden seat. Adults and children were equally touched. Fifteen minutes later we were outside, looking over the entirety of Paris from the highest vantage point, a hazy Eiffel Tower sketched in the distance.

As we made our way back down by the same tram, Gran said, "You know, weather like this makes me think of your Dida's Pear Brandy Liquor – Kruškovac."

"Oh, you're so right!"

"Well, Dear," added Gran, "We French may have champagne, but I became quite partial to Dida's Kruškovac, and," Gran chuckled, "It had some kick to it."

I laughed. "Do you know, to this day I can still recall the recipe for Kruškovac. It's imprinted on my brain."

As Gran and I made our way back, the smell of something sweet, prompted Gran to say, "Do you remember, the cakes, they just kept coming. Your Nana could whip up a storm of sweet-treats!" Nana had the skill and devotion of a master pâtissier.

With my apartment around the corner, even at Gran's tourist-pace stroll, it took less than five minutes before we were both crammed into the suitably small 1920s lift.

That evening Gran and I feasted on what was a poor facsimile of Nana's Easter Sunday suppers.

"Arrh!" Someone bumped my shoulder with his oversized computer bag, and I was shocked back to my seat in the café. The villain in question sat behind me, two tables up, no apology or even mild acknowledgement of my shoulder's existence. I tried to stare him into an apology, but he looked through me as though I didn't exist. I was tempted to wish a hex on him, but if you'd seen him, you'd agree someone had beaten me to it.

I'd seated myself outside so that I wouldn't miss Ilija, just in case he thought it was a different café since there are so many in Hardware Lane. I watched the passing parade. Very serious looking blue, black, and grey-suited men clinging to smart-phones while staring at their pacing steps. And pencil-skirted, stiletto-heeled women, some clutching Prada bags or puppies, or puppies in Prada bags, while others grappled with takeaway lattes and phones, and anonymity.

The business crowd was, thankfully, also punctuated with the odd *Nouveau-Grunge* and a spattering of Emo-Goths. They were kind-of cool. I looked down at my casual garb. Grey shirt, blue jeans, black sunnies and sneakers, and I wished I had their flare for visual dramatics.

When I looked up again, there he was!

Christ, I'm pathetic.

At a guess, I'd say he'd have been mid-to late twenties and tall, did I mention I like tall? He seemed a full head above everyone else. His hair, now free to bob with his steps, was as dark as his bushy eyebrows, with a slight unkempt wave. I watched his bounce-like stride. All he needed was a well-placed tattoo and a bass guitar, and he'd be perfect.

He was hot. Some might say too pale. Not me, I preferred pale. I'm pale, the sun was never my friend and I'd become quite disillusioned with it. I knew we needed the sun, but the sun and I had a true love/ hate relationship which usually ended in blistered skin the shade of boiled crab-claws.

Ilija waved as he got closer, and I gulped away a slight flutter. Ilija possessed that irresistible sexy-dirty-hot-look. The one which suggested he was a little wild and makes women swoon as they imagined they could be the one to tame his restlessness and yet also secretly desiring never to quite tame it. *Bad-boy-needs-saving.* It was in his walk, his smile and within the snow-crystal-like flecks, dancing in his stormy eyes.

I got up and suggested we go inside. As we took a four-seat table to ourselves, Ilija dropped his backpack into the spare seat and slumped into his own. A slight waft of pleasant-smelling cologne prickled my nostrils.

Oh! His cologne; sandalwood and...vanilla? No, it was something else. That familiar aroma played with my memory. He was light-handed with his cologne, enough to notice, not too much to offend. He was the first man, *ever*, whose aftershave I loved. Most made me gag, this one made me melt.

I could instantly see how much more at ease he was away from his boss. This only made him more attractive. After ordering two massive mugs of coffee, Ilija and I wasted no time in getting back to the journals. Though, it was not as easy as I'd anticipated. I couldn't get over the difference in his mannerisms when removed from ugly-shirt-boss. For one thing, he smiled a lot more. We continued to speak Croatian between us.

The next few journal instalments, though interesting, were not noteworthy enough to mention, however, then we read:

24th July 1914

These past two weeks have seen Papa's personality change so much, that is when we are even able to see him, and, last night I overhead Mamma and Papa arguing. I wish I knew over what but I can guess. It's this war; this

73

war that everyone says we must be part of, that everyone says is necessary; but how can it be necessary? How is killing good or right?

After church, I heard the old men whispering that God will be on our side, but this makes no sense to me at all? Is our God not the same God as the Germans? Is it not the one and same God of all? And if we are all His children, is it possible that God has favoured children? And loves Russians more than Germans? Or are German mothers and fathers saying the same to their children?

Or is this a bigger Cain and Abel? Brother against brother while God watches his children kill each other? What frightens me more is the good brother died and the evil one lived.

I cannot talk about this to the Big Pair for they only scold me and Maria, Oh silly, beautiful Maria, she has become too boy-crazy to make any common sense at all.

Dear God, why can't you just make the Germans go home?

It is only with you, Madame Diary, that I don't mind sharing.

Although neither of us had any idea who or what *Big Pair* was, the rest of the entry was very telling. A young girl, perhaps twelve to fourteen years old, could not understand how planned killing could be a solution to world peace.

There was no getting away from the simplistic train of thought, but it did get to the heart of biblical doctrine. How can anyone who believes in one God of all, also believe God could support a war of brother against brother?

After the page was translated, Ilija jumped in with an idea. "Why don't you create a spreadsheet and record dates and names and so on?

"We already have terms like "big pair' as well as names like the Frenchman Gilliard and a sister called Maria. And we also know that they must have been quite religious," added Ilija. "They have mentioned God, the Bible and church several times so religion plays a big part in their lives."

The next instalment was very eye-opening as it included a small painting and some critical information:

28th July 1914

Oh, what a day! What a wonderful, wonderful day!

Maria and the Big Pair could not stop looking at the soldiers, but I could not stop looking at the tremendous dancing and riding Cossacks. Are they not surely the most brilliant of all of Russia's Imperial Army!

And we were all together, all of us, Baby, the Big Pair, us two and Mamma and Papa and even Papa's own Mamma in her jewels and feathered hat, how elegant she looked. Thank goodness it wasn't too windy or else she might have lost her feather.

Oh, what a laugh it would have been to watch the soldiers scurry about after Grand-mamma's feather, though nothing could be more exciting than the riders, sword in one hand, reins in the other, dagger held between their teeth, riding as wild-things possessed!

Papa sat with General Pavel most of the day but at least he smiled, and it was a real smile. Baby smiled too. It felt like an early birthday party for Baby.

God is good today.

"Marica, look at this drawing. This little artist has drawn from her memory. Look at the detail, the rider in full gallop, the horse sweating. This is a watercolour of someone who was trained."

Ilija looked at me. "Your little authoress has tutors and tutors cost money." He shook his head. "She is wealthy and ..."

"And?"

"And, I don't know what to say, this is no ordinary young lady? The reference to jewels and fashion, they were well off."

I quickly Googled the name 'General Pavel' and came up with several options, so Ilija suggested adding the absolute of 1914. The result shocked us. The best possible match was the Russian General Pavel Rennenkampf whose First Army invaded Eastern Prussia in a full-scale offensive on August 17th, 1914. August 17th Gregorian calendar.

If this was the same General Pavel then the author of this journal was linked, at least through the army, to the Russian Tsar, the Imperial Army and God only knows what else.

Michel brought us refills, giving me the first opportunity to introduce Ilija to Michel. I figured if we were going to use Michel's café as our meeting place then they should at least be properly introduced. Gran would've been pleased to know I did sometimes follow social protocol.

When Michel wandered off to serve the next table, Ilija pulled out a packet of cigarettes. He offered me one.

"I do occasionally have a cigarette, but I don't think I need one today, my head is already spinning."

As a casual smoker, I was not immune to the pleasures of a cigarette, but not without at least two or three glasses of wine. I didn't admit to anyone the secret stash I kept for emergencies.

Ilija got up to smoke outside. I watched him puff away and wondered if his mouth would taste of coffee or cigarettes. I willed him not to taste of cigarettes. Stale cigarettes triggered memories of Uncle Steve and those thoughts had no place here. I focused on the aroma of the coffee.

With Ilija finishing his smoke outside, Michel walked over. "Your new friend seems interesting," he said in his strong French accent. "You are good friends?" He asked.

I shrugged.

"Oh? *Quelle surprise.* You look very close. And very good together, *non?*" Feeling my cheeks burn, I blushed at the suggestion and quickly focused on the almost empty coffee cup, causing Michel to chuckle, which only made my face burn more crimson.

Ilija drew on his cigarette one last time before stubbing the butt in an ashtray and making his way back into the café.

We continued with the journal entries.

30th July 1914

It was Baby's birthday today.

I feel so sorry for him.

For almost a year he had planned his party. "I will be in double digits" he repeated time after time as each month rolled closer. And now all his wonderful planning, his expectations of laughter, presents, a house full of guests, music and Cossack dancing are for naught. No one talks of anything but this awful war.

"That's a birthday. Did you add that to the spreadsheet?"
I nodded.

Papa insists there is nothing to concern ourselves about, but we read the paper and we all hear the whispers - the Germans are not backing down as Papa said they would. And now talk of weapons, recruiting and strategy fill our home.

Baby's party has no-one but Monsieur Gilliard, nanny Derevenko, our sweet Doctor and his wife, Grand-mamma and us. Not a single Godfather, not even his favourite Cossacks. Papa says they could not be spared as they were either already at the front or are in training...all those strong handsome riders not even one week ago are now marching; perhaps toward their deaths.

"Did you add?"
"Yes, I added the name Derevenko."

How can God be so cruel as to make Baby so fragile and deny him so many pleasures? If there is a God.

Mamma put on baby's favourite necklace, the one with all the rubies. Baby loves to see Mamma's skin and eyes offset with sparkling rubies and I must say, the Big Pair looked ever so pretty today as did Maria; though no soldiers to flirt with or impress.

Happy Birthday, Baby – my wish to you, that your next birthday is a day of fun, cakes and playing games and no war, never war again.

God, please, if you are there and you can hear me, please let Papa be right. Please let the war be over by Christmas and bring my uncle home to us, safe. Please let me again be allowed to love granny. Please.

As I typed Ilija's translation, I felt a little ill. This young girl, so desperate for her normality to return. I understood her need for normality. I didn't understand war but I understood fearing the loss of a happy life.

I was drained and so was Ilija.

"Add that 'baby' is fragile," instructed Ilija.

I was glad he reminded me as I'd almost forgotten.

Then we read the next entry:

4th August 1914

The war is real now.

Russia is at war with Germany.

Granny is now the enemy of Grand-Mamma.

My great-uncle is no longer my relative.

Papa called us all into the great room and sat us down to tell us what was happening. "Today, General Pavel Rennenkampf's First Army has invaded under the orders of General Sukhomlinov."

Papa wanted to lead from the front but was persuaded otherwise. I think perhaps Mamma was the most persuasive. Uncle Nikolai is going in his place. As Papa is sure the war will not last long he told us to expect our uncle back by Christmas.

Papa says our army is too strong, too mighty and will force the Germans back in one sweep as we are already more than one million soldiers strong. "And when the recruiting starts, there will be many millions more."

I did not want to question Papa but, why would we need more soldiers if we are already strong enough?

I think perhaps Papa is lying just a little to protect Mamma.

I connected with this young girl, baffled at how quickly her life had spun off its axis. Doubting her faith, watching her beloved Imperial Army set off to war as her father wished he could join them. It must have felt as though her world was imploding. Like me in so many ways, after Nana and Dida died, and Mother moved to Brittany.

Ilija sighed and I flinched. "She must have been completely afraid," I said.

"I am not surprised your authoress started this journal. She needed someone to confide in. Her journal became her secret friend."

Ilija looked at the time on my laptop. It was already past noon. As he had his English class starting at two, we both decided to order lunch and attempt a few more pages.

I flicked to the next page and asked, "When can we get together again?"

The page was short. Ilija looked it over and translated in a matter of minutes. Mostly about Maria complaining about a dress.

I flicked over to the next page.

Ilija said, "I wish we could do this more often, but I think between work and school I have every Tuesday morning and perhaps the odd Sunday, depending on other things?"

I was disappointed. One morning a week and the occasional Sunday.

"Marica?"

"Hm?"

"You know we have something very special here, don't you?"

I felt he was right but, as we started to work through the pages, I also felt a little guilt. Her words were so intimate and personal, was I intruding? Had she ever intended anyone to read them? It was odd. I felt I was betraying her in some way. But I also felt bonded to her.

Ilija said, "We cannot stop now; we need to acknowledge her story."

Part of me wasn't so certain.

Ilija touched my wrist. "Marica, if we stop now, we have already invaded her privacy, we owe it to her to at least hear her story to the end."

I didn't necessarily agree. "Why's this so important to you?"

Ilija did a kind of head rock, shoulder to shoulder. "It's fascinating. I mean, don't get me wrong, it's great to spend time with you too, but seriously, it's kind of like you've found this little hidden treasure, and well it's all a bit exciting. Like I told you, Dad worked for a time in Russia, so it's a little personal for me too. But mostly it's just the intrigue, or maybe the idea of intrigue."

I played his words in my head as I considered whether I'd be as invested if it was the other way around. I was pretty sure I wouldn't have been but then I was also pretty sure I was a little odd anyway.

"These are your journals so you can do whatever you want, but I have to say this, I think we owe her the respect to listen to her story.

"Marica, in some ways you have uncovered a kind of tome, and together we are unwrapping its treasures. We cannot take one or two treasured moments, the ones that best suit and then bury it up again, as though the rest has no value."

Ilija was still holding my wrist. I wriggled my hand free. I saw a slight flush of colour come over him as his eyes looked down to his hand and my wrist, and his fingers loosened their grip.

A second later, both sets of eyes focused on the journals. Ilija did have a point about hidden treasures. Or did he? I honestly didn't know.

"So," he said as his hand slid back to his side of the table, "Next week, 8.30am."

He reached for his wallet. He intended to pay for both of us. This would not do. I was sure I had more disposable income than him. "Let's both pay our share?"

By the look on his face, he was genuinely surprised. I quickly blurted, "I'd feel better if we each paid our share, that way we can become friends without money getting in the way." Truth be told, I intended to pay for both of us, given I'd asked him to meet me. This was the first time I'd felt a cultural clash between us.

Ilija shrugged, unconvinced, as he returned one of the notes to his wallet. Grabbing his bag, he leaned down and gave me a peck on the cheek, much to the amusement of Michel, and with only a few long strides disappeared into busy Bourke Street.

The warmth of the kiss remained long after his image drifted into the mass of the lunchtime crowd. But I knew I'd made a dreadful mistake. Ilija was from Europe. The rules were different. A man paying for a woman's meal or drink was expected, even if it wasn't a date. I'd all but buried any possibility of romance between us.

I replayed the scene in my head and each time it ended the same way. I bit my lip as I imagined what should have happened, but it still came out all wrong. *You're being an idiot!* I said to myself. I'd fucked up royally. I hoped he still wanted to translate for me.

CHAPTER 12

Easter Memories

As the Grand Prix and Labour Day long weekend both passed, I got to better know my author and my translator. Both equally fascinated me. After the bill-paying coffee fiasco, Ilija's body language changed. He remained friendly as always, but a distance now existed. And even as the romance of the journals swept us both to a place one-hundred-years-ago, the spark I thought was there seemed to have wilted for Ilija. We continued to pay our equal shares for every coffee and meal, and I continued to have fantasies.

As Easter got closer, I started to feel odd, like a sense of wrongness loomed. I put it down to memories of after Dida had died and Nana was already ill, but an ache within me was not simple loss or childhood memories.

I felt frustrated and annoyed. As I couldn't work out what the hell was wrong with me, I instead concentrated on the journals, and on repairing things with Ilija.

One bright but coolish afternoon, Ilija suggested he'd like to go to Melbourne Aquarium. "Would you mind coming with me?" I'm not sure why he didn't simply go alone but I figured it was an opportunity to further repair our friendship.

We wandered around the aquarium and talked. The conversation drifted naturally between topics of family, his and mine, and his future plans. "If I can get a real grip on some of the unique qualities of pace and syntax within the English language, it'll make me a better teacher down the track," he said. "Truth is, Dad always imagined I'd be an engineer like him. I'm just not that into the whole build-a-bridge thing."

When we got to the Mini-Minor car that had been converted into a fish-tank, complete with several schools of fish happily darting between the seats, Ilija laughed. "Dad would've loved that; he's got this thing about making something outta junk." He took several photos and then asked if I'd mind taking one of him.

"Now it's your turn," he said as he positioned me. As he moved back and forth looking for the best angle, I couldn't help but wonder what the caption of a photo with me in it, would say. A woman with three kids walked past us. Ilija asked her to take our photo. Ilija wrapped his arm around me and smiled. I'm not sure what the expression on my face looked like because next thing I knew he was poking me. "Sheesh, a smile already, it's just a photo."

I felt completely clumsy, not knowing what to do with my arms. The woman kept repeating, "Get in closer," to me, indicating with her hand to snuggle into Ilija. "Otherwise, you can't see the Mini with the fish," she added.

I finally put my arm around him and, as I was wearing almost flat sandals, my head fitted perfectly into the joint between his arm and chest. It felt good, right somehow. Ilija was squeezing me into him and I responded by hugging back. The woman took several snaps before handing back Ilija's phone and saying, "You two look really good together." She looked around and past us before adding, "No kids yet?"

I dropped my hand from Ilija's waist and blurted, "Oh, no, no, we're just friends!" As soon as the words left my mouth, I wanted to swallow them back up. My pathetic half-grin toward Ilija caused him to laugh at me.

Putting his phone back in his pocket, he thanked the woman before adding, "I tink I am nott prretty enough forr herr," and he laughed again.

The woman leaned in so that we'd both hear. "Don't bet on it." She grinned at me and added, "Have a wonderful day."

After that day we often went for walks between translating pages and talking about the author. Ilija and I would sometimes meet by the Yarra and walk up to the cathedral and over to Young & Jackson's. Ilija was fond of the famous painting of 'Chloe', but I have to question if it was for the artwork or the beauty of Chloe's nakedness. And sometimes, when some hot little bitch smiled too eagerly, I'd move closer to Ilija, staking my claim. I'm not sure if Ilija noticed. If he did, he said nothing. Truth is, if he'd made a move, I wasn't sure how I'd react. The only thing I was sure of was I didn't want anyone else to have him until I knew what I wanted. And yeah, it was wrong, but I didn't care. With him, I channelled Mother a little too much.

Our conversations crisscrossed between the journals and his plans. He'd talk about spending some time in the UK and then returning to Croatia to teach English and Russian. "Because it'll make me a better teacher if I can draw on personal experience with colloquial terms and phrases," he'd say.

My standard dazed reply would be an "Um?" In some ways, I felt guilty that I wasn't assisting him in better improving his English. We almost always spoke in Croatian now. As for my author, for now, I just continued to collect information and record the facts as they came through.

Ilija was fast becoming that person I'd call or text whenever I had news, even news which had nothing to do with the journals. Aside from his plans, I'd learned he lived on his own in a very small studio, which, as it turns out, was covered in unwashed clothes that day I suggested we meet there. I didn't believe him at first, but, after a while, when no girlfriend appeared, I guessed he was telling the truth. Either that or a one-night-stand was still sleeping it off. *Whatever.* He was officially single.

Sometimes I'd get the feeling he was about to make a move, ask me back to his place, or something, but he never seemed to act on it. I started to think it was all imagined on my part, even if Michel constantly taunted me with his looks or remarks.

On the home front, Gran and Tom were getting along exceptionally well, so much so that she invented an entire family history for him. Tom didn't mind. He became quite fond of the idea of having traced his fabricated family tree to a relative of Sir Thomas More. Why she picked Sir Thomas, only she knew. Perhaps there was a Tudor special on TV the day she created Tom's past. Gran's logic mixed with her ability to concoct stories was amusing. Though she would not have gone to so much trouble for someone she didn't like. I don't know why it hadn't occurred to me until Sir Thomas More became Tom's long lost relative, but, if she could create such elaborate lies then could she not also keep one?

I decided it was time for Gran to meet Ilija, though, for my sake, Ilija promised to keep our true reason for meeting a secret.

On second thoughts, perhaps we all kept secrets, and this was the true legacy of my family.

Of course, Gran thought it a terrible idea. "What on earth will we talk about?" she insisted. "He can speak English, can't he?"

I decided to add more lies to those already told, saying he was also taking art classes with me, hence our meeting. As it happened, Ilija's mother was a naïve artist in Croatia who worked primarily with wood, creating three-dimensional carvings which hung on walls.

"Yes, he can speak English. Goodness! Gran, if I didn't know you better."

86

Gran gave me one of her fire-and-ice stares.

"Well, you can talk art," I replied.

"Art?" demanded Gran. "What would he know of the arts?"

"His mother is an artist."

"Oh, my Dear, *saying* one is an artist and actually being a true artist are two entirely different things."

As Easter was only a few weeks away, and Ilija was alone in Australia at a very important time to Croatian Catholics, I thought it would be a nice gesture to have him join us. Besides, it gave me more reason to plan the *'Marica Easter'* as I happily called it.

I felt sure Ilija would feel home sick. Even though Gran wasn't Croatian, she had come to love Dida's traditions. Before everyone died on me, the entire family came together for Easter.

I remember with a mix of pride and bemusement how Nana and Gran held court at Eastertime. We celebrated Croatian style, while speaking French, and living in suburban Australia, and, in memory of Pop Colin, would have his bagpipes take pride of place in what was once his seat. All the while, a pot of Earl Grey, or sometimes Lady Grey, was set to infuse for tea and cakes after dinner. All this was done in a country where Easter fell in the Autumn not the Spring.

It sounded like a joke, but it was wonderful.

Those few Easters, when Nana, Dida and even Mother were all still alive, remained in my memories so strongly, that I decided we'd reinstate as many as we could of our family traditions.

I invited Ilija to join us.

The weekend before Easter, he came for Sunday lunch. At first, the conversation was stiff but Ilija possessed the kind of charisma that drew people to him. There was an innocence mixed with an understated class which I saw on that first day, and which Gran recognised. When he arrived, his hair was all bouncy and shiny, freshly washed. I wasn't sure if it was coincidence or an effort to impress Gran. Either way, my impression of him as a quasi-rocker didn't fit the clean-hair look.

After lunch, as we sipped on a glass of particularly good port, Gran said, "So, Marica, have you told this young man what adventures you have in store for him?"

She had no intention of letting me answer. "I dare say not. Well, I certainly hope you enjoy a feast because I fear if you don't you should run for safety now."

"Gran!" I demanded. "Don't scare him!"

Gran chuckled. "I should think that a strong sturdy young man can hold his own against an old woman's ramblings." She looked hard at him. "If that is all it takes to frighten him then?"

Gran surveyed Ilija's face before adding, "He seems more than ample of character to comprehend the meaning of my little attempts at humour?"

Ilija wasn't sure how much of what Gran had said was real. "I lovving to eat so in nott badd...yes?"

"I should come clean," I admitted. "Perhaps I should tell you a little story which might explain why Easter means so much to me."

"I vould lyke to hearrr."

Gran grinned as she happily refilled all our glasses and waited to for me to retell the same story I shared whenever I got nostalgic for Dida and Nana.

"As you know, everyone has times of the year which bring back the best of memories. For me it's Easter. I know most would say Christmas, and I do think Christmas is wonderful, but I prefer my Christmas with snow. I mean, let's face it. Christmas in Australia, I don't know what's worse, soaring temperatures making big, rich, roast-dinner meals unpalatable, or the swarms of flies ensuring the great Aussie salute remains alive, or sweaty armpits and skin that smells of sun-block."

Ilija stopped me. "You vill be saluting Orssies?" He had no idea what that meant.

"No." I tried to correct his English and explain in one action. "It's a saying because there are so many flies in Australia that swiping them from your face is like an official salute."

He laughed. "Oh, vell, is good to know, you know?"

"Easter, whether it's in Spring or Autumn, is great, no matter where you live. Yes, chocolate eggs and whatnot, but also so much more."

I took a sip of my port as Gran said, "You must admit, Easter is much more about family than Christmas, all tradition and not about presents."

"Just before I started high school we moved in with Dida and Nana. I don't remember Dad but with Dida Nik, Dad lived in him and me. Those were some of the happiest days of my life. Dida Nik was such a character, always singing and making stupid jokes, which were funny because they weren't. And Nana was such a lady. And she learned how to combine the best of her French and Dida's Croatian culture into this magical festive day.

"So, the Thursday before Easter Sunday was the day set aside for egg-painting. Weeks before, Nana saved onion skins. The brown ones were the best, but the red ones also worked well. Early Thursday morning, Dida and I would go out into the garden to collect small leaves, while Mother brought out several pairs of their torn pantyhose, which was her contribution.

"You see, Nana's coloured eggs had become somewhat famous in the neighbourhood. At Easter time, more people than normal popped in for a coffee, particularly our Australian friends. We all knew why they were there. As the neighbours touched and caressed each egg, admiring unique leaf patterns stencilled on each shell, Gran poured coffee, or tea, from porcelain pots into Wedgwood cups and passed them to eager hands, always accompanied with a cake-plate and linen serviette.

"On the table, with the ochre, amber, or chestnut- brown coloured eggs, sat at least one three-tier platter, piled high with an assortment of cakes. Sweet homemade biscuits filled with aromatic silk-like fillings that glistened and tempted."

Ilija leaned forward, picked up the port bottle, gestured to Gran, who happily accepted the re-fill, and did the same to me before filling his own and saying,

"I know dis ting vit da cakes, my madder's cakes, hum!"

"Nana always prepared a small sample set of sweet-treats for drop-ins. So many varieties, some flavoured with nuts, others laced with alcohol and still others with caramel or secret treats inside. Many formed to resemble little mini fruits. My favourite was peach-looking ones. It took hours. And so many other varieties.

"And we always dyed extra eggs to give to the neighbours, so no one left the house without a plate of Nana's biscuits and a few select coloured eggs. It was so magical, and everyone, even Mother, was happy."

I stopped babbling and looked at a bemused Ilija and a proud Gran. A flush of crimson blush heated my face. "I thought it would be nice to have a tribute to our old Easter tradition?" My face must have been the colour of beetroot as I considered how childish I must have sounded.

Gran grinned. "Well, Marica, after that cake and painted eggs story you'd better brush up on your Nana's recipes!" she joked.

Ilija filled my glass and winked at me, which helped dissipate the heat in my face. It was going to be a good Easter and I felt certain my Dad, Dida, Nana and Pop Colin were all watching with a smile. Maybe even Mother. I knew she too loved Easter.

CHAPTER 13

The truth about Maurice

A few days before Easter I went shopping. I'd promised a traditional Croatian Easter and now I was going to have to either eat my words or do my best to replicate my Easter memories. Gran, out of respect for me and for the memory of Dida and Nana, agreed to fast with me on Good Friday. That meant a visit to the fishmongers as well.

As I drove Gran's car, the one she bought just after Mother left for Brittany, it occurred to me how strange it was that I, born in Australia, was now driving here on an international licence. The gearstick, the steering wheel and the traffic were all on the wrong side of the road. Even the traffic lights were wrong, set so high. What numbskull thought lights so high up was a good idea anyway?

Although I was still becoming accustomed to driving in Melbourne, I have to say that the streets of Paris and Parisian drivers prepare you for anything!

But at least the streets, and especially the parking spots, in Melbourne were easier than Paris. No need to gently nudge or even bump the car in front, there was room enough for everyone.

And although I didn't own a car in Paris, whenever I visited friends or Mother and Maurice, I'd hire a car in preference to catching a train. Trains were cheaper and the train service in France was excellent, however, it didn't option unexpected stops or last-minute drop-ins. Like my friend Arnaud, who lived in Paris, while his family had a 34-hectare property in Cognac, where, as you'd expect, they grew Cognac grapes. The family property was more than three hundred years old. The house, a grey-stone long building with its low ceilings and massive fireplaces, was as welcoming as his family.

The property was stunning. Half was planted with grapes while the other half was a mix of rolling valleys marked with hedgerows, interrupted by wild passages of woodland and happy little creeks.

Or my other friend Marie-Christine, whose family lived on the French-Swiss border in a traditional Swiss-chalet style house, complete with masses of exposed beams, rendered walls and pretty flower boxes, all this and a view of Mont Blanc from their balcony. My January/February week-long stays with Marie-Christine resulted in my becoming a fair skier. Not great, but not bad either. It also resulted in me seeing what a real family looked like.

One year I and another student, whom I met in a history class, decided to make a long weekend into a week-long stay, first in Nice and then to Monaco – the land of Princess Grace! That was also my experimental week. She was openly gay, and I was openly distrustful of men. With her, I had sex with emotion attached. It was the first and only time I'd experienced anything close to sex and love together.

Though I knew I wasn't gay, I was in desperate need of love. I owed a lot to her even if I didn't ever tell her. Our relationship, or affair, or fling, I'm unsure what to call it, lasted past that week. I ended it, just as I'd ended every sexual encounter. Though this time, I hurt someone who deserved better. People do get attached, and sometimes you lose a great friend for the sake of a night or two of lust, and intimate company. Sometimes you lose a little bit of self-respect too.

Gran's car was almost ten years old but hadn't even clocked 50,000KM. She rarely drove and when she did, it was mainly around the local area. I often questioned why she'd buy a new car well into her 70s. I was starting to suspect this car was always intended for me, perhaps for my eighteenth.

Victoria Market.

Stallholders shouting, row after row of vegetables, the seemingly boundless numbers of delis and freshly baked bread and meat and fish, it brought it all back. Strangers nudging me as we all crammed to be served. Stallholders yelling words my then young ears could not comprehend, but Nana could. The smell of smoked pork sausage and pickled cabbage mixed with pastries and fresh coffee. It was as though I was fourteen again.

Thankfully not much had changed at the Market. Stallholders here valued their place, handed down from generation to generation, each unique stall making up the tapestry that was the Queen Victoria Market. And I loved it.

I quickly moved between the merchants and the hordes, recalling the stalls Nana went to, knowing instinctively which sausage to ask for. It almost felt as though she was still with me. I gave in to the craving and treated myself to Vic Market doughnuts and coffee before returning to my car.

A strange feeling started creeping up from somewhere deep. I'd felt its presence a day or two earlier but ignored it. Now it was much stronger.

I got in the car and it just happened.

Crying.

Uncontrollable crying.

Me. Alone. In the middle of the Queen Victoria Market car park. In the middle of the city with the smell of fish, fried foods and fresh bread, everything about those few years of happiness came flooding back and the release was a torrent of tears. In the middle of preparing to re-live some of the best memories of my life, I was miserable.

Back then the world made sense, and the love around me was real. When I was genuinely happy, with Nana Marguerite and Dida Nik, and with Gran visiting almost every day. When I was safe. It all came exploding from within.

* * *

Being a heavy smoker all his life, Dida was already suffering the effects of emphysema when Mother and I moved in with them, though no one told me. Everything was hidden from me. I had no idea where Dida Nik found the energy for our 5am fishing trips. His love for me was greater than his pain, I guess.

Within two years, the emphysema was playing host to another disease; cancer. It was much more ravenous. The Autumn I turned fifteen was the last Easter fishing trip Dida Nik made. That Winter I wept.

For the funeral, Nana decorated the house in Croatian flags and photos of Dida as a young Legionnaire. He looked so handsome. Just like Dad, or was it that Dad looked like him? Well, they were identical, except the eyes. Dida Nik's were a dark steel-blue and Dads were hazel-green.

At the age of seventeen, Dida Nik fled the communist regime of the former Yugoslavia, rather than succumb to the forced conscription into the Serbian army. Many Croatian men did the same, and, without language or completed formal education, crossed the border into Austria and then down to France, eventually finding a new home and family within the French Foreign Legion. After a career filled with awards, Dida became a French citizen, soon after meeting Nana. Just before the uprising in 1972, Nana and Dida, with their four-year-old son, emigrated to Australia.

I remember it so clearly. Everyone cried uncontrollably, even Gran, at Dida's loss. Everyone except Mother. Not a single tear. It made me wonder if she refused pain the luxury of winning or if she truly felt so little for others. Even then, right after Dida's death, I think I knew my haven was eroding. Nana followed Dida less than eighteen months later. I was barely sixteen and already four members of my immediate family had left me.

At Nana's wake, the only sense of disappointment Mother seemed to show was for the lack of decent food on offer. "Look at this," she whispered. "Why did they not simply just provide soggy sandwiches and cold sausage rolls?"

I was ashamed for her. "Must you be the centre of all attention, even at a funeral, even at *this* funeral?" I demanded in an angry whisper.

"Really, Marica," she'd proclaimed with feigned interest and a cocked brow. "When will you realise the world is made up of that which happens and that which can be avoided. Death happens, poor catering *can* be avoided."

Cold. Oh good God, how cold she was!

"I would appreciate if you didn't speak right now," I said as I clenched my fists and my stomach. The distance between Mother and me was tangibly evident. I'm sure I loved her; I just didn't like her and rarely respected her.

"Must you persist in this taciturn attitude?" she asked.

I didn't reply, I was too busy looking at the genuine sadness, the sincere tears from everyone, even Gran, everyone except Mother. She by this stage, had moved on to non-verbal commentaries on how the other mourners were dressed, rolling her eyes and doing the 'half-point' at what she perceived as bad fashion sense, using either her prayer-book or a below standard canapé as a pointer.

She was my mother and I loved her, and, in her way, I think she loved me, but her total lack of consideration frightened me. No, it was more than that, it was as though she was devoid of human compassion, yet she understood what compassion was when she required it to be directed at her, or when she manipulated it for her advantage. You see, Mother was too busy to even pretend to cry. During the service she'd noticed someone of interest and now, here was her target again, in Nana's house, commiserating with some of Nana's friends. A tall, still handsome stranger in a very well-cut dark-grey suit, perhaps in his late-forties, who seemed to have come alone.

"Come." Mother's hand grabbed me with the force of a mugger. We went into her bedroom, where she set about selecting a more appropriate dress to change into, one that flattered her still perfect figure, and showed a glimpse of her cleavage, while still befitting the proper dress for a wake. Her new uniform was a pencil-thin dress in gunmetal grey with a slight ruffle of fabric on both the V-line neck and just above the knee. She teamed this with a stretchy (read hugging) jet-black cardigan, black tights, and black boots with killer heels. The heels served a dual purpose. Not only sexy as hell but, given her natural stature and the addition of a heel, she could easily measure her prey's height when standing beside him.

"Do you think my make-up needs retouching?" she asked.

"What for? It's not as though you've shed a tear or even sweated a drop of pain or anxiety."

"Hush!" I understood Mother's tone, she did not need to finish with, *you stupid girl.*

When Mother morphed into Huntress, her eyes changed colour. No longer their usual crystal blue, they seemed to become opaquer with a violet hue reminiscent of a young Elizabeth Taylor. In fact, in many ways Mother resembled the 1950's icon, same alabaster skin, same feline sex appeal and enchanting eyes.

As I watched, Mother puckered, pressed, smudged and tissue-blotted her lips in dark crimson-red, before repeating. Echoes of her motherly advice to me as a teenager drifted in my mind.

I don't know why you are so intent to ignore your God-given gifts, she'd say. *Yes, you could be a stiletto-heel taller, blame your Nana for that corrupted gene, but still you have more than a passable figure, decent skin and lips most plastic surgeons only dream of replicating...*

I watched Mother continue to preen and pat her hair and neck and lips, especially her lips. *Lips are essential,* she'd say to me, *a snug skirt, large sunglasses, well-chosen hat and plump velvet-red lips can get a woman almost anything.*

She blotted one last time, ensuring she'd added enough colour to leave a planned branding on her victim's cheek. There were other single middle-aged women there; she wanted ownership tattooed as soon as possible.

"I knew I should have dyed my hair for today!"

Her mock self-scolding was designed for my reply of *you look beautiful* but I couldn't bring myself to play that day. "Yes, I agree, funerals are such great places to meet new men." I paused for effect. "And you have a captive audience."

I waited for her response, but she wasn't playing. "As funeral social protocol necessitates, he'll stay for a minimum respectful period, mustn't miss an opportunity to prance and pounce, right?" I added.

All the reply I got was her left cocked eyebrow reflected in the mirror. But I was on a roll. "You really must make best of your ensnared prey. What do you think is the acceptable obligatory period for a stranger to remain at a funeral wake?"

Gran may have argued that their eyes were a different shade, however, no one could argue they wielded their ice-stare with equal impact. I saw Mother's eyes blacken. "What do you think will become of us if I do not secure our future!"

I wanted to scream, *you could get a job, we could remain here in Nana's house and live like normal people,* but there was absolutely no point in arguing with Mother when she had a man in her sights, and I did not want to turn Nana's wake into a yelling match, so I said nothing.

"Oh, give me that!" She dislodged the atomiser I'd been playing with.

"Ouch," I muttered at the force with which she wrenched it from me.

"You're hopeless! Can't you see?" She rolled her eyes. "Can't you see we must be rid of this place?"

"Nope," I snapped, with as much indignation as I could muster. Though I marvelled at her self-belief. For all her faults and shortcomings, self-confidence was not one of them. While most women her age were becoming concerned that men who were their contemporaries were now chasing women closer to my age, mother knew her strengths and played to them. And men, whether younger or older, were still unable to resist her charms. While women, younger or older, were unable to eclipse them. Even as I dismissed her pursuit of a man as superficial, I admired her confidence.

She swung back to look at her reflection again as she said, "Marica, women have few virtues which all men value, and a sharp mind and quick tongue are not necessarily two of them."

She added a sweep of blush to each cheek before adding, "And while I still have what they want, I will take what I need from them."

"What's the French equivalent for skank?"

"The French are not so dull as to need a word for 'skank' and frankly I would have thought you better informed also."

With admirable dexterity, Mother pushed the mascara brush in and out before removing the excess and brushing her already jet-black lashes, then drawing back her view from the mirror before leaning in, her nose almost kissing her own reflection. If I wore that much mascara I would either end up with those ugly black gluggy clumps in the corners of my eyes or Panda-eyes. Once, I managed to stab my eye with the brush.

"Do you think I should add more liner?"

She was aware she looked stunning, but vanity had always risen above cleverness in Mother. She was beautiful. She knew it, I knew it, and everyone knew it, though this never stopped her canvassing for compliments. And she seemed to require confirmation more and more often. Perhaps she was coming to realise time was indeed running out? Perhaps, when standing naked and alone in the bathroom, the evidence was all too clear. Alone, with her artillery, maybe she'd noticed that her greatest assets were falling victim to gravity and discolouration. A tell-tale sliver of silver among a mane of golden-brown locks made everything so much more desperate. Or perhaps I was creating a depth of character which didn't exist because she was my mother and I needed reasons to love her unconditionally.

She rose from her seat, patted her dress free of creases and, with the skill of Mata Hari and pheromones of a doe rabbit, she lingered at the top of the stairs until her intended victim looked up. Although I had inherited many of her features, except her eyes, I didn't inherit her predatory nature. Or perhaps I did, but after seeing Mother stalk each next victim, the hunt repulsed me.

Once her prey's gaze belonged to her, she began her descent, emphasizing each hip swing by crisscrossing her legs down the steps. I defy anyone to attempt this without looking down or falling. She could. And there was no denying, even as her fortieth birthday had rolled around, more than once, she still possessed the skin tone and figure of women half her age.

That's how Maurice became my fourth father figure.

CHAPTER 14

Mother

Maurice was a distant relative of Nana's and, as luck would have it, was in New Zealand on holiday when news came of Nana's death. Feeling it only appropriate, given the proximity of Melbourne and the South Island, Maurice flew over for Nana's funeral. Within a month of Nana's death, Mother had left me with Gran while she got to know Uncle Maurice better in France.

As Nana and Dida's only grandchild, the family home was my inheritance. Nana Marguerite, it seems, was cleverer than Mother had given her credit for, ensuring the property remained in trust until my thirtieth birthday. Everyone knew Mother's taste for the good life. Nana had more than once shouted lines like, "I know you'll probably buy yourself a fancy Ferrari or something just as pointless, with the sale of this house, when I die."

As fate would have it, Mother found Maurice and didn't need Nana's house to ensure her future. They were married in Brittany, without me there. Six months later, I was again ripped from my home.

* * *

Looking back, now, here in my car, with tears stinging my skin as much as the memories stung my perception of everything a loving parent should be, I felt more certain than ever that there was no need for Mother to pull me from Gran. She did it because she could. She could have at least waited until I finished high school. I could have visited her in France. Perhaps if I had, our relationship might have been better, distance making the heart growing fonder and all that.

Mother wanted to impose her power, and in doing so forced me to abandon the hope of a family. I guess I hadn't realised it earlier, because I didn't want to. Perhaps part of me also wanted to believe Mother couldn't be without me.

Given I could speak French, the transition was relatively smooth. And even though Maurice and I were never close, he was a good man who seemed to genuinely love Mother.

My first few years in Brittany were not exactly perfect. There is a chasm of difference in understanding French learned from a grandparent and knowing enough for school studies. The only thing that kept my grades reasonable was the timing of the school year. By the time I began school in Brittany, I was close to finishing the same school year in Australia.

In truth, I don't have negative memories of Brittany. Between the lovely beaches and stunning countryside dotted with mills and flooded with postcard picture-perfect valleys, you would be hard-pressed to find a more captivating place. However, I was a teenager, wrenched from her friends and school, dragged to the other side of the world, and I felt disjointed and orphan-like. And quite frankly, I didn't care if my langoustines were caught in the Atlantic Ocean or the Mediterranean Sea. I wanted a life with friends and parties. I wanted to get my licence and do the rites of passage every teenager in Australia does.

Things improved when I was accepted at Université Sorbonne

Nouvelle, in Paris. I quickly found new friends, other students fascinated with Australia and keen to practise their English. Initially, I moved into a student dorm. However, with savings accumulated from renting Nana's house, I had a decent nest egg with which to splash out on renting my own place. Finding my apartment would complete my transformation.

Freedom! I remember that feeling of possibilities.

So, when I happened on an apartment on Rue Livingstone, with stunning views of the Sacré Coeur in the Montmartre district, how could I say no? It even had two balconies and was furnished and came with a resident cat named Odette. Admittedly, for the first year, Odette, with her effortless disinterest, her azure blue eyes and silky grey-silver fur had more style than I did. I'm sure I saw her roll those purebred eyes more than once. Often, as I watched Odette sitting and grooming herself on the balcony, I longed for her effortless sense of regal dignity. Damn cat.

But views of the Sacré Coeur aside, it was the lifestyle that captured my heart and my imagination. Every season created its own magic. Christmas decorations and festivities the likes of which I'd never seen, all over the city and especially the Avenue des Champs-Élysées. Autumn leaves cradling each street and carpeting the entrance to the Tuileries Palace. Spring blooms at The Palace of Versailles and the extensive lush green Summer gardens peppered with fountains and extraordinary statues. Even the streetlights in Paris were works of art.

Yet it wasn't just the architecture, or the gardens and not even the history of the City of Lights. Paris had me. She became my surrogate mother, embracing me with more affection than Mother had ever demonstrated.

As I sat in the car park of Queen Victoria Market, sobbing uncontrollably in Gran's car, I had to ask myself if I'd somehow given Paris more credit than I'd realised. Embracing her as I believed she'd embraced me. Paris loved me. My new friends loved me and the men, well the men were more than a little fond of me.

It's no coincidence Frenchmen have the reputation they have. Seriously, there is no equal to a Frenchman. Not only hot but also without a skerrick of fear or shame. A Frenchman will set his mind on a woman as though she was a target and track her until his prey is within capture. Yet they seem to do this with an innate knowledge of that fine line between amorous attention and stalking.

To Frenchmen, every woman is beautiful, no matter if she is short or tall, slim, or voluptuous, blonde or brunette. With that sort of attention and mental mindset, is it any wonder French women hold themselves in such high esteem?

Now, my tears slowed to a few loose droplets.

I had it all planned out. After my thirtieth birthday, I'd sell Nana's house and buy a small apartment in Paris, or perhaps even offer to buy this one if I could afford it, teach English and be happy! I had romantic delusions of living a bohemian existence, painting the Seine, drinking coffee in Montmartre and catching the risqué shows at the Moulin Rouge. I was quite a talented water colourist and could become a private tutor to those wanting to improve their English language skills. Then fate called on me, determined to play with my emotions and life.

Drawing gasps of oxygen, I felt the last of the tears trickle down my face. From somewhere deep in my handbag, I found some clean but crinkled tissues and attempted to remove the evidence of my breakdown. Gran did not need to know.

Thankfully, I was not fond of caked-on make-up and was able to, with some swipes and careful pats, restore my face to something close to hiding evidence of crying. Well, almost everything. My eyes were still bloodshot and puffy.

Perhaps if Gran asked, I'd say I got some grit in them. Yes, yes that would work. *More lies.*

CHAPTER 15

Two Old Men and a Still

Ilija arrived with two bottles, one of champagne and the other, Kruškovac, which pleased Gran no end. No fishing trip aside, after my private breakdown I rallied myself to be happy and derived pleasure from painting eggs and preparing the lunch table. My biscuit selection was not nearly as varied as Nana's nor as visually perfect, but I was pleased with how everything looked. Gran also did her bit, baking a French-style torte, which surprised me no-end; I wasn't even sure she even knew how to turn on the oven. We started with a glass of Kruško-vac before Ilija pulled out first Gran's seat and then mine. This must have worked a treat because, after that, I couldn't stop Gran from chatting. She told many stories, some of which I'd never even heard. The walk down memory lane mixed with fine alcohol loosened Gran's memories.

Then she got to the one that always made me laugh. "Do you remember the story of the still?" she asked.

Ilija's eyes lit up as he opened the now chilled bottle of champagne. "Dis you must tell me pleazz!"

"It seems when you combine one grandfather from Scotland and another from Croatia, it is only a matter of time before a home-made still ends up in someone's backyard." Gran's smile stretched across her face.

"By the time your parents were engaged, your two grandfathers were already the best of drinking buddies; two middle-aged men getting together to drink scotch, beer, wine and Kruškovac." Gran stopped, and then added, "Well, your Pop Colin was much older but when he and that Dida of yours got together!" Gran's voice hit a note somewhere between a squeak and a shriek.

"Well," she said. "The step from drinking buddies to *illegal-owners-of-a-still* buddies was not much of a stretch.

"A friend from Dida's days in the French Foreign Legion was staying with Dida at the time. Now armed with a third, to make a troublesome trio, building the still was only half the fun. It needed testing. Besides, they already had orders far-and-wide for their homemade brew!

"So, the three alchemists were in the middle of making that Rakija – plum brandy – of your Dida's. The brewery was in full progress with its pungent fragrance permeating the entire neighbourhood. Anyone with half a brain would have known the smell. Completely distinguishable. Aside from the nasty old woman who lived to Dida's left and the nice old man who was their neighbour to the right, everyone at that time was from various parts of Europe. Most were pre-ordered customers, and the rest didn't care.

"In the backyard, between the veggie garden and the chook-pen, stood the still, in full production. By that stage, your two grandfathers had quite the local reputation for homemade spirits! That's when the knock at the door came, two young, uniformed policemen behind it.

"Well," Gran slapped her knee, "your mother went into shock, convinced we'd all be sent to prison; she remained prone to overdramatic panic to the last.

"Dida Nik, Pop Colin and Dida's friend all stood together on one side of the threshold, the two officers on the other, with me and your Nana in earshot and your mother locked in her bedroom while your father stood behind Dida Nik."

"Your father did his best to remain calm but Dida, that sly old fox, bamboozled those officers! He pretended not to understand English and what he did say, he said with the strongest accent. I swear to this day I'm not sure what he said! Your Nana and I just looked at each other and held our hands over our mouths to stop ourselves from laughing!

"And then Pop Colin jumped in... with his Scottish accent exaggerated tenfold and asked what he could do for the officers. You' have never seen two police officers looking so bewildered in your life!" Gran laughed again.

"As it turns out," Gran's voice had cheekiness to it. "They were looking for Dida's friend. It seems he hadn't paid a speeding fine and, after tracking him down to your grandparents' home, they issued him with a court order because the matter had gone so far.

"After the bewildered officers walked off, and then drove off, I don't think we ever laughed so loudly, even your mother! The officers didn't know what the smell was and put it down to 'foreigners and their weird food.' They left without asking a single question about the smell!"

As Gran told the story, I recalled reading what the ancient Greeks believed. When we talk of our loved ones departed, we bring them back to life. Perhaps there's some truth in that. Gran and I hadn't shared that story with anyone in such a very long time that it was a kind of relief to have it free again. It was obvious Ilija thoroughly enjoyed every word, chuckling often and when finished, he rubbed his eyes free of tears.

As late lunch turned to early evening, Gran offered Ilija to stay for supper, but he generously declined, wanting to return home so that he could call his parents to wish them a Happy Easter.

"But, vould liyke to tankk you forr making feel me att home, I vill neverr forrget vonderful food and the even betterr stories, must be telling today my fardder dis v-one forr still!" Ilija said graciously.

Gran, true to form and just as Nana would have done, prepared several doggie-bags, Gran style. None of this silver foil stuff for her, everything was wrapped as though Ilija was headed for 1900s picnic. "You can return the plates and containers to Marica the next time you see her," she said.

Ilija smiled his hypnotic smile, thanked Gran and joined us in one more drink before warmly hugging Gran goodbye and placing a very proper peck on my left cheek, the second warm touch of his lips on my skin.

As Ilija left, I felt more determined than ever to learn the family stories of my authoress. She had a life, a family with its traditions and rituals. Whoever she was, she deserved to have her history acknowledged and embraced.

And while I was still uncertain what to do with the knowledge, I was concluding that fate-, *oh damn you fate-*, which so often played tricks on me, was now offering me the opportunity to free the suppressed memories of someone who lived and loved and who, when WWI came, seemed to lose everything. I needed to know what happened to her. That's when another thought hit me: what if both journals were not by the same person? We knew she had siblings and family. What if someone else continued to tell her stories as Gran and I were telling Dida's?

"Well," Gran interrupted my thoughts. "I must say, your young man seems quite well raised and did you know his mother is an artist?"

Let me think, did I know Ilija's mother was an artist? Hum yep, I'm pretty sure you heard it from me. "Gran, he is not my young man, he is a friend who happens to be a young man, there *is* a difference."

"Really. How so? Tell me, Marica, is he a young man?"

I rolled my eyes. "Yes."

"And did you invite him to our Easter lunch?"

"Of course. I invited him."

"And would you agree with our party of three, the two of you were best known to each other?"

"Well, yes... but that doesn't..."

"So, as the guest who joined us on such a sacred day was not associated with me, then it falls that he was your guest, and therefore, as your guest is a young man. How else would you suggest I should have referred to him?"

"As Ilija."

"Really, Marica, why must you complicate everything? Unless there is something which you think your grandmother and only remaining living relative should know?"

I gave up and said nothing.

"Well?" she insisted.

I could've argued but there was no point. "I'll go wash up before supper."

"Very good, Dear, very good. Oh, and your sweets were quite excellent, Nana would have been proud."

As I washed the dishes, I could not get Nana's happy smile and Dida's incredible laugh out of my mind. Dida. By now he would have broken out the ukulele and be singing a traditional Croatian song. In quiet moments, when Gran and I were alone, she'd bring out old photos. Pop Colin armed with bagpipes, Dida Nik with ukulele and Nana Marguerite at her piano.

Nana stopped playing her piano when Dida died, selling it so as not to be reminded that their sing-a-longs were over. But Gran never forgot. The other night I went to bed early. Gran was already in her room. As I walked past, I heard her hum a tune. It wasn't just her humming that stopped me, but also the melody. One I'd heard many times from a piano or a ukulele. It only now occurred to me that the story of Gran dismissing Dad as *that tradesman* may have been more to do with frustrating Mother than Gran's true feelings.

CHAPTER 16

The Truth About Dad

After Ilija left, Gran had an odd look on her face. I was familiar with most of Gran's expressions but this one was new to me. She gestured to the sofa by the far wall in the sitting room and invited me to join her.

"Dear." She paused and I heard her sigh. "I think that young man has taken to you in a very deep way. I can see it in his eyes and the way he watches your every move."

I remained silent. If only she knew how little he was interested ever since the bill-paying-coffee-incident.

She sighed again. "Marica, the stories we told him today, they are stories which only connect to family or those close to us, people who knew your Dida and Nana, or people who are bonded to us and want to know more."

I wasn't sure what she was implying.

"While they are amusing and fun, even given his Croatian heritage, they could not have been nearly entertaining enough to warrant such responses from him; unless he was either falling in love with or had fallen in love with you."

I stood up. "I think you're wrong. He misses his own family and home, and the stories..." I didn't finish my reasoning because I recognised it for what it was, protesting too much.

Gran held me in my place simply with her gaze. "Deny it as much as you like, but it does not change the fact. He is enchanted by you. Like your mother, you can beguile and bewitch any creature. But unlike her, you do it unknowingly. The question therefore must be, do you feel even a little for him of what is abundantly clear he feels for you?"

"Gran," *here comes the justification*. "We've have been working very closely together. I'm helping him with his English, and we have more than one mutual interest. I think you're reading more into this than exists."

"Am I?" Sometimes Gran's questions were not questions. "Sit down, please." Adding the word 'please' made it sound like a request. I sat down at the other end of the sofa.

"And I think, perhaps there is a mutual feeling that you are doing your best to deny. So, I have to ask, why? He is someone who seems worthy of you and is your equal in character and intelligence?"

I almost fell off the sofa hearing that.

"So, why do you dismiss what is evident?"

"Gran, even if what you say is true, about how he feels about me, I mean, it's pointless. He'll be leaving Australia soon, so what is the point of trying to develop something which has no future even before it begins."

Gran huffed. "Oh for goodness sake, Marica! I am not asking you to run off and elope with him. I am suggesting you open yourself up to the possibility of happiness."

"Happiness?" I demanded. "What is happiness? From everything I've witnessed and experienced, even if you find happiness, it is so fleeting and never outweighs the price of loss. Everyone who I love dies!"

"Dear, just because your mother died young, does not mean you will."

111

"Seriously, Gran, there's Dad, Dida, Nana, Mother and then there's Pop Colin who I didn't even get to know, and what about Gran-Gran and ggYves? How can you say people don't die around me? HOW?"

Gran patted the space between us. I hesitated for a moment, but she had that stare, that glassy icy stare that I was yet to learn how to refuse. I shuffled over, trying to act indignant.

Gran put her arm around me as she said, "We all have to die. Some die too young. Sadly, in your life, there have been more than a few and many more than your fair share, but you can't stop living just because you are afraid others around you will die before you."

"And what if *my* future children die before me?"

Gran was about to try to say something, but I stood up, put my hand between us and said, "No! I will not go through more death. I'm not as strong as you. I just want things to stay the same, why can't the world stand still for a while?"

"Marica." Gran's voice was serious, and it stopped my self-loathing cold. "You can't be afraid of life, otherwise you are not alive, only existing."

I felt the same feeling as in the car park overwhelm me, only this time I held back the tears. "What if I am more like Mother than I care to admit? What if my life will mimic hers?"

"Where on earth did that come from?"

One tear escaped. "Sometimes." I sniffed the other tears back to the recess behind my eyes. "Sometimes I can hear Mother's words in my mind. Sometimes I find myself being selfish and inconsiderate of others."

"What nonsense!" demanded Gran.

"Well, you said it yourself, I can enchant and bewitch just as Mother did, so-"

"So what!" Gran's voice echoed in the darkness of the empty house. She took a deep breath, straightened her back, and steadied her voice. "Just because you possess an enchanting personality does not mean you are your mother."

Gran reached out her hands toward mine. I took them. Her hands were warm and soft. Even the aged creases were somehow soft.

"Marica, my darling, you are sweet and loving and wise beyond your years. Perhaps this is because of what you have experienced or perhaps it is something innate within you, but it is there. And you are not your mother."

She lowered her eyelids a little before looking lovingly back at me. "I loved your mother and perhaps because I loved her, or perhaps because she was the daughter I never thought I'd have, both I and your Pop Colin indulged her more than we should have. I think maybe her personality was always prone to vanity and selfishness and we fed it instead of being temperate. By the time she was a young teenager her characteristics were already formed and beyond my influence. For this I partly blame myself."

It was the first time, *ever*, Gran had spoken this way. It was also one of the few times I had seen Gran vulnerable, but it changed nothing. Whatever Gran's regrets regarding how she raised Mother, the truth was evident- Mother and I were more similar than she was willing to admit.

Gran was right about one thing. Ilija was a decent person and deserved someone equally so. I had too many ghosts haunting me and he didn't need to be part of that. If Gran was right about Ilija's feelings for me then that only made my situation more delicate. If she could see it, if Michel had noticed it also, then it was up to me to ensure I didn't encourage him. Regardless of my attraction, I was not going to repeat my mistake of destroying a friendship for sex, even sex with emotional benefits.

I watched Gran's hands slip away from mine.

"It's getting chilly; I think I'll light the fire."

Gran didn't move as she watched me leave and hadn't moved when

I returned with kindling and a few larger logs. Gran remained silent and still as I coaxed the fire from a single flame to a glowing mass of yellow gold. She didn't say a single word as I put the larger pieces on the flames, went outside and returned, arms burdened with a mass of misshapen logs. Not a word. Not until I clapped the dust and bark remnants from my hands.

Then the thunderbolt. "Your father didn't die in a car crash."

She stopped me cold. In one second, I flushed with heat and my knees trembled. I swung around 1-80. "What?!"

"He died as a result of a street fight."

Fuzz filled my head as anger made my throat feel like it was closing on me. Inside my head, I could hear shouting. I shut my eyes for a second. Behind my lids, I was throwing one of Gran's cut-glass crystal vases at Mother's silver-gilt-framed photo. I opened my eyes, sucked in fresh, cold air and found some of my voice in the silence that was now a chasm.

"I'm sorry, WHAT?!" The rest of my sentence was still churning inside my lungs, coated in mucus and hatred.

A high-pitched ringing in my ears drowned out whatever Gran was saying. The next words I could make out were, "We all decided to keep the truth from you."

What was she talking about, what the hell was wrong with her?

"We?" I gulped my hurt into a fit of rage. "Who the fuck is WE?"

I'd never sworn at Gran. It did nothing. Her voice was monotone and robotic. "Your grandparents, mother and me, we thought it was better for you to believe a drunk driver killed him than to know the truth."

I pulled up a tapestry-covered chair, took a deep breath and tried to settle the nausea in my stomach. I shook my head. A poor decision as I was already close to fainting. The action had me almost topple into the chair. Gran reached out to steady me, but I pulled back.

I found the seat of the chair, dropped my head between my legs and, without looking up, ground out the words through my teeth. "What are you talking about?"

The first sound from Gran was a sigh. This only angered me more. My mind fell to the girl in the photo, Gran-Gran's birth certificate and the journals. I slowly lifted my head, and, in almost a whisper I said, "For God's sake, how many secrets are there in this God damn family?"

Unimpressed with my blasphemy, even though her face shouted at me, her voice remained steady. "I think perhaps it's time you knew the truth."

Truth! I thought, *Interesting concept in this family.*

From the corner of my eye, I could see the port bottle and my glass next to it. I got up, steadied myself with the chair and filled the glass to its rim, drank half of it and again sat in front of Gran, before I said, "What is the truth?"

Gran reached out again but I swung away from her hand. She let it drop, as though it was a limp, wilted flower and an instant of regret pinched my spine. Gran placed her hand in her lap, looked around the room and then out into the still, wintery half-light before making eye contact with me. Her eyes held no strength now. "It was your mother."

"Sorry?" Her voice was fragile, triggering another spasm of guilt through my body.

"I was babysitting you the night it happened." There was a tremble in her voice, as though she was about to break out into a shiver. I'd never heard Gran sound feeble, breakable.

"Please, what happened?" I whispered.

"All of it, no matter... I think it's time I knew?"

"Your mother, being the person, she was, liked to go out to the city and loved being the centre of attention. Your father, for the most part, was able to cope with her vanity and also able to keep some grip on her endless spending. But the payoff was that every Friday evening they went out. *Every* Friday evening."

So far, I was not seeing the issue. Sure, Mother liked the attention, and I could imagine her being a handful but one night a week out with your husband, so what? My look of confusion must have been evident because Gran added,

"It's not the going out but the alcohol and the personality when she'd had a few too many drinks."

I started to recall the odd time I'd seen Mother drunk, how she acted. I remembered my eighteenth birthday in Brittany, how she'd flirted with my male school friends. At one point Maurice forced her into their bedroom and locked her in for almost an hour so that she'd sober up before she did more than the table-dancing she'd already performed. I felt a whirl in my stomach and a ringing in my ears. My body was preparing me for something bad. "What did she do?"

"We don't know all the details but from the police report..."

Police report. Police report?

"...and the bartender's account and what we could piece together, your mother had dragged your father to a rather interesting bar and was making a bit of a spectacle of herself, and several of the equally drunk men were happy to accept her silly advances. Your father decided she'd taken it far enough and insisted they return home."

OK, OK prepare yourself, Marica.

"It seems your father had gone to the men's room and then paid their bill but could not find your mother. After some searching, he found her out in the side-lane being groped by two men, one of whom was already-"

Gran stopped. I saw the tremble in her lips.

"Oh Marica, it seems one was behind her and the other with his pants down and she half-conscious with her skirt around her hips. They were... oh Marica."

116

Gran's eyes filled with tears and her pain made my heart ache while also reprising memories of Uncle Mike. I started to feel ill, not only for the disgust of my mother but also the revival of all too vivid revolting memories. From somewhere beyond the rising bile in my stomach I mustered the courage to ask, "Was she aware of what was happening? You said she was half-conscious, they might have dragged her out, and?"

Gran shook her head. "Your Nana and I tried to piece this together. The bartender said he saw her go out with both men and one was groping her even before they walked out the door, but then, she was almost passed out when your father discovered her, so we never knew, and your mother couldn't remember." She bit her lip, "Or perhaps she didn't want to remember. It must have been horrible for her too. She never spoke about it to me, not once."

I wanted to believe she'd had one too many drinks and wandered out into the fresh air, unaware of the men, unable to stop them or call for help, but I also knew Mother thrived on male attention; still, if she was barely conscious then how could she be responsible for her actions, or my father's death?

Gran forced the most unconvincing smile I've ever seen. "When your father saw the two men he started screaming and punching all at once, but there were two of them, and they were drunk, and only one of him."

"Where was Mother while this was happening? Are you saying she stood, did nothing, while my father was beaten to death?"

"It's a bit sketchy, but from what we could piece together, she started screaming when she realised the two men were kicking and punching your father. She fumbled her way back in the bar for help, but she was so drunk she struggled to walk."

The tremble in Gran's lip had spread to her fingertips as she said, "What we do know is..."

117

I looked at Gran, willing her to tell me my father didn't die in a filthy back-alley with two drunks who were about to rape my mother.

"...Sometime between your mother getting back into the bar and the police and other people arriving, your father's head was smashed against the brick wall and he fell to the ground."

I wanted to disown Mother. I wanted to shout profanities at Gran, Nana and Dida for keeping the truth from me but I couldn't. I understood. I don't know how it all made sense at that moment, but it just did. The person I wanted to throttle was already dead and the only other person I could hurt was already in pain.

I understood.

In the dark, with my elderly Gran, who rarely cried, in a room filled with memories and lies, I got it. Why so little was ever said between Gran and Mother. Why Mother often found herself busy when Nana, Dida and Gran told stories of Dad.

"He was pronounced dead by the time they got him to the hospital." Gran brushed a tear into submission.

I stood up but braced myself with the chair. I understood, but understanding didn't make the cut less deep. My voice eluded me. Sound eluded me, but for the ringing in my ears, which had returned. I could see the ghosts of Mother's eyes fixed, on me, fixed, imprinted, and marking me like I was the daughter of Cain. I wanted to know the rest, or did I? Part of me feared asking.

Gran's hand came out to me, as though slowed down in some sort of time vacuum, leading me back to sit beside her. She was still talking, what was she saying?

The ringing became less as I concentrated on Gran's mouth moving.

"... And we didn't know how to tell you your mother's actions were the instigator of the scene which caused your father's death."

My mother's actions! My mother's actions, always her actions. She

118

took everything from me, Dad, innocence, a home, the ability to trust and even love. Gran was still talking, her hand on mine.

"How could we, you'd already lost your father; how could we destroy what remained of the relationship you had with your mother?"

My voice returned, poisoned and acidic. "What relationship?!" I spat at Gran. But the venom lasted only a second. I crumpled, hot tears on hot flushed skin. I whimpered, "What relationship?"

Gran reached for the box of tissues by the sofa, the TV tissues for those soppy movies she loved, offering me several, as well as a warm loving hug. I sat on the same sofa every member of my family had sat on at some stage, family ghosts sharing the space with me. In the darkness, with my inner monsters, I felt crushed. I sat for; I have no idea how long until I realised darkness had completely fallen outside. I didn't even notice Gran was still with me. Sitting silently, waiting for me to catch up, to absorb the loss and the pain and the lies, the lies, the lies, those God damn lies!

I heard her voice, soft, touching me inside. "Marica?"

I winced and flinched, unintentionally wounding her. I didn't want soft, I wanted to pound something, smash something. I felt the sharpness of the overhead light sting my eyes and the touch of Gran's hand to mine. She was holding a glass of water. I remember drinking it, I think. Or did I imagine that too? I'm not certain. It doesn't matter. I continued to sit as memories, repressed, real, and imagined, floated and mixed in the cauldron that was now my mind. My head was like the drawings in the journals, some bright and cheery, such as those Easters with Nana and Dida or the recent walks in Paris with Gran, others were smutty and dirty like Uncle Steve or cold and damp like Uncle Mike and the numerous others who didn't even warrant a name.

And death. And death. And death.

Hours passed.

119

I said nothing.

Gran said nothing.

The fire went out.

The house said nothing.

Then Gran's voice. "Dear?"

I was frightening her. I needed to say something. I ordered the symphony in my head to be quiet and braced myself. "Why?" I asked. I understood keeping the truth from a toddler but not the rest. "Why tell me now? Why now, and not sooner, or never?"

"We wanted to, so many times we intended to, your Dida, Nana and me. But then your mother would do something, marry someone, moved somewhere new. Each time we wanted to tell you, there seemed to be another potential disaster waiting to happen and with each year that passed it became harder."

"Harder?"

"The relationship between you and your mother." Gran's voice was pleading for me to understand, its tenderness softened me to listen.

"Dida was ill for a very long time. I was much older than Nana and Dida and the three of us, we feared if we were to die, you would have no one but your mother. We couldn't find the courage to risk what remained of your relationship with her. We couldn't bring ourselves to leave you all alone."

She was right.

Gran was right.

What else could they do?

Or was she?

Think, Marica, think.

If I'd had a child, I would have done the same thing, I was sure. Yet at some point, I would tell my child. I felt my tongue swell as it attempted to form words. "But why didn't you tell me later, when I was old enough?"

"After your Nana's funeral, your mother wasted no time in taking you away."

I clamped my confusion and stored it with my resentment and hatred, hidden deep in a black pit I never opened but always knew was there.

MOTHER! She took me away not only to hurt her own mother but to protect herself from me learning the truth. *I HATED HER.*

It all made sense. The numerous times I suggested we visit Gran in Australia, which never happened. I couldn't even comprehend who, or what, she was.

Damn! That's it! Maurice. She wasn't afraid of me finding out at all.

I was the weapon by which to injure Gran as much as I was the instrument through which she might have lost Maurice. These last years, as she felt middle age creeping up behind her, she must have lived in fear that Maurice would learn the truth and leave her. With her fearing she'd all but lost her charms, Maurice could never find out. I was never the prize; I was never even in the running.

"At least I know now," I said at last.

"Marica?" Gran's voice, still soft, but not soft enough. I needed silence not softness.

"I might go lay down for a bit," I said.

Locking myself in my room, I retrieved my secret stash of cigarettes, emergency ones, and puffed through half my supply, until my tongue tasted stale, my throat stung, and my head swirled from the excessive nicotine. I slumped on the bed, half a cigarette between my fingers, an alcohol-like buzz swishing in my head and curdling my stomach. I drew back hard and deep on the cigarette, and then exhaled the poisonous gas in clouds of grey and white about my head, wishing that, somehow, by exhaling the cigarette smoke, it would take with it my toxic thoughts.

121

I started thinking about a parent's love and if Mother had ever felt anything close to it. At some point I heard Gran knocking on my door asking, "Are you all right, Dear?"

I pretended to be asleep, which was kind of childish.

"Marica, whatever you may think..." She paused and I feared there was more. I couldn't take any more. I feared that Dad wasn't even my father. Perhaps that's why Gran always referred to him as *that tradesman*? It had crept into my mind, but I forced it into submission and now Gran was at my door, with more words.

"Marica, my love," she whispered, "Are you asleep? Perhaps you are or perhaps you simply wish you were, and perhaps that makes it the best time to say what I am about to say, because we can both pretend I did not say it."

She took a breath and I held mine as I waited to hear I was the daughter of one of Mother's interludes.

"The young man is in love with you—"

Wait, what? Is she talking about Ilija?

"—At least a little. I know this is perhaps not the right time to talk about these sorts of things, given everything, but as you said to tell you everything, then I shall."

I let out the air through my nose, clenched the doona cover and listened. Part of me was paying attention and the rest was thankful that she hadn't said what I'd feared most.

"If you feel the same way."

She paused. "I think you do. Perhaps I'm wrong to say this now but I will blame my old age. Us old folks can't be sure we'll be around tomorrow, that's my excuse for bringing up your fellow."

I heard her sigh again before saying, "Eventually all truths, all pasts, resurface. And sometimes it's too late to change the outcome."

I remained quiet.

Gran knocked again. "Marica?"

122

Gran murmured something I couldn't make out before saying again, "Dear, are you awake?"

I lit another cigarette and waited for her Russian soldier footsteps to tell me she'd given up. A moment or two later the *clip-clop-clip* told me she had.

CHAPTER 17

Secret's

As Easter Sunday evening turned to Easter Monday. Gran attempted to approach the subject of Dad's death, but I froze the conversation with, "Gran, thank you for telling me but I'm not ready, not ready to talk about Dad, Mother or Ilija."

I was determined more than ever to remove myself from any possible romance. If Gran thought that by telling me Dad's story, I would somehow feel freed, she was wrong. Yes, the truth helped. It helped cement my resolve. All that mattered now was the journals.

I decided it was time Ilija saw the photo of the little girl. I knew the photo and journals were linked, and somehow both were linked to Gran. Now I wanted answers. If Gran could keep the truth of Dad's death from me, then she could keep many other secrets.

Because it was Easter break there was no school, but as Gran already assumed there was more to my friendship with Ilija and was encouraging me to pursue it, I thought I might as well use this to my advantage. And I wanted distance, physical distance from Gran. It wasn't her fault, and she did what she had to, what she believed was right, but I needed space.

This time Ilija and I did meet at his place. His studio was small but well set-out and allowed for an obvious division of space and a reasonable-sized table, which Ilija also used as a study desk. He made us traditional Turkish-style coffee and served me my cakes, which I thought was cute. And even though the revelations of the previous evening were almost more than I could handle, being with him did help.

We spent the next four hours reading, writing, typing, and giving each other odd looks. The journal told of large parties and classes for needlepoint as well as archery for the authoress's younger brother. It spoke of elaborate dinners, Summers spent by the seaside and Winters in St. Petersburg surrounded by crystal chandeliers, great works of art and velvet drapes. References to Paris fashion as well as royal palaces.

This went on and on for pages, and I could not resist any longer. "Ilija, I have something to show you." I pulled out the frail photo which now rested within a clear plastic envelope.

Ilija looked at the photo, examined it carefully, read the back and then kind of stared at me before he said, "Do you know who this is?"

I shook my head no.

"Where did it come from?" he asked.

"I found it in Gran's attic," I mumbled.

Reaching over for a textbook sitting at the end of the table, he said, "I've been looking at the facts we've collected, I wrote mine down here, but you have a copy on your laptop, right?"

"Yes."

"Do you mind reading out the list?"

I opened to the spreadsheet.

Big Pair
Maria
Monsieur Gilliard

General Pavel
Baby
Papa
Mamma
Cossack

Ilija then had his list, which included all the above and a few other details such as the names Olga, Tatiana and the name of a nurse. He then flipped several pages of his textbook and pulled out some loose sheets with photos before saying, "Look at this."

I drew the loose photo prints closer to me. Ilija placed my little photo against one of the others and asked, "Can you see a resemblance?"

I could, but I wasn't ready to say it just yet. "Well, it's a photo of that time. Everyone looked the same in a way, it's the fashion." Even as I spoke, I knew I sounded unconvincing.

"Where did your list come from?" I asked Ilija.

"The internet."

"And the pictures?"

I paused before finishing my question, "From the internet also?"

Ilija nodded.

"What site?" I was pretty sure I already knew the answer.

Ilija got up, poured two glasses of whiskey, neat, and pushed one toward me before saying, "Drink."

"I don't drink whiskey."

Ilija shook his head. "Drink."

I brought the glass closer to my nose and almost immediately withdrew it, imploring, "I can't."

"Don't smell it, just get it down."

"One gulp?"

He nodded.

"Straight?"

He nodded again.

I screwed up my nose so that I couldn't smell it as I gulped the foul poison that is whiskey.

As I let out an "Arrrh" and scrunched my eyes, Ilija finished his glass and with a slam of the glass to the table he said, "Right." He twisted his textbook to face me, flipped back the pages to the one with the list and said, "Read it."

What he had before me was a summary of the Romanovs. The Tsar and his entire family, who were all assassinated in the European Summer of 1918. I started reading some of the facts, even though I knew them very well. Why was I reading something I knew? Because I needed time to think.

There was a French tutor called Monsieur Gilliard, the two older daughters were playfully known as the Big Pair and the two younger ones as the Little Pair, and Baby. Baby was the pet name the family gave to Alexei because he was the baby of the family and because he needed to be babied due to his haemophilia. Everything seemed to fit, and everything seemed to confirm my suspicions, but I wasn't prepared to accept it just yet.

"Well, what about the dates, the birthday of Baby, and the other dates? Did you check them also?"

"I've checked all the dates and they match, every single one of them," confirmed Ilija.

I sat, trying to find a better explanation. Ilija was already up, getting both of us a glass of iced water. I drank it as though I'd not had a drink in a week before drawing breath and strength to ask, "And the photo?"

Ilija sat down and fumbled with the little photo for a while before saying, "I think it might be one of the sisters, though I'm not sure. The message on the back mentions one sister. Maybe it's a cousin?"

That made sense.

Wait, no, no it didn't, no, he couldn't be suggesting that—

"So...so are you saying that these journals were written by...?"

"...By Anastasia Romanov, yes."

"No, wait!"

"But it can't be?"

I pulled out the second journal and flipped to the final pages, those in Frenglais and demanded of Ilija, "Look! Look at the dates!"

The journal had entries that went well beyond 1918. In fact, beyond 1927, and therefore these could not be Anastasia's.

Ilija flicked through the back pages and seemed genuinely frustrated. As he couldn't read French, I turned to the last page, in English. "Look at the date," I demanded.

He did.

"Read it!" I demanded again. "It was written by the authoress of the journals, that's what it's telling me."

Ilija read every word. He took his time, perhaps reading it more than once or perhaps reading slowly due to the uniqueness of the cursive script.

He looked up. "I don't know what to say, except everything fits, everything tells me this was written by the youngest sister, but yes, I have no explanation of this?"

I shut both books and hid the photo between them. We were both confused. Ilija got up again to make us another coffee. We both sat silent for several minutes, the silence only broken by the question, 'How many sugar's do you want?"

I asked to use the bathroom; because I needed fresh air and cool water, but neither helped. When I returned, Ilija was sitting, waiting, two coffees in front of him.

"What now?" he asked.

I sipped the coffee in silence for some time before I allowed logic to float to the surface. "It can't be her because let's face it, she died long before the diary ended."

Ilija nodded in agreement but I could tell he didn't agree, so I pushed for his theory. "Well, it just can't be, can it?"

Ilija sighed. "I don't know what we have here. Maybe you're right. The photo of the little girl might be your authoress and perhaps as you say, she is some sort of relative to the Romanov's but..."

"But?"

"But, that still doesn't explain why the authoress used all the same pet names as the Romanov children and had a tutor with the same name. That cannot be a coincidence?"

He was right, but so was I. Anastasia died in 1918 and the authoress of these journals remained alive for some time after that.

"And?"

"And what?" I asked.

"Marica." Ilija's voice softened. "You must have asked yourself who did all this, the journals and this photo, how did they end up in your gran's attic?" Ilija sighed again. "How could your gran not know about the journals or the photo?"

His questions were the very same questions I'd been asking myself, but then Ilija added a new one I'd tried not to consider. "Besides, didn't you say your gran loathed anything to do with Russia? Why would anything from Russia be any connection to her?"

I felt numb and Ilija must've felt the same way because he broke the stagnant air by saying, "Are you hungry?"

I wasn't, but I thought a walk in the city might help clear my thoughts. Though I knew it was not entirely possible, I hoped perhaps some reprieve from them would be enough for the moment.

We found a little place off Little Collins Street where Ilija proved he was every bit the typical male, devouring a meal which could have fed a small developing country, while I played with a plate of overripe tomatoes and too salty feta. In fairness to the café, there was likely nothing wrong with the salad and had more to do with my numbed tastebuds, from whiskey and shock.

I ordered a triple-shot espresso, and Ilija an iced coffee, and as we waited for our drinks, I opened the subject again. "What now?"

Ilija shrugged. "I think we have to have faith that if we keep working through the rest of the journal entries, we might find the real secrets?"

"Real secrets?" I asked.

"Look, whoever the authoress is, whether it's Anastasia or someone very close to her, the journals will eventually tell us as long as we keep working through."

It made sense, except now a new idea was forming. What if the journals were fake? I knew nothing of the type of people Gran-Gran knew while in Paris. What if this was some sort of fun parlour game she was part of? What if the picture was a real photo but the inscription formed part of the game?

I mean, in some ways it made more sense than the journals being genuine. Gran-Gran was quite wealthy and would have moved in circles where inventive parlour games formed part of the social culture.

As I silently probed the holes in this new hypothesis Ilija broke in with, "But, while the possibility of discovering lost journals that belonged to one of the Romanov children is exciting and could, if we can prove it, make you, well both of us, rich and famous, to me..."

Ilija stopped but I insisted, "Go on!"

"Well, to me there seems to be a much bigger mystery, the one which links all this to your gran. Sure, the rest of the world might not think that's such a big deal, especially when compared to the Romanovs, but I see it differently."

If it's even real, I thought.

Our coffees arrived as Ilija focused his train of thought. "Look, whether I'm right and these journals were Anastasia's, or you're right and they were written by someone close to the Romanovs, or if we're both wrong and the authoress is of no historical significance, it's irrelevant when it comes to the personal significance to your family history."

There at least we agree, I thought. *Even if they are false, where did such detailed information come from if not personal knowledge of one of Gran-Gran's friends? Damn!* I thought, *I'm back to where I started; someone Gran-Gran knew, someone linked to the Romanovs.* God, I could hardly bring myself to even think it, perhaps a cousin or other relative of the Tsar?

"I know you want to know who she is," he said, "But most of all, why was it in your gran's attic and who is the authoress to your gran and the photo, and why the lies about where you're great-gran was born?"

I listened as I sipped my espresso.

"And if there is a family history, which was supposed to be a mystery, the little girl in the photo and the little authoress of the journals and the little old lady who professes her *Frenchness*, are more closely linked than you could have ever imagined."

I interrupted Ilija. "No! No, they can't be linked. At first, I thought the photo might have been my great-grandmother, Gran-Gran Ana but it's not her. The features and the dates don't match, which means the journal is not Gran-Gran's and the family tree might just be coincidently linked to Imperial Russia. I believe that."

"Fair enough," said Ilija resignedly. "But you cannot give up on your authoress or your girl in the photo just because you keep getting more questions than answers!"

We finished our coffees and returned to Ilija's apartment.

The walk back gave me time to think.

I'd come to trust Ilija and I was ready to test that trust.

"Ilija," I said with some authority, "I think you have a point; the answers have to be in these journals."

As I grabbed journal Volume one, I asked Ilija if he had a spare USB. He retrieved one from a small cane basket on his bookshelf.

I copied everything we'd saved so far, including the spreadsheets, to the USB and said, "I need to know the answers and I can't wait any longer, so I've decided to leave Vol-one with you. It's all in Russian and you can work just as fast without me as you can with me.

I'm going to start making sense of the Frenglais pages and see if I can't work out what was happening after the war and perhaps who wrote those pages."

Ilija asked, "Do you think Vol-two was written by someone else?"

"Maybe? It makes sense, I mean if you're right about Anastasia?"

He wasn't, I was certain. A secret like that, well it couldn't be kept – besides, Anastasia's body was found in 2007 so he couldn't be, but still, more questions than answers, Ilija was not wrong about that.

"And the handwriting, it's not the same...is it?"

Ilija winced and I nodded. That was hardly a strong argument. Individual handwriting changes from teenager to adult even in perfect conditions, add in a revolution and war, it wasn't even worth considering.

I let his new theory ferment for a moment. "I mean it's possible that the first volume was written by Anastasia but then when the Romanovs were imprisoned in 1917 when their French tutor was refused the option to stay with them, it's maybe possible that the journals were given to him and he got them back to France?"

"Yep, yep, possible, except their tutor was actually Swiss-French," Ilija corrected me.

"OK, so, that only makes it more possible, doesn't it? What if he took the journals? And this little girl in the photo was somehow related to the Romanovs surely, and their tutor would know their relatives? And if this girl was a relative of the Romanovs and perhaps a friend of my great-grandmother then the link would exist?"

"Except that still doesn't explain why your gran dislikes anything to do with Russia?"

Before my headache got any worse, I got up. "But I think your idea of approaching this from two angles has merit," he said. "And I'd be happy to try."

Ilija opened the door and leaned down to hug me, except he wasn't letting go. Well, certainly not quickly enough, and when he eventually did free me his usual peck on the cheek seemed a little too closely aimed near my mouth. Trouble was, I only half-minded. Yet we were working together. I needed to keep my distance, at least until I could process this new information and form some sort of opinion. In my head I had a quick conversation with fate. *OK, are you having fun yet?*

"Great, as if there's not enough going on." But secretly, I couldn't deny part of what Gran said about Ilija's feelings for me, and it made me wonder - what if? I'd all but accepted a chance of a relationship between us was over after my mess-up at Michel's all those months ago. But that hug. It was more. I wasn't imagining it. Or maybe I was. I decided to intentionally misunderstand the implication of his overly long hug and headed home satisfied that our new plan would reward us with information much more quickly.

Gran met me at the door with questioning eyes.

"Gran," I said, "I'm not upset any more, but I'm just not ready to talk either. I love you but I just need a bit of space from the subjects of Mother and Ilija."

That evening, I opened a new page on my laptop called Vol-two, eager to start the next stage of this mystery.

"Oh, Gran!" I muttered, "Wouldn't she love to know about the hug."

CHAPTER 18

Could It Be?

I woke up early, feeling emotionally lethargic. So, I did what I do when I want to waste time but fool myself into believing I'm doing something of value. I started with coffee and then checked my emails.

I saw Ilija's email instantly, with a hard-to-miss uppercase subject matter: *PLEASE READ*. Thinking it might be his version of *War and Peace* explaining the overzealous hug, I successfully ignored it. Obviously. I wasn't interested. Arrh! OK, that's a lie, I wasn't ready.

Instead, I read all the rubbish emails, checked my Twitter and Facebook updates and replied to all-and-sundry, all except Ilija's email, glaring at me in thick bold, challenging me to open it. I was such a coward sometimes!

Then came the text messages. After receiving the fourth, I dared myself to read them. Three simply said 'read my email - important'. The last said, "Are you up yet? Read your email and call me ASAP".

It was clear I could no longer put off reading his email to me. Hum? Evidently, I could, by making another coffee and bacon and eggs on toast for Gran and me.

Breakfast time was skilfully controlled by me. When Gran got *that* look I'd interrupt her intention with a generic comment.

"How many pieces of bacon."

"Coffee or tea?"

"We're running low on jam."

"I'll have to arrange for a wood delivery."

I had several dozen of them. More than enough to avoid last night's topic.

By the time breakfast was over, Ilija had sent another three text messages. His badgering was beginning to annoy. I wasn't fond of being pushed and pushed.

After breakfast, I took what remained of my coffee, huffed at my email account and opened the damned email.

Couldn't sleep. Started translating many of the pages. Haven't stopped all night other than for coffee & cigarette breaks. When you read the attached, you'll know why. Call me, we need to talk urgently.

Ilija

16th September 1916

I joined my sisters to help at the hospital today and now I have come to understand why they always look so sad when they return home.

I did not expect the stench of stale blood to hit me so powerfully, only countered by the antiseptic smell of death.

So many soldiers.

So many.

And I never thought I'd say that those who had died may well be the lucky ones but it is true, for how can any man feel complete after he has lost his eye, his leg, his arm or his courage?

And how can I help him find it when I cannot even help him find food for his hungry child?

Before this day was over, I will have cried for the deserved life of every man and woman.

Though I didn't understand an empty belly or the chaos of war, I understood crying for a deserved life. Even so, I was struggling to see what was so urgent. I kept reading.

28th October 1916

When I was younger, I believed freedom was measurable by the respect of our neighbours to remain within their boundaries. Now I have come to understand that it's limited more by the restrictions of our combined histories and the preoccupation of the paradox of the philosophy of freedom and the reality of repeating past histories, and freely suffering the same fruits of our labours.

I couldn't help but admire her philosophical thoughts as much as I was beginning to admire her. Here was someone who had lived a very privileged life and likely never had to want for anything or consider anyone, yet she now could put such thoughts together. I was a little jealous of how deeply she could think. But still, what was Ilija on about?

21st November 1916

Today I hid some food in my coat pockets. Not for my sake but for the shockingly slender nurse, whose protruding shoulder blades, evident even through her uniform and thin gaunt face, were failing to mask false hope.

She spends each day helping the dying soldiers in the hope that someone somewhere is doing the same for her husband long since missing.

Tatiana tells me...

I gulped down the name as common in Russia. It just could not be.

...she is a mother, yet I have no courage to ask how many of her children still live, perhaps because I know it is none. I wish my meagre gesture of smoked ham and hard cheese could have come sooner but I knew her not a year ago. I also wish it could nourish her hope, but I fear nothing can do that, perhaps not even for me.

I confess I find it more and more difficult to reconcile eating while so many of my people starve.

To a Russian, there is a difference between starvation and poverty, and the difference is tangible. Poverty means no meat, no pork sausage but a mother can still feed her child with porridge, boiled potatoes or bread and cheese.

Starvation is simple to quantify, it is when a Russian mother can no longer bake enough bread for her hungry children.

And yet if one were to ask the Bolsheviks, they will deny all. It seems starvation is another disease, which does not infect Mother Russia. Perhaps they should meet the skinny nurse.

I asked her what gives her the courage to rise each day, the answer shocked me. She is just waiting for even one letter, even that letter if it must be. For death in itself is a kind of freedom for both soldier and family alike.

Freedom in death.

The thought made it all so real, these words, pages, these pictures of moments of hope in pages of desperation, that I wanted to cry. People today pay homage in memory to 'the unknown soldiers', and rightly so, but what of the unknown mothers, children, grandfathers? Who will remember them? Who will even know? Even in this journal, the nurse has no name, no identity. It's just sad.

But there was a name -Tatiana.

24th December 1916

It is Christmas Eve and I have nothing to celebrate and only one wish to beg of God, please bring sanity back to Europe.

2nd March 1917

Today Papa is no longer Tsar and neither is my little brother ever to be...

Wait... what?

I read it again... and again. Part of me knew, even in open denial I knew, but still, to see it in words? Did Ilija translate it wrong, should it have been *Papa no longer works for the Tsar?* Or maybe *Papa tells me we no longer have a Tsar?*

...I have nothing to add for I fear what is to come, so much that I cannot even be honest with myself.

29th March 1917

I was told that my birth was marked by a special sign, which is why my second name is Nicholovna yet if this is so then was I born for this? For these times? For this turmoil?

I felt fear mixed, with excitement, mixed with relief and disbelief.

...Every day there is more and more word of our White Russian's and the evil of those Bolsheviks. I fear we are truly all destined to suffer the assassin's bullet.

April 14th 1917

Man has moved as far from God as is possible when brother will no longer protect brother.

Papa has just told us we are not to travel to England after all. What was once almost certain as the government of Britain offered us exile was reversed by no other than the King of England himself.

I am still confused why this would be for King George V is not only Godfather to Alexei but also cousin to Papa... yet we are to be left to... to... the mercy of the Bolsheviks, to a people who do not even understand such a word.

I feel shame for King George, we may be disposed but he is the one in dishonour, shame on you I say and I hope that our blood will stain your unwashed hands...

Papa remains both diplomatic and ever faithful to his people.

He neither blames Lord Stamfordham for advising King George V against offering us asylum nor does he believe his people will raise anything more than an angry shaking fist against him.

I remain much less hopeful and I must admit Alexei now believes we are all ruined.

It was true! Or was it? I mean, really? If it was true, then these were the words of the Romanovs, the last words of the Romanovs, hiding in my Gran's attic.

17th July 1917

The Russian army is all but shattered and our country in ruins.

What the revolution has not destroyed, God help us, the War is obliterating and now, Papa tells us, Kerensky has become Prime Minister of a provisional government, but I ask myself a provisional government of what? and of who?

Those who demand the return of our Imperial Russia or the Bolsheviks? Or perhaps something in between or even worse, something new and yet to attack what remains of our land and our people?

To have an effective government, provisional or not, one must have a nation.

August 25th 1917

I write to take my mind off the situation even as I have nothing I want to write.

We have now been moved to Tobolsk in the Urals, for our safety we are told. God save me from my 'saviours' I say.

As we travelled, like little more than cattle, I watched our country crying. Villages razed to the ground, where once prosperous farms stood, now the only signs of life, desperate people scavenging like vermin among the rubble. Old chimneys the last remaining trace of once flourishing farms and bountiful harvests, rising like guards, reminders of a better past and a proud Russia.

Dead. Everything is dead.

I couldn't stop reading. Reading and re-reading, trying to take it all in, and trying to work out if what I was reading was real.

...Dogs are barking as gunshots pierce the howling wind while cinders crumble what remains of buildings once housing smiling well-fed children.

Though the former Governor's Mansion offer's comfort, we remain little more than caged animals, allowed the freedom of our enlarged pens while armed soldiers patrol and our letters are read ...for our protection.

Alexei's Doctor still has some measure of freedom and medicine is freely available, but Monsieur Gilliard feels uneasy in our new home and often speaks French to avoid every word being recorded and misinterpreted.

Yet Papa still holds hope Prime Minister Kerensky will protect Russia from Lenin, –who in private moments, Papa calls the Devil's Son.

27th October 1917

Word has reached us that Prime Minister Kerensky's government is no more, the Bolsheviks, led by Lenin, are now in power; God help Russia and God help my family.

Papa is now forbidden to wear his epaulettes.

Papa says it will all work out in the end, however, I no longer believe this, even a little. Perhaps I must learn to have faith.

23rd December 1917

There will be little to celebrate this Christmas.

Orders have been given to our guards that we must reduce our cost of living. Our coal has been reduced as has our food supplies and even our Doctor's supplies are becoming limited.

I remember when I had food and freedom and could offer it to others, now I must beg for both. I remember the nurse, does she still live I wonder?

Comrade Lenin, take from us coal if you must and I will simply warm my hands with an extra pair of gloves. And take if you must my pork and potatoes, I shall simply eat more bread and even if you take from me the warmth of the sun you will never take from me the soul of freedom.

I ached. I knew they did not have much more time to live. What twisted over and over in my head was how they found any strength to not wish to die? As I read, I realised how selfish I was. I blamed Mother and even God and fate for my miserable life yet look at what this woman was living through, looked at her courage. What were my moments of self-pity compared to her real sorrow?

1st March 1918

We are now officially on soldier's rations.

There will be no more butter, no coffee, nothing that Lenin and his monsters consider to be luxuries. They have removed ten of our staff also for we do not need them, so Comrade Lenin tells us. Does it seem we have too much already? Too much of what? Fear? Death? Yes, these we truly have too much of.

Mamma protested; are we now to dig and plough like peasants for our potatoes, yet I have greater fears, I can dig and plough but what are we to dig for if there is nothing to dig up?

Papa tells us there is hope.

Last night we heard the gunfire of White Russians and believe there is every chance we will be freed before the end of Spring.

143

How resilient is the human spirit to be able to endure what they were enduring and still think of hope? I wished I had a fraction of her bravery.

15th April 1918

Today they were removed.

I have no hope left, not a single degree, for yesterday Papa and Mamma were taken from us. We have no way of knowing what will become of us or what will become of Papa and Mamma or our dear sister Olga.

We only know that they have gone from Tobolsk to Yekaterinberg.

Will I ever see them again?

I'd always been fascinated by this period of history, but this was the first time I felt the history. I started to imagine their lives, a chess game, Black B5, except Black was now Red – the Red Army - Red B5, working toward exerting pressure on White E4 Pawn. Lenin, eating up all the Whites.

28th April 1918

We have received word from Yekaterinberg.

My poor parents. Now they sometimes do not even have tea for breakfast as the soldiers use up all the hot water.

The food is so poor that Mamma is often ill. Dr. Botkin pleaded for the food and conditions to be improved but the Kommissar has no regard for them.

I heard our guards laughing as they spoke of how the Kommissar and guards helped themselves to Mamma's and Papa's meals, picking what they liked and leaving the scraps as though feeding dogs from the table, and boasting that they'd had enough and could now be given to my parents.

Thank God for Dr. Botkin and his wife, for without them how would my parents live?

I gulped away what remained of my disbelief. These weren't forged, or some parlour game. Were they written by Anastasia? It was difficult to believe but it certainly looked like it. Whatever the case, the facts were spot on.

5th May 1918 Easter Sunday

Today we were allowed to be visited by a priest and four nuns to enable us to hold Mass Service for this of holiest of days.

Mamma had prepared presents before she was taken away, and Maria distributed to our servants what we could but the greatest gift came from our people for they have not forgotten us!

The village gathered and gave to us food enough for a feast! Yet, how are we to feast when we have no word for Mamma or Papa?

We remain in a great state of anxiety, fearful for our parents but even more so for our brother for he still cannot walk and Dr. Derevenko can only do so much. But Alexei cannot be moved or he will surely die and while he remains unwell we remain parted from Mamma and Papa.

Though now it may not matter if Alexei is well enough or not to be moved for the river is again ice-free and I fear the act of kindness from the villagers has only angered the Kommissar's. Will they move us again?

I had to let my thoughts catch up. Part of me was still unwilling to accept what I was reading. Thinking back to my history lessons, were there two doctors? As I freed another cigarette from my emergency stash, I tried to recall. Yes, yes, two doctors. One was married, the family doctor, and the other specifically hired to care for Alexei.

11th May 1918

We are all becoming more and more anxious for our dear parents.

Reports continue to come of their treatment. And this stress has caused Alexei to be flushed with fever. His temperature remains high and now he is weakened from another injury and further loss of blood.

31st May 1918

Seven days ago, they replaced Colonel Kobylinsky and all his men with a mixed guard of Letts and sailors. These newcomers show the hatred of us openly.

Rodionov, who replaced Kobylinsky, seems to take pleasure in tormenting and humiliating those under his rule, both us and even his men. Now we are subjected to a daily rollcall. Seating us in a row and it begins, "Are you Tatiana Nicholaevna?" then he asks, "Are you Maria Nicholaevna," etc. while he jokes, "There were so many of them, how am I to remember either their names or their faces!"

Sentries are now posted inside the house and all the doors must remain open.

Our servants are no longer allowed out but for very rare occasions.

Nanny Nagorny took a bunch of radishes from the garden the other day but was searched and was very lucky not have been court-martialled.

Poor Nagorny.

1st June 1918

We have been commanded to pack, for tomorrow we too will be moved to Yekaterinberg.

I am happy to be again embraced by Mamma and Papa but fear that Alexei is too unwell to be moved.

God help us!

2nd June 1918

Monsieur Gilliard was forcibly removed from us as the skies flooded with rain and the Bolsheviks shouted "Only Russian's! Only Russian's!

Tatiana's little dog crouched deep in her handbasket sheltering from both rain and fear as she pulled and pushed her brown suitcase with Alexei's nanny Nagorny carrying my brother and somehow finding enough force in his knee to help Tatiana push her case.

I understand how the dog felt yet I fear the little puppy's future is brighter than ours.

As we were shoved into the train carriages, some women threw flowers at us, but they were rudely pushed aside by the soldiers. One, who dared turn to face the soldier, had the handle of his rifle thrust into her chest. I watched her crouch over in pain as they shut the cattle-carriage door, and locked us in.

7th June 1918

Our new prison is the two-story house of Nikolay and our daily walking pen is little more than a dog-cage.

13th June 1918

The world has gone mad.

The White Czechs captured Chelyabinsk and in Petropavlovsk they shot all twenty members of the local government.

Our prison guards have now removed almost all our servants, only Doctor Botkin, his wife and nanny Nagorny remain.

Dr. Derevenko was summoned by Kommissar Avdeev to be informed that he would only be allowed to enter the house we now shared, under strict medical conditions and would remain in compounds outside our prison.

Even under Lenin rule, doctors held positions of power and therefore Dr. Derevenko was given both freedom and orders in the one breath. It seems he is now a Red Army Doctor.

We still have Doctor Botkin. Losing Dr. Derevenko was very upsetting to Alexei, but at least we have Mamma and Papa back, yet, something is wrong with Papa. For the first time, Papa seems to have lost his faith in fate.

26th June 1918

One of the soldiers who guard us passed a message to Doctor Botkin which he sadly shared. More than two thousand White Russians were captured, stripped of their weapons and rank, their shoes and metals removed, hands tied and then shot.

Russia, has the Devil truly stolen every portion of your heart that now, one Russian kills so easily another?

Doctor Botkin said the guard was brought to tears as he told of the massacre, yet we remain prisoners waiting, I think our own riffle-fire.

Bile rose from my stomach. Their murders were only weeks away.

28th June 1918

I am now forced to write in secret for we are allowed so little freedom and I fear, you, my sweet journals will be taken, read and burnt, – and that I could not bear!

Now sentries are posted even as we use the lavatory, and follow Mamma and all of us, watching every step. It is so embarrassing for us when Madame Becker visits each of us every month to have to explain and for Mamma to have to prove our bleeding, our rags, inspected by the grey uniform nurses with grey faces and black souls.

Though it seemed obvious, I didn't want to believe, but a quick Google search quickly confirmed 'Madame Becker' was what the sisters called their periods. As a woman, I felt sick at the lack of privacy.

29th June 1918

Everything is taken from us; everything.

We have only five forks to seven people, all our money is stolen and almost all our jewels have been taken from us; everything.

30th June 1918

Alexei and I have noticed Doctor Botkin and Papa whispering when they think it safe to do so.

Dr. Botkin somehow managed to obtain for us to have an hour in the garden each day and today Olga said she saw the Doctor and Mamma look at each other strangely several times.

And I saw him take a cigarette from a guard yet Doctor Botkin does not smoke. Is it possible there is yet some hope?

I felt so much for them! I'd read and re-read their history in books, but this was different. This feeling wasn't sympathy, it was empathy. They were only days away from their deaths and all this young woman wants is the simple right to hope until the end.

1st July 1918

Alexei, my sisters and I are convinced something is happening.

Both Mamma and Papa have spent every hidden moment they could find in discussion with Doctor Botkin, and Alexei has not missed how his nanny has kept a closer eye on the guards as though anticipating something.

Doctor Botkin once again was seen sneaking off to have a stolen cigarette with the same soldier and, for no reason, the Doctor's good wife began to dance as nanny clapped the Polka and even Papa jumped like a Cossack while Mamma hummed as she danced around us. Why do they dance? Is it madness or something more?

Whatever is coming, I pray they are not risking everything for nothing; we must all live or otherwise we should all die.

11th July 1918

The ritual every day.

Every day.

Every day, the Commandant and his young assistant make us show all our jewels, the few we were allowed to keep, as the young assistant notes all down.

Every day they say to Mamma, why do you have this and that piece?

For how long have you owned it?

Where did it come from?

And she answers every time the same:

"I do not know. I have two bracelets from Uncle Leopold, which I cannot take off, and each of the children, the bracelets we gave them, which cannot be slipped off, also my husband's engagement ring, which he could not take off."

15th July 1918

The Commandant and all his men are now gone, replaced, why? No one knows or perhaps no one is willing to tell.

The new Commandant came with our jewels, sealed them up in our presence and left them on our table. He said he would come every day to see that we have not opened the parcel.

At 10.30 am. Workmen appeared outside and put iron bars in front of our open windows while from the outside they white-washed the glass so that we could not see even the sun, but for the hour allowed.

Do they imagine we shall climb out or get into touch with the guard! But Mamma seems to be even a little pleased for she said, "While we cannot see out neither can they see in."

I was ready to vomit. 18th July was the date the Romanovs were murdered. Ilija and I were reading Anastasia's last words, her last moments and thoughts. We were discovering her as only her family knew her, and I had no idea what to do with this information. I'd invaded her thoughts and yet I also felt as though history had denied her the dignity of truth.

I was at last certain it was her. I had no idea who wrote the entries after their deaths, but this was her, it was too genuine not to be. I didn't know whether to cry or scream, but Ilija did. He was tired of waiting. My phone was buzzing with his name.

"Hello."

"Have you read it?"

"Just finished."

"And?"

"And you were right, it must be Anastasia. Either that or a very convincing forgery?"

Ilija would have none of it. "You know it's real."

"Probably."

"No, not probably, it is real."

"Well, even if it is, that still doesn't answer who wrote Vol two?"

"That's one of the reasons why I've called you, to see if you've read any of the second volume?"

"Haven't had a chance," I replied.

"We need to get together and work out what happened in that journal, who finished it, who got them to your gran's house and how?" he said.

"I know."

I was full of clever replies that morning.

Finding my thoughts, I asked, "How far did you get with Volume one?"

"To the end," he replied.

"OK, so the rest of the answers are now with me," I said.

"Looks that way, will you have time to look at it later on today?" asked Ilija but before I could answer, he added, "Wait, the first bit, it's still in Russian, right?"

I grabbed Vol-two as I said, "I think so?" And after quickly checking, I added, "Yeah, looks that way, about a third is still in Russian."

Ilija said, "Right, I'll come over and get Vol-two from you and do the first bit and then you can do the French stuff, OK?"

I nodded instead of replying so Ilija asked again. "OK?"

"Yes, OK."

"Marica?"

Gran's voice interrupted our conversation, and I said, "Gran's calling, I have to go."

"OK, see you in an hour," said Ilija and before I could reply he'd hung up.

"Marica," Gran called me again. "Are you up in the attic or your room, Dear?"

"Hum, I'm in my room, I've got a bit of a headache," I replied, knowing this would bring out the maternal instinct in her.

I heard a knock at the door just before she peeped around the corner. "Is it a headache or a migraine, Dear?"

"No, it's just a headache."

Gran disappeared behind the door and I knew within five minutes I'd be served herbal tea and a rainbow selection of head-cold and painkillers. I also knew the internal pounding would not end until I'd had time to take in the email I'd just read.

CHAPTER 19

The Tom before the Storm

Flipping to the last page I read it and re-read it, looking for some clue.

1st Jan 1933

This will be my last entry.

You have been a dependable confidante and reliable companion for so many years and through more lives than I sometimes care to remember; yet it is time, dearest Journal, for us to part.

When I began this journey with you, I was so young and naïve. I knew nothing of love and hate or even of life and death, yet it seems we both have lingered too long in death. I feel it is time to let life breathe in complete freedom.

I do not know if I shall ever visit you again, yet I know I cannot bring myself to read you ever more. The pain of those first entries' memories, where I was able to feel happiness without fear, I think perhaps they hurt the most. Is it not true that the death of innocence is the very worst kind of death?

Good-night sweet friend, some secrets are perhaps too much, even for a time.

But it gave me no more answers.

I started flicking through the pages of Vol two, and that's when it struck me –- there were virtually no pictures or sketches. *It must be someone else who wrote this one*, I thought. It made sense, perhaps smuggled out and given to a distant relative, maybe the girl with the vacant eyes?

I flipped back and forth, trying to familiarize myself with the Frenglais and unique cursive script, trying to find clues in the other pages, but I was too worked up to be able to concentrate and made out only a few odd words.

A little over an hour later Ilija arrived at Gran's doorstep, which amused her no end. And, just to make sure there wasn't a single person I knew who hadn't met Ilija, Tom turned up unexpectedly with several brochures and a new suggestion.

The conversation went something like this:

Gran: "Hello, Ilija, what a pleasant surprise to see you so soon again?"

Ilija: "Yez, sorry to intrude, Marica has book I vanting to borrowing forr few dayz-"

Gran: "And it couldn't wait even one more day?"

Ilija: "Vell?"

Gran: "No, I understand, study is very important, but I am surprised you didn't remember it when you were here on Sunday?"

Ilija: "Vell...?"

Marica: "Yes, sorry, Gran, we got so into story-telling that I forgot to give him the book."

Gran: "Of course, I understand."

Ilija: "I must go, I tink? Sorry?"

DING DONG DING DONG

Gran: "Oh, that'll be the door. Marica, show your, hum, friend to the kitchen and put the kettle on while I see who else has popped in."

Tom: "Hello, Marica, sorry to interrupt but I had an idea and thought you would probably be home, but I see I've interrupted something?"

Gran: "No, not at all! This is Marica's good friend Ilija who was here for Easter lunch but seems to have forgotten something and came back already..."

I'm sure you have the picture now. Tom shaking Ilija's somewhat sweaty nervous hand while I fumbled for words and Gran muttered little jibes while having a private chuckle!

Ilija wanted to leave as much I wanted him to. As I ushered him out the front door, I knew that sharp-tongued and eagle-eyed Gran had her cornflower blues fixed on both of us.

Doing a 1-80 swirl, I found Gran and Tom in the kitchen whispering over coffee mugs and cheesy grins.

Gran, pretending they'd been talking about the renovations, said calmly, "Tom came to suggest we plaster off half the room, put in two doors to serve as storage and make upstairs much more formal and neater. And I think it's a very good idea!"

Without giving me a chance to reply, Tom added, "I know it'll cost a bit more, but you have some wonderful pieces of furniture and artwork." He paused and, looked at Gran and continued. "We found a few additional paintings, plus all sorts of family photos and knick-knacks and you could create a kind of gallery while still having a huge attic space hidden behind the doors?"

I had to agree that Tom's idea sounded clever. But when I brought up cost Gran said, "I think we can find the money as long as Tom is willing to be fair with his prices?"

Not wanting to look rude, I searched for the right words, but Gran jumped in, saying she would pay for it herself if need be.

Gran surprised me yet again when she suggested Tom call his "lovely wife" and see if she'd like to join us for a late lunch. "As I'm keen to meet her and also very keen to show her what a wonderful job her husband is doing."

When Tom indicated they already had plans with his team, I thought that was that but, as usual, Gran confounded logic and all preconceptions by extending the invitation to the entire team. Let me repeat that, *Tom's Team of Tradesmen!*

I had no idea what had come over her, a houseful of tradesmen? She must've been feeling ill! And I wasn't altogether sure we had *that* much food leftover.

I said to her again in French, "We don't have enough in the house for that many people and it'll be..."

But she stopped me with a combination of smile and stare, adding in English, "Oh, I'm sure we have more than enough, Marica. What about the ham and those smoked sausages we haven't even opened? And we must have a dozen eggs remaining?"

As Tom made several phones calls, I sensed I also felt sure Gran was up to something.

Tom's wife was more than happy to comply, anything to avoid having to cater for hungry tradesmen. She even offered to bring the trifle she'd prepared, which Gran graciously accepted before asking me in French what on earth was trifle?

I just rolled my eyes. We both knew she knew what trifle was.

"Do you think perhaps your friend Ilija will want to join us?"

I rolled my eyes back the other way.

CHAPTER 20

One Little Photo, One Massive Lie

Tom's wife, Susanna, a truly tiny little thing with whippet-like limbs and thin pale lips (she couldn't have weighed more than fifty kilos), could not praise my Gran enough, which instantly made them best friends.

Susanna was a teacher and, even better, she taught English Literature which naturally made her suitable company. While Gran paid tribute to Tom's talents, Susanna, ever gracious, praised Gran's beautiful house and stunning gardens.

I busied myself in the kitchen with the first of the dirty dishes. Several times I overheard Susanna using phrases such as, "So what is it he does?" and "Do you think he's..." and could only assume the topic was my Ilija.

Andy, the apprentice, brought his girlfriend. I couldn't help but notice how physically suited the two of them were. Andy, without a bucketful of dust covering his face, was every inch the typical surfer-type, as was his equally blond surfer-chick of a girlfriend who spoke with way too many "like-you-know-like" phrases, much to Gran's raised eyebrow dismay.

Even though they were nothing alike in personality or education, clean Andy bore a striking resemblance to photos of my Pop Colin as a young man. Gran must've seen it too.

One of Tom's other men brought his wife and two small daughters, one dressed in lilac and the other in sunflower yellow with ribbons in their hair matching the bows on their dresses. The girls, thrilled with the hide-and-seek, fairy-tale-like enchanted garden with its little secret corners, didn't remain clean too long but Gran didn't seem to mind, perhaps because she wasn't the one who would need to clean them. Or perhaps it was nice to have the garden so admired through the eyes of a child again. They saw magic and adventure where I now saw weeds and overgrown hedges. It'd been a very long time since I'd crept and crawled through hedges and scrubs into dark and mysterious corners where only blue wrens and fairies live or jumped in and out of toadstool rings.

The girls laughed as they played tag and even a scolding mother couldn't maintain her disapproval as the little girls charmed both their parents with scruffy hair and dirt marks covering a multitude of freckles, while presenting a bounty of the first of Autumn colour with outstretched hands and captivating smiles.

The impromptu party was in every way a success and even managed to draw me away from Ilija's translations. I knew I should've been beyond happy, but I wasn't. I think I wanted my authoress to be somebody but not *that* big. Now she was somebody who belonged to everyone. Mother's shadow, by way of my selfish nature, was on parade again.

I genuinely believed the girl in the photograph was directly linked to the author of the journals and both of them were linked to Gran-Gran's secret life back in France. But, with the authoress being Anastasia, even if the girl in the photo was related to us, a Princess of the Russian Imperial Royal Family *and* member of my family she could not be. This realisation devalued *my* journals. I knew they had more open market value but to me, their intimacy was eroded. So, Gran's party was exactly what I needed to put a bit of space between the journals and me. However, as I have often repeated, Fate seemed to take exceptional pleasure in creating havoc where there should be none. Just as I was starting to enjoy myself the phone rang.

"Marica, it's Ilija. I have to show you something and it cannot wait."

"What is it?"

"I've found something in the journals; honestly, this cannot wait, I don't even believe it but it is what it is. Please we must talk now."

I remained reluctant. "Can you email me?"

But he'd have none of it. So, I excused myself, retreating to my bedroom where I asked again, but he was insistent we needed to speak face-to-face. Eventually, he wore me down and I agreed to meet him at his place in an hour or so.

I was already off the phone by the time I re-joined the party in the conservatory. As I walked in Tom, Susanna and Gran all stared at me, which made me uneasy. I held up my mobile phone as I started to say, "Sorry, I..." but I stopped mid-sentence as Gran's grin was now shared by Tom and Susanna. Clearly, I was a topic of conversation and they weren't placing bets on the identity of my caller.

I didn't bother explaining. "Sorry, I have something to do. I'll try to be back in a few hours."

The three of them just stood, staring. Tom saluted my leaving by raising his glass as Susanna broke her stance taking three steps closer, before saying, "I'll help your gran finish cleaning up, go ahead, have fun with your boyfriend."

My what?

Oh, what the hell, I couldn't be bothered!

The entire drive to Ilija's place I just kept repeating Susanna's words in my head. Who was she? I'd never met her before. Who was she to make assumptions? And Tom! Tom was just our builder, who was he to judge my friends let alone extend that judgement to his wife!

As I stepped out of the lift, Ilija was waiting for me at the lift doors, which was strange. "What is it?" I asked.

Ilija rushed his words as though we were in some sort of vocabulary marathon. "I started working on a few of the pages, and most of them were short and sweet, talking about the lack of food and poor water supplies, that sort of thing. Other pages talked about her sisters' depression and her mother's refusal to accept reality."

Ilija ushered me to his door as he sucked in a chest full of oxygen before starting the marathon again. "There were also a few lines about Rasputin's murder, not much. Then I got to an entry, a long entry dated 15th July 1918. Written just a few days before they were assassinated."

Ilija caught his breath as he unlocked his apartment door and began his ramble almost instantly. "It went on for several pages and the handwriting was not very clear, so I read it four or five times."

He stopped.

It surprised me because he just stopped.

"Yes?" I asked, "So what did it say?"

Ilija pointed to the table as he offered me some orange juice, which I declined. He then flipped the kettle on before saying, "So, as I said, I re-read it to be sure. You know, it's one of the last entries in Russian, so I guess I should've known it would be significant, but I could never have imagined what I read, never, never, never, never!"

"So?" I was becoming frustrated with him. I mean, seriously, how many more revelations could there be?

"What have you read now?"

I leaned over where he pointed and started to read over his notes.

I slumped my head back down to re-read.

Ilija had a cigarette in his hand, but I declined. I felt ill enough already and was afraid the cigarette would make it worse. He drew back on his cigarette. I watched it cinder with a red edge against the white paper and reflect in his brilliant, mystic grey eyes. He drew in and then blew out.

"Do you get it? The photo, it's the little girl! It's the little girl!"

I kind of gave him a strange look because I hadn't read that. Perhaps I missed it, so I started reading it for the third time, this time out loud.

15th July 1918

I do not know how to write this but I must, for today I have discovered the lie that all of us have lived with and indeed the lie that I am about to live with, perhaps for the rest of my life, be that one day, one year or more...

Living with lies, this too I understood only too well.

...Papa called us to the kitchen and, as Doctor Botkin and his wife kept watch at the shadows beneath our doors, Papa showed us a photograph of a little girl with long cherry-blonde hair and pale eyes.

None of us had seen this little girl before so, given our current position, it seemed very strange that of all the things my parents managed to hide, a photograph of a little girl who we were sure was a stranger should be one of them...

"Photograph of a little girl, are... are they... talking about my photo?"
Ilija nodded.

...As the good Doctor and his wife watched the sentries' shadows Mamma said, "This little girl is called Anya-Katarina and she is someone Papa and I have known for almost fourteen years."

The five of us looked at each other because we'd never seen her or met her and yet she knew our parents?

Then Papa said, "She is someone very special to Mamma and me, and very special to your Grand-Mamma also."

The Doctor's wife remained sentry as Doctor Botkin approached. He was about to tell us a story, one which would change everything, changing, our lives and hers. One which even as I write this I cannot believe and yet I must.

So he began by saying, 'Almost fourteen years ago two babies were born, one a boy and one a girl, both beautiful babies but both small and fragile. No one expected twins.' The little boy was stronger and suckled immediately but the little girl would not eat nor would she sleep. No one knew how to appease her, not her parents, her Grand-Mamma, not even her doctor. But there was a bigger issue, you see; her parents were known to many and the birth was keenly awaited by thousands. Their parents were nobility, royalty. The public wanted to rejoice in the news of a new Prince, after all, there had already been four Princesses and a Prince was needed for the throne to be passed.'

I gulped away the disbelief and took a slurp of the coffee. "Is the photo of my little girl a photo of a missing Romanov sister?"

"Just read on."

'...Will the world think the long-awaited and desired boy to be also ill? Will people see it as a bad omen? This crown did not need any more bad omens.

That eve, nothing was said, yet everyone prayed the little Princess would live. But she became weaker, not stronger. Then more disaster fell on the babes.

The next morning, instead of receiving news that the little Princess was recovering, the family Doctor diagnosed the little Prince with haemophilia.

Everyone was convinced that Anya-Katarina would surely die, and should she do so, then her brother's disease would be discovered. This could not be. This could not happen.

So, a plan was hatched, one which would protect the Prince, little Anya and her entire family.

With the help of the family Doctor, their Grand-Mamma and Grand-Mamma's faithful companion, two births were recorded that day. One to the Tsarina, a beautiful son named Alexei and the second, to the child's real Grandmother's primary handmaid who was in her mid-forties, married but childless. A little girl named Anya-Katarina. And to ensure no one would ever discover the truth and given the handmaid was French, the date of birth was recorded using the Western European calendar rather than the Russian Orthodox, thereby ensuring the brother, Alexei's birthday was the 12th of August while his twin sister was recorded as thirteen days apart...'

My hand was trembling, as was the journal.

'She was thin and gaunt and showed definite signs of suffering from haemophilia, though perhaps not as seriously as her twin brother, yet for a woman, it can be worse because womanhood brings regular bleeding.

'Everything was arranged. At first, she lived with her adopted parents in Moscow. Her real parents made secret arrangements to see her whenever they could.

'But, as she got older it seemed she may yet survive so further arrangements needed to be made. More permanent plans for her future.

'Her adoptive parents and she were sent to Paris where a substantial home for her as well as a healthy bank balance and secure future including education, were organised.'

Paris! Things were falling into place. I hadn't told Ilija of my great-grandparents' apartment in Paris. Anya must have been a friend of Gran-Gran's family in Paris.

'To everyone's surprise the child prospered. But as she improved, her real family's fortunes began to reverse to the point where they were all imprisoned and soon they expected little from life. Yet her real parents found some solace in knowing at least one of their children might yet survive.

'But things began to change for little Anya also. As she reached womanhood, she became quite ill one Winter and soon was suffering from whooping cough and a bout of pneumonia. Between this and her monthly menstruations, her condition became serious.

'The first year it was not so bad but with each cycle, she lost more and more blood and became less and less active until it was clear to her doctors and *her adoptive parents she would not survive to full adulthood. The child, now a young woman, knew it also. The beautiful secret it seemed was to die with the beautiful Anya.*

'Her adoptive parents told her the truth about her lineage and her real mother and father and her four sisters and brother. She deserved to know...

I needed a moment to think and catch up. I put the paper down, took another gulp of coffee and then put the cup down too.

"What's wrong?" asked Ilija. "You have to keep reading," he insisted.

He was right, but I felt I needed to share the Paris apartment story with Ilija.

Ilija listened. "Still, if your great-grandparents were only servants, why would such a story be shared with them and not a living member of their own family?

"And, it still does not explain what your great-grandparents did to deserve the apartment?"

'As she became weaker and weaker she also became aware of the plight of her real parents and siblings. Soon she feared for them more than for herself.

Then, one day, she was asked a question; the answer required of her to do the greatest thing anyone can do, place her life at risk to save one of her siblings. The request was made that much more unfair because she'd never known her real family.

Even so, she knew she would not live long and, therefore, after many weeks and evenings in quiet prayer, she agreed.

So now we needed to find a way to make possible a swap...'

"Wait, what?"

"Where have you read to?" asked Ilija.

"To the line about *'make possible the swap'*. What swap?"

"Read on."

...One which would replace one daughter for another right under the gaze of Lenin's hellhounds, and there was only one choice, it had to be, the Tsar's youngest unknown daughter would replace the Tsar's youngest known daughter.

There were only three years between them and even though Anya was thin, she was tall enough for one to pass as the other and, without realising the Bolsheviks had given us the opportunity through Dr. Derevenko's visits.

'Over the coming days, we will come to check on Alexei and bring two nurses to check on the condition of the four sisters. One of the nurses will be Anya. While the pretend physical examination was taking place, I would take Anya's nurse's uniform and walk out with Dr. Derevenko and the other, older nurse, Anya's adopted mother.

'One of the guards who longed for money more than Lenin's praise and who found irrational death difficult to suffer had already been paid to let me out by doing nothing other than not inspecting her too closely. They were sisters so there remained resemblance, but one had light hair and the other dark, eyes needed to remain shut to the truth.

So it must be. One daughter's life for another's. If one lives so might the others, and if not, at least the truth will be known.'

I started to think this was too wild to possibly be true. Perhaps these journals were fake?

'If all goes to plan and if God helps us, we will all make it and again embrace. If not, then we must trust in God and never breathe a word of this.'

When the doctor finished, Papa only added, that he loved us all.

I was to become a sister that I'd never known or never seen. I was to take her life, her name and even her birth date.

I tried to argue that it could not be so, but Mamma's tears and my sister's comforting hugs helped reconcile the decision I was now forced to make. Even so, I struggled with our fates.

Baby said, "if one lives, we all live and if you die we are already dead. Do not take away from us the last bastion of hope which remains simply because you cannot be brave enough to not die with us, please!"

I can only confide to you, my Dear Journals, the pain I am feeling now. How can it be God wishes one to die for one to live?

I understand nothing of man or the Heavens; nothing.

By the time I'd finished reading, Ilija had poured two glasses of wine. We sat in silence, drinking the wine and just staring at each other. I needed to read it one more time before I could fully grasp this new entry, which not only changed my reality but history. This frightened me. These journals no longer belonged to me, they belonged to the world, and I didn't think that was fair.

Ilija had almost finished his cigarette by this stage. I gestured for him to offer me a drag. I sucked in the poison and let the nicotine swirl in my head.

I'm not sure how much time passed, before I found my voice. A hoarse sound grunted out. "How do we know it's my photo?"

"Because it fits, it just fits," he said.

And he was right. The evidence was mounting and if this were a trial I'd have enough to convict.

"Did you say the Russian bit is nearly over?"

He nodded as he refilled our wine glasses.

"Well, I don't think there's much else to say but I hope your floor is comfortable because I think we are about to pull an all-nighter!"

I flipped the pages. "Have you read these pages?"

"I wanted to wait for you, I wanted us to read them together," he said.

16th July 1918

We have just been told to expect Dr. Derevenko and two nurses tomorrow afternoon for a complete physical.

I am frightened.

I don't want to go but I don't want to stay either.

Papa says I must keep calm.

He gave me Anya's photo and told me to keep it safe.

Mamma said they will always love me.

Baby said not to be sad for them as they will get to know our other sister and I will not.

As Ilija read out the words I cried. What a sad thing to have to live through and what a horrible choice to make. Live or die and to live knowing others must surely die.

"I feel so sorry for her," I said as Ilija flipped to the next entry to find a pen and ink sketch of the Grim-Reaper. The Grim-Reaper with the face of Lenin and the crown of England and all it said at the bottom was:

The Devil Wears Many Crowns & Takes Many Forms but Remains the Devil.

17th July 1918

I write this as we travel through the village, it is mid-afternoon and I cannot believe how wonderful the sun feels, even on my parched, scorched Russia.

My new mother has said but ten words to me.

No one knows me.

No one cares.

I cannot believe it worked.

How can she not hate me?

Dr. Derevenko says I must keep quiet, not even speak for fear of saying the wrong thing.

Dr. Derevenko says we are yet unsafe.

If the guards realise the swap, my entire family will be dead and so will we be for we are still in Russia.

The cart is bumpy and rattles and yet makes my stomach churn even more. My new mother hugged me, but it was not real, forced, I feel so cold inside. How can she even stand to look at me?

I cannot stop thinking about Anya, my sister, or is it me that I am now thinking of and Anastasia is already dead? No! Dear God, forgive me for thinking this; not dead! Not dead!

Anya; oh Anya, I am so sorry,

Anya, with your beautiful cherry-blonde locks which I got to touch but for a minute as sentries paced outside.

Anya, whose voice I don't even know; our combined and shared fear stopping all but the faintest of whispers.

Even though she is younger than me, she is a little taller and much thinner, yet our eyes are the same, always the same, pretty cornflower-blue pools looking back at me...

"Wait!" I stopped Ilija's translation. "What did you just say?" Ilija looked at me before repeating: Even though she is younger than me, she is a little taller and much thinner, yet our eyes are the same, always the same, pretty cornflower-blue pools looking back at me...

And then, as though needing to qualify his translation, he said to me, "Cornflowers are little blue flowers which often grow wild. Their colour is kind of a purple-blue, unique."

"Yes. Yes I know."

Ilija mumbled something like, "It's just such a beautiful and unique way to describe an eye colour."

But all I registered was that Gran and I needed to talk. Soon. "Sorry, Ilija, go on."

...Even though she is younger than me, she is a little taller and much thinner, yet our eyes are the same, always the same, pretty cornflower-blue pools looking back at me, and I into hers.

She hugged me. My sister I never knew, and may never know, hugged me and I felt both her warmth and her thin frame, and my shame. I hope that one day she and I will hug again but now I must stop for we are coming to a checkpoint and I must cover my face as well as my identity.

18th July 1918

Dr. Derevenko has been very clever and I thank God for him, for without him we would never have made it through the checkpoints.

I don't know who he paid or how he arranged it but his papers have allowed us to survive this new ordeal.

Dr. Derevenko says we will be on a train before nightfall.

My new mother, oh dear God what do I call her? And what must she think of me? And how can we live together when she must..., she must hate me? My new mother just stares at me.

18th July 1918

I scribble this as Dr. Derevenko makes the final arrangements and as he hands me and my new mother over to a stranger. I don't know who this man is and I pray he is a man of honour.

Dr. Derevenko tells me that this man is a former Imperial Guard Soldier and will give his life for mine, even if he does not know who I am; or does he? So many secrets, so many spies, so many lies.

When I asked who the old man thought I was Dr. Derevenko said I was a former servant of the Tsar's daughters who was already threatened once and if I remained in Russia I would surely be raped and then murdered and that I travel with my mother who is French. And we must find our way to France.

18th July 1918

Dark has fallen and the train rattles, I hope we travel toward safety, but I do not know.

Dr. Derevenko has parted from my new mother and me. He said he must disappear for if our plan is discovered he will be tortured to obtain my location and then killed.

He is right, I know, but I feel completely alone even with this woman beside me, I feel so alone, we, now mother and daughter, we, both strangers, she, having lost the daughter she raised, and I, having lost everything.

The old man and I have not spoken; perhaps it is for the best. He just stares at me and I stare back yet I am not looking at him, I see only my sisters, Papa, Mamma and Alexei. I see us at the seaside with Olga shielding her face from the sun while Alexei's nanny carries him into the rocky hills so that he can feel a little freedom.

I see Maria painting the seascape and Tatiana running her toes in the water while I collect seashells.

That's what I see.

I am so tired and must sleep.

19th July 1918

I woke this morning as we pulled up to the border of Russia and Prussia and as I am still in Anya's nurse uniform I was asked to help with some injured soldiers while the train prepared to move on.

I am grateful for the time I spent with my sisters in the hospital for it allows me to not only play my new part but also help these poor young men who are all but dead around me.

One of the soldiers was staring too much, it frightened me, but my new mother knew what to do, telling him some story of a lost husband and missing children and emotional breakdown – he let us pass.

I write this as the old man attempts to find us some bread. When he calls out to me, I don't recognise Anya as my name, yet I must quickly learn.

We are headed for Berlin. There we will find a large number of our White Russians who will help us to France.

We are passing another ravaged village, another broken dream, another handful of soldiers breathing but as dead as I, one smiles, another hands me a newspaper...

...OH DEAR GOD. NO!

I cannot even write and yet I must for if I do not write I will scream and everything my family suffered this last eve will be for nothing – for they are dead, dead, dead! All of them dead!

All of them dead!

I hate Russia for her abandonment of us and I loathe England for her cowardice!

I must free myself from this place, God! I must forget everything I have loved and all that has been lost – yet I will never forget this hatred, I will never again be Russian as I am ashamed for you RUSSIA! Ashamed to have ever been called RUSSIAN!

"Can we please stop for a moment?"

I needed fresh air. Ilija's apartment was part of the Temple Court building on Collins Street, oddly enough built not long after this period, in 1924. His apartment faced Bank Place, which was some-how poetic. Bank Place could have been anywhere in the world -- in Paris, in Moscow, or in Melbourne. It was intimate and narrow with buildings of an era from the early 1900s. Some had been 'face-lifted' but all remained true to their original era. Painted seats circled trees, while pretty 1920s lampshades lit up the small cluster of cafés.

Ilija didn't have a balcony and I needed air and space. I needed to breathe. It wasn't late, but, being Easter break, very few people were around, which suited me.

Autumn had just begun to kiss the city of Melbourne with the odd crimson and gold floating among mostly green leaves, and although March had been warm, the evenings at last blessed us with soft cool breezes. And a soft cool breeze was what I needed.

Ilija instinctively knew I needed space, offering me his spare set of keys as he said, "I think we could do with a drink and I'm out of wine. I'll meet you back here when you're ready." He walked out without looking back.

I watched his long, long, lanky strides and his slightly wild, slightly greasy hair bounce in time to his strut. Tall, lanky and a cross between a rocker, an artist and a lost-in-time beatnik, his broad shoulders looked even broader from behind, especially offset against those skinny bass-player-like hips and legs.

I knew he was attractive, but I'd not noticed just how much, simply because his personality was that much more beautiful than anything physical.

As soon as I heard the lift go down, I also walked out and found my way to the middle of Bank Place and slumped onto one of the green seats, which were wrapped around the pretty deciduous trees. All I could think about was, *I need a cigarette.*

I sat in stillness, surrounded by silence. I have no idea how much time passed.

Ilija either knew where I'd be or he saw me in his travels or from his window, I wasn't sure. All I knew, at some point he was with me, a bottle wrapped in brown paper in one hand and a packet of cigarettes in the other. He put the bottle down beside me and offered his hand, which I willingly accepted. Warm, safe and comforting.

His hand reached around to my shoulder and his hug was all-consuming and I didn't care if it lasted for one hundred years. A tear freed itself. One solemn tear for Anya and all of them. I turned around, my back now firmly fitting into Ilija's chest as he lit up two cigarettes and offered me one.

We sat smoking together, without saying a word until the last cinder of each smoke died. Ilija reached down for the bottle and I moved free from his warm chest. Together and yet still apart. Part of me wanted him, most of me feared him. We returned to his apartment.

I couldn't bring myself to read any more, not straight away, so we ordered pizza and made useless small talk. The entire thing was completely surreal. Neither of us mentioned Anya or Russia or France or even Gran. Truth be told if you asked me I wouldn't recall anything of that conversation other than we both agreed pineapple does not belong on a pizza.

After almost two hours of pointless nothingness, I found the energy to open the journal again. The entries were about Anya, the new Anya, her first days in Paris, her loneliness.

Not today, not today, I almost begged Ilija as I said, "I will read these again, but not today."

He took the journal from me, and translated in silence, re-writing the words in English. As I looked at them, I was grateful his English was not perfect, because it would be easier *not* to read them if I struggled so.

"The next date was 27th Easter 1921." Ilija interrupted our silence. "It seems after her initial arrival in Paris, Anastasia didn't write again for almost four years," he adds.

The entry was very telling. During those four years, Anya/Anastasia had adopted the Roman Catholic date calendar because the 27th of March 1921 was the Catholic date for Easter Sunday.

178

27th March 1921

Easter Sunday – and my first day as Anïs-Katarin, I now have a new name to go with my new date of birth and my new parents. Grand-Mamma made it all possible.

I am neither 21 nor Anastasia and not even Anya – I am no one – I am obscure and unknown – and I am free to remain imprisoned in my cocoon of lies and regret.

Anya's foster parents have both now passed away, and, but for Dr. Derevenko, who went missing not long after the Tsar's family was killed and Grand Mamma, no one else knows the truth.

The Tsar's family. Even writing this makes me want to laugh and cry at the same time. How shameful it is to deny who you are. Yet, that is to be my life now. The Tsar has his four daughters, son and wife buried alongside him somewhere, and I have my parents buried in a graveyard outside of Paris. Grand-Mamma still writes to me but always in code. Brother is sister and sister is a brother. This is something she did with my foster parents and Anya. Even the photo, which I still hold, the reference to her sister's eyes was a reference to Baby.

Grand-Mamma Maria says that one day the truth will come out, but I do not know what the truth sounds like any longer. The truth: my life is one of the endless lies.

I didn't want to read any more. But Ilija persisted. "Brother is sister," he said. "Do you understand?"

I didn't.

"Brother is sister! The photo, brother is the sister?" he said again.

My mind caught up, *brother is sister*. It was too much.

It wasn't late but I felt tired, so very, very tired. And I didn't want to go home; I didn't even want to call Gran to let her know. I kind of wanted to punish her for her part in perpetuating this deception. She must have known. She and Gran-Gran had spent their entire lives in a false reality and managed to drag everyone into it with them.

Everyone.

Nana and Dida, Dad and even Mother; and now me.

Everyone.

"I feel as if I should get some sleep," I said.

"You can have the bed, I'm not too tired and I can always crash on the couch."

Still fully clothed but for my jumper, shoes, and socks, I slumped onto his bed as I watched him call someone. Whoever it was, they were speaking in Russian. I could only understand a few words, words common to all Slavic nations, but there was not nearly enough to even guess the conversation. And my fatigue made me care even less. I assumed it was some friend from his English classes and drifted off to sleep as he rambled on.

Around three or four in the morning, I woke with Ilija, also fully clothed, wrapped around me, and I didn't mind. I needed the reassurance and it felt so good having his arms wrapped around me and his wisps of loose hair resting over my forehead. I closed my eyes and slept.

CHAPTER 21

Gran's Garden

I woke to the sound of a teaspoon stirring in a cup and the smell of crumpets, but I had no appetite. Ilija forced me to eat at least half a crumpet but I must say the coffee was very welcome. As I sat with a hot coffee in hand, Ilija went to have a shower. I was extremely grateful he didn't ask anything, but then again he wouldn't, he always seemed to know *that* line.

When he came out, I was thankful he didn't appear in some cliché obligatory white towel wrapped around his waist, a caricature of a 1980s soft-porn star, though even with his super dorky Superman print boxers, he still looked a little too good. Even freshly-washed-clean, he still looked sexy-dirty-hot. Still, I couldn't help but wonder if his lack of t-shirt was a sign of being exceptionally comfortable in his skin or a subtle attempt to gauge my interest. Hooray was all I could say to the tattered, rainbow-coloured towel he was using to dry his hair. It was something I'd expect a child to own and helped make the situation slightly comical and me less self-conscious. Even so, skinny chicken-legs aside, I guess my admiration of his more than a little fine body must've been obvious because Ilija grinned and, feeling my ears burn, I blushed.

The more he held me in his stare the more feverish I felt, sure my normally pale face was a bright hue of crimson-pink. I decided to make a run for it. It's not that I wasn't interested, or that I missed his interest, it was more the state I was in.

"I, I, thanks for breakfast, and, and last night, well not, well, you know what I mean." I attempted desperately not to make contact.

The grin on Ilija's face remained. His confidence excited and annoyed me simultaneously. He walked to his door, unlatched the lock and opened it, all in only his boxers.

His still wet hair trickled water droplets past his shoulders and back. I wanted so desperately to lick those droplets free, and then just keep going, tasting every rippled muscle and soft pillow of skin. Another embarrassing flush overcame me as I stuffed the journals and printouts, everything I could grab, into my backpack.

Ilija was still standing at the door, one arm reached over his head, creating a human arch for me to pass through. With his height evident against the doorway, I slipped past him without even needing to crouch. I stood just on the other side of his threshold, his arm still over his head. I could smell his cologne. Sandalwood and, and, bergamot, that's what it was! For months I'd registered something in his cologne. This morning it was fresh and clean. And I knew the scent. He smelled like Christmas and Nana's afternoon teas.

He was staring at me. Perhaps it was my silence or maybe I looked like a weirdo sniffing him involuntarily.

"Sorry, I didn't mean to stare, it's just, well, this will sound strange, it's your cologne."

Ilija's arm weakened above my head, bending at the elbow. He'd misunderstood.

In one action I stopped his hand from dropping and said, "No, it smells good, great." I watched his lips form a slight smile. "It's got bergamot in it, right?"

"Most people don't even know what bergamot is."

"Gran and Nana," I said as I looked away, sure this would be *that* moment. "The two of them would have this high-tea tradition and Nana loved her Earl Grey, the tea leaves have bergamot in them."

I adjusted my backpack, hoping to give him time to make a move. We stood for what seemed like minutes but was only seconds.

"Oh," he said, "I haven't had Earl Grey tea, I just like the smell."

That's it?

"Well, I guess I'd better head off."

Nothing. He did nothing.

Maybe I read the signals wrong.

I blurted, "Well, thanks for—"

The rest of my sentence was lost in his perfectly timed, soft, slightly open-mouthed peck on my lips. I could feel the softness of his coffee aroma lips and the hint of hot breath behind those lips. I pulled away just a little and then pushed into him. His cheek brushed mine as we both drew breath, and then kissed even harder. He was everything I'd craved. He was warmth and love and passion and safety. He was more than sex or lust, his kiss was the key to what I hungered for, my need to belong without fear.

As I pulled away, I felt a sudden regret. I wanted him to make a move, yet now I just wanted to run away. It was too much. My ears flushed red. I was desperate to get out, especially once Ilija's smart-arse grin returned. I'm not sure if he liked the kiss, or maybe it was the look on my face.

My body heated up. Not the good pre-sex hot. This was *I'm-so-embarrassed* hot. I fumbled for my keys, avoiding his eyes and wondering how one little perfect kiss with perfect soft lips could make me tingle so much. I knew the answer. I think I hated him a little.

As I rushed off down the hall toward the lift, Ilija shouted, "I'll call you."

I turned around when I got to the lift and pressed the button at least a dozen times, then looked down the hall; he was still standing there. I waved this pathetic wave before the lift doors opened and I rushed through them.

I got into my car and took a deep breath. I knew I'd never felt so much from so little. One kiss. *Damn him!* It was perfect. I tried to focus my frustration on Ilija but I couldn't deny I was frustrated at myself. Why, why was this happening again? Someone I could love, someone who, given different circumstances, could make me happy; maybe, except he was temporary. He, too, was going to leave me.

The drive home was spent flipping between Anïs-Katarin's journals, thoughts of Gran's life- long deception and Ilija's kiss, and my kiss, or was it *our* kiss? I'd been thinking about how I wanted to taste his body just seconds before and I didn't pull back.

"Jesus, Marica!" I shouted at myself as I hit the palm of my hand against the dashboard, "Gran, Anïs-Katarin, concentrate on them, not some random hot guy who'll be nothing more than a pleasant memory soon enough!" I was still shouting.

"Right!" I nodded. "That's it, one damn tragedy at a time."

By the time I'd got home, I'd managed to manipulate the kiss into nothing, and if it was something, it was Ilija's something, not mine. *He* kissed me first. *He* made the first move. Whatever happened, would be his fault.

With my mind finally on Anïs-Katarin, I wanted to hear it from her, from Gran, that Anïs-Katarin was my Gran-Gran Ana-Katharine. I couldn't imagine a life where, for almost twenty years you're known as Anastasia, then for three or four years, your name is Anya only to be changed to Anïs-Katarin and eventually Ana-Katharine. I also wondered if the last change was to better fit into Australian life or was it another attempt to remove herself from her true past. After all, Great-Granddad ggYves didn't change his name to Iain or John or whatever.

There were still a lot of unanswered questions. I wanted to hear Gran's version. I wanted to know if she knew, or if she too was misled.

Gran's house was built by my great-grand-father Yves. Gran-Gran and ggYves, so the story goes, left Paris in November 1928 and arrived by boat in the Australian Summer of 1929, though to this day I have no idea why they decided to move to Australia. It did seem somewhat random, especially given the tale of ggYves' successful business in Paris, not to mention their seemingly fabulous apartment. But now things were falling into place.

Back in Paris, ggYves was a goldsmith. He must've been very good at his craft because Gran inherited some incredible pieces. For some reason, they decided one day to up stakes and travel to the other side of the world where they knew no one. And while Gran-Gran could speak English quite well, ggYves struggled, and even with his understanding of German, which resulted from working with large numbers of German Jews in Paris, English was difficult for him.

From the little I have been able to piece together, they came to Melbourne, where ggYves found a job with prestigious Hardy Brothers Jewellers in Collins Street, Melbourne. He was fortunate enough to have been given excellent recommendations by his Paris connections and Hardy Brothers could not have cared less about his accent, only his skills with setting emeralds and diamonds.

Initially renting, it wasn't long before Gran-Gran saw an opportunity. She wanted space and a garden, somewhere she could sit and read and even paint if the mood took her, but ggYves was reluctant. Even so, Gran-Gran usually got her way! *And as Gran said, the sale of the apartment gave them liquid assets.*

I kept thinking, adding up, rejecting one idea and forming another one. There, in the car, outside the house that started all this. It was like a cross between a puzzle and a poker game.

Melbourne. A world away from Europe. Cashed up. Educated. Survivor.

Gran-Gran, the original re-inventor.

There was a new development in the eastern suburbs among the apple and pear orchards. The blocks were large, and the development was only a few minutes' walk from a tram stop, so even ggYves couldn't complain. *Gran-Gran, the manipulator, Mother's grandmother, is that who Mother learnt her art from?*

The development was in the suburb of Surrey Hills and Gran-Gran saw the opportunity, but she held off for she sensed a change was happening. People were making too much money on the stock market; it was only a matter of time before the extremely exhilarating elevator ride up would need to come down. And the higher it got, the faster it moved, the further the fall would be. Banks were throwing investment cash at developers with little or no additional financial backing and Gran-Gran knew this false reality could not last. So she waited.

Gran-Gran the stalker, the huntress. Mother the stalker, the vixen.

Gran-Gran could afford to wait. GgYves was making decent money and they had liquidated many of their assets, transforming them into easily transportable and ever valuable gold coin.

Happiness is a fat pocketbook.

When the stock market crashed on Wall Street in October 1929, the first ripple of doom happened as small investors, who'd thrown all their cash into stocks, now had 10c to the dollar, if they were lucky.

Then came the bigger investors, those who were now struggling to keep banks from repossessing homes and boarding up businesses. This resulted in job losses, and that in turn resulted in speculative investments, such as developments in outer eastern suburbs, facing bankruptcy. That's when Gran-Gran struck. While other people were praying they'd have a job to go to tomorrow or lining up in soup kitchens, Gran-Gran made an offer to the developer, buying four adjoining blocks – early 20th-century size plots, not the small half-block of the modern world, but big, fat quarter-acre blocks. And Gran-Gran bought four of them, for the price of one. The developer could not refuse the irresistible clink of coin, even at a quarter of yesterday's value. *Gran-Gran, the savvy negotiator.*

Family legend has it, she said to the developer, "This is what I am willing to offer and not a penny more. What you must decide is, is it sufficient. For if not, I can spend my money elsewhere, but can you find another buyer elsewhere?"

Gran once repeated to me her mother's words. "The rest was easy. People had neither money nor work. I have seen the desperation of poverty before and well know how to both survive and manipulate it."

How to survive and manipulate it... words which could have come from Mother's mouth.

With one in three people jobless, even ggYves lost his position but Gran-Gran didn't fret, reportedly saying, "We have more than enough funds to sustain us and now you will be able to better oversee the building of our home."

Paranoia, stemming from a past of being watched, mustered and herded?

No one explained to me where this phobia stemmed from and how it didn't pose a problem in a Paris apartment. Family idiosyncrasies, I'd assumed. Now it was falling into place.

She had the house plonked snap-bang in the middle of the four blocks with a barn to one side and a garage to the other. High cream-yellow sandstone fences edged the entire parameter; Gran-Gran preferred solid materials and didn't trust simple wooden fences would keep out the dingoes. There were no dingoes. There weren't even kangaroos, though the great possum-rose-bud-eating-plague was, from by all accounts, akin to a natural disaster. A large cat and numerous traps solved that 'catastrophe'. The same cat fixed the problem of parrots feasting on her apples and plums.

Fruit trees, self-sufficiency, exactly what one would expect from someone who'd felt hunger and seen starvation.

The front fence was evenly pierced with dark wrought iron window peepholes, to ensure all her neighbours could enviously glimpse her picture-perfect house and postcard-pretty garden as they wandered by. The front double gates were also wrought iron, ever closed.

The same sandstone, mixed with redbrick, was the material used to build the house with the very traditional Australian tin roof, leading to a bull-nose veranda, which hung a full two metres over the entire edge of the house's circumference. The same elaborate wrought iron design as was in the fence decorated each veranda cornice. At each entrance and window, massive sandstone plinths and doorway arches created an image of strength and wealth, as did the house's matriarch.

Aesthetic beauty, uniformity, signs of someone with education and culture.

Inside was a formal lounge room, a small snug, a formal dining room, a library and a large kitchen-meals area, which opened onto a stunning cut-glass conservatory.

Outside, a very functional decked area effortlessly led the eye to the strategically placed rotunda, overgrown with a wild entanglement of white and pale, pale pink roses. On either side, two straight-as-arrow pencil cedars stood like sentinels. The garden was designed by someone with an eye for design and knowledge of seasonal colour, *someone who'd been raised around beauty...*

It was also carefully conceived to give the onlooker something to look at from every angle, but also something to strive toward because you couldn't see the entire garden from any angle. This not only created the illusion of endless space but this delicious feeling of being on the verge of discovering a secret entrance to another world or dimension. I know because that's how it felt to me as a child.

Magic... she was bringing back the magic of a lost childhood...

Whilst Nana and Dida's garden was also beautiful, it was much smaller and much more functional. As a child, I loved Nana and Dida's garden, but I adored this one.

From the front gates, the purpose of the white- pebbled driveway was to lead those lucky enough to gain entrance into Gran-Gran's *'ode to Monet'* on a journey. As for those resigned to admiration only, an enticing glimpse of heaven. Considering the design with adult eyes, it seemed obvious.

It was starting to all fit, memories of Paris and France, memories of hunger, insecurity, Gran-Gran's garden was her entire life story.

Thinking about it now, I was a little disappointed for not connecting the brilliance of shape and design, which could only come from a specific type of lifestyle and study. Ample fruit trees, a walnut and chestnut tree as well as numerous hazelnut bushes. Her extremely productive vegetable garden was almost half of one of the blocks. As for her chicken pen, which she managed to also make attractive by placing a picket fence on the outside of the chicken wire and then underplanting with an herb garden, it took up what remained of that side of the garden.

Not that she worked in the garden, other than to pick ripened tomatoes, dead head rose bushes or collect the odd egg. "That's what the help is for," Gran often quoted her as saying.

Of course, it was. To her, servants were as natural as a mobile phone to me.

From Gran's stories, they built their house and planted their garden for next to nothing. "What were these wretched souls to do? Many had no money, no jobs, and no food, and a garden full of fruit, vegetables and eggs was quite valuable."

Gran said that during WWII's ration period, sometimes her mother paid people with little more than eggs, potatoes and cabbage, though the day ggYves brought a goat home so that they could have fresh milk nearly brought them to blows, with Gran-Gran exclaiming, "I will not have that foul beast in my garden, do you hear me, sir! Remove it or remove yourself!"

The following weekend Gran-Gran arranged quite the garden party with *goat-on-the-spit* as the main meal.

How had I missed all this? HOW!

Gran was born in June 1931. Two years later ggYves started his own jewellery business. As Gran would say, "I never knew the pain of an empty stomach. Even though WWII we had vegetables and eggs and chicken every Sunday. Life for me was never really a great struggle."

Gran-Gran ensuring her daughter wanted for nothing. Did Gran-Gran spoil Mother to the point of expecting everything?

I was not sure what happened to ggYves, none of us was. For some reason, even though he was older, he couldn't sit back and let his beloved France be decimated, so in 1941 he enlisted. With fluent French being a huge advantage and some sound knowledge of German, it was clear where he'd be sent.

On the 24th of December 1943, Gran-Gran got the telegram. They didn't celebrate Christmas that year. His body was never recovered.

So much sense now. Why Gran always acted as though she was better than everyone else. Why Mother believed she should not be denied anything. *Mother! Mother must have known!*

But then I rethought it. If she'd have known, she would have been even worse to live with. *Still, Mother must have known something, surely?*

Both the vegetable garden and the chicken pen were long since gone. I certainly have no recollection of them. Dida and Nana supplied the entire family with ample supplies of both fresh eggs and vegetables, so perhaps there was no need.

190

In their places were planted a thicket of silver birches, under-planted with daffodils and lilac-coloured hyacinth heralding Spring's arrival each year. The rest of the old veggie patch was now covered in pine trees with a blanket of pine needles beneath, which supplied us with and Autumn feast of pine mushrooms, as well as opportunities to try and catch fairies as they danced among the red toadstool rings. I never managed to catch one, but I swear I saw one or two when I was little.

I'd driven the car into the garage and got out. The crunch of cream pebbles heralded my approach. I could smell the linden trees, their dried flowers making wonderful herbal tea and even better-tasting honey. My crunching on the stones disrupted a pair of resident ring-necked doves. I loved the sound of their coo-cooing. I loved everything about this garden and now I understood so much. Where the money had come from, where the inspiration had come from, and where we had come from originally.

CHAPTER 22

Riddle Me This

I was ready to talk to Gran.

I had both journals in my backpack but wanted the old cigar box also. I wanted to see Gran's reaction when she saw it. Some time ago I'd moved it from my bedroom to the garage. Gran didn't drive, had not for several years, and she did not dig *that was for the help.* No chance of her looking in the garage.

Quickly I retraced my steps back to the garage, crunching pebbles under my feet. The toolbox. Then the cigar box and back out. I put the journals back into their box, added the photo, mustered up my courage and walked around the back. As I walked in through the kitchen door, Gran was sitting, waiting. Her sunken face and strained eyes betrayed she'd been waiting for some time.

Sitting beside her at the kitchen table, I placed the old cigar box, its contents returned, plus some additional sheets, some of Ilija's translated pages printed, and in particular the last few entries, on the table between Gran and me.

I was about to start talking when Gran interrupted with, "Yes. Before you ask, the answer is yes."

"Yes to what?"

"In the box, what you have in the box, the letters or whatever they are, yes they are Anastasia's."

I felt sideswiped or ambushed or something.

"And yes—"

I'd not said a word and yet she knew exactly what I was about to ask her.

"—Your great-grandmother was once was called Anïs-Katarin, Anya and ... Anastasia."

Outsmarted. I was no match for her.

I took a deep breath. "So you know about the journals?"

"No, well, not until last night I didn't." She looked away and then looked back. "If I'd known about them I would've burnt them."

She glared at me with her cornflower blue eyes. "That's what you should do, burn them."

"Last night, what do you mean last night?"

"Your friend, or boyfriend, you know, Ilija. He called me last night to let me know you were tired and would stay the night. He worked it out, and I guess he suspected I'd know Russian. You fell asleep as he quickly gave me a rundown about the journals, though I understood him to say letters. My Russian isn't nearly as good as his, and then—"

She stopped long enough to tell me she was still choosing her words carefully.

"—All he needed to say was that the two of you had discovered the truth about our true family name and tomorrow the great-grand-daughter of a princess will need answers."

I was furious. It had taken me a few moments to absorb Gran's words, but they finally sank in. Not only had Gran ambushed me but Ilija was how she did it. My mind was screaming, *Kiss me and stab me in the back all within a few hours!*

I felt the anger feed crimson into my cheeks but held my tongue and my purpose.

193

"Journals, you say?" asked Gran.

Without replying, I took out the photo of the little girl who I believed now to be Anya and pushed it toward her.

Refusing to touch it, she lashed with her acid tongue, "Where did you find this?"

"In one of the boxes, that first day I was up in the attic," I said.

No smile, no emotion, just a monotone voice blurted, "I thought it was lost." Then as if she had a change of heart, she took it in both her hands, touching and caressing the photo's creases as though summoning a three- dimensional living creature to appear.

She knows who the girl is.

Another pendulum swing of emotion. "Throw it away, she is no one," she said as the photo fell from her fingers back to the table.

But this time I was ready for Tornado Gran. "This is a real person. A real person!"

"And she is the reason you and I live!"

"She is also the reason *only* you and I live." Gran's voice spat poison.

"What?"

"It is her legacy, the real legacy, which has haunted all of us, her and her sisters. They prevented us from having anything resembling a normal family."

I didn't understand.

"It is also her fault that I could never be truly honest with those I loved and could never be free of the past. Everyone has a right to the pursuit of freedom; everyone except our family!"

The venom in Gran's words stung me. I started to get the feeling I was all too eager to victimise and blame before I'd finished getting all the facts. Ilija still had a lot to translate, perhaps I'd rushed ahead.

But I maintained my indignation. "So, you're blaming Anya's selfless act on what, your own few moments of sadness? Really? How many times have you told me you knew nothing of real struggle, even through the aftermath of the Depression and WWII?"

"Marica! You are twisting my words! There is a chasm of difference in never feeling an empty belly and never filling an empty soul!"

"Empty soul? What does that mean? Weren't you happy with Pop Colin? Are you saying you regret your life? What part do you regret most, your daughter or me?"

Gran's face showed the first signs of softening. "No, you were never my regret. You were my greatest treasure and my greatest fear."

"Fear?" I was stumped. "Fear of what?"

"Of the day I might have to reveal everything to you. The day you too may be faced with a sickly child, one with the family curse of haemophilia."

God! I'd forgotten all about that. I was so busy looking for reasons to be angry that I forgot the one big secret of the Romanovs' legacy – haemophilia. I shook away my momentary weakness as I was determined to make Gran pay for the lies. "So what, are you saying you kept all this quiet because you thought someone would discover we might be carriers of haemophilia?"

Gran opened her mouth to reply but I stopped her.

"WOW! Now that's unbelievable! And so that's your excuse, you didn't want the neighbours to know someone in our family some generations back once may have had haemophilia?"

"Not *may* have had – did have!" she pleaded.

"OK, yes everyone knows Alexei was a sufferer, but that's like..." I worked it out in my head, "...my great-great-uncle. Seriously, you'll need to come up with more than that."

"Not just him," said Gran.

Those three words caught me off-guard. *Not just him*. Three words.

I was attacking an old woman in her eighties about something that happened even before she was born. In many ways, she was as much a victim as I.

No, no she wasn't, I thought, she'd known the truth and could have told me so many times, even as she told me the truth about Dad. She may have been a victim, but she was also equally to blame.

I found my strength. "Who then?!" I demanded.

Gran's eyes glassed over. I started feeling sorry for her, but I didn't want to give in, not this time. I wanted all the answers, *all of them*. I calmed my beating heart and softened my voice a little. "So, we're both here together and I'm ready to listen, tell me now."

Gran motioned to the photo. "I think this is the only photo which exists of Anya." Then she added, "Now that you know, what are you are planning on doing?"

Calm, she was way too calm. *How can I shout and demand and break her if she remains this calm?*

The tone in my voice held. "I don't know exactly. I'll probably start with yelling at Ilija for warning you and then I think we'll talk about what happened between 1918 and 1921, and between 1921 and 1928."

Retrieving journal Vol-two, I flicked the pages to the next entry and added, "And finish with these fears of yours."

Not allowing her opportunity to sway me, I pointed to the pages as I said, "Look, 1921 and then barely another entry between then and 1928. I'm sure Ilija will help me work it out, but it might be quicker if you tell me."

Gran stared silently at me.

"There's no point in keeping the truth now. Between these final journal entries, my imagination and a quick search on the internet, I'll work out the truth, but I'd much rather hear it from you," I said.

I assessed her body language before adding, "Even now."

Gran got up. I thought she was about to walk out but instead, she suggested, "Well, if we are to talk all day I am going to need a very strong coffee."

Coffee? Really? Was she making excuses or time to think of a new lie? I nodded OK.

Something was wrong. Gran went from defiant denial to resignation too quickly. Something more, how much more could there be? What else was she hiding, keeping hidden in this house, garden, and her head? Her suddenly agreeable attitude to my discovery was unnerving me.

Were the journals a complete fabrication? After all, she'd managed to fabricate an entire fake history for Tom the builder.

Maybe she wrote them! An only child, with a mother who preferred the company of her flowers and fruit trees to other people. I'd recreated and fabricated an effective imagined past with Dad, why couldn't she have done the same thing, but through journals? There was no way of knowing how long the journals had been in the attic, eighty or forty years; their look would be almost identical.

The more she stood silent, waiting for the coffee percolator, the more my new hypothesis made sense. She'd lost her father, missing in the war, perhaps this was her way of passing the time and when he never came home, it would have served her well as a way to keep her mind occupied. But then I realised, no, she would still need someone to write the Russian pages. What the hell else was she hiding!

CHAPTER 23

True Lies and the Lines In-Between

As Gran put two very large mugs of coffee on the kitchen table she asked, "How much do you know?"

"I know about Anya and she and Gran-Gran changing identities and how Anya was left to die so that Gran-Gran could live," I said, though the suggested edge to my voice bordering on sarcasm was unintended.

Without letting Gran interrupt, I added, "And I think I understand why Gran-Gran hated Russia and even England so much, but what happened in Paris and why did she and ggYves move to Australia? And did ggYves know and—"

Gran stopped me. "Fine," she said as she lifted her hand to stop the bullet-spray of questions. "I'll tell you what I know, and we'll work out the rest together."

Too obliging.

"OK," I said.

"First, your great-grandfather had no idea of who his wife was, that's how your Gran-Gran wanted it. She wanted nothing to do with Russia."

I nodded and kind of waved my arms for Gran to continue.

"In 1921, the year your Gran-Gran was turning twenty-one, by her sister's birth certificate, she was about to turn eighteen. Anya's adoptive father died a few months after she joined them in Paris and resumed Anya's life. While she was still legally a minor, her 'mother' also passed away. This made things rather complex.

"However, Great-Great-Grandma Maria, being the clever woman she was, insisted on becoming Anya's godmother and when she realised her former handmaid was quite ill, arranged to become Anya's legal guardian. As Anya was the Duchess' ward, it fell to the Duchess to ensure her protection until her legal age of twenty-one. Anya/Anastasia detested having her dead sister's name and insisted she should be allowed to change it. The Duchess arranged for Anya-Katarina to become Anïs-Katarin, a close French translation." Gran took a sip of her coffee.

"Great-Great Grandma Maria put Anïs-Katarin through university and ensured she'd never want for anything financially, but melancholy often overcame Anïs-Katarin. No matter what was tried or where she was sent, your Gran-Gran could not shake the ghosts of her siblings and parents."

Gran took another sip. "Then in 1925, that stupid fraud, good God what was her name?"

Gran bit her lip, but I knew who she was referring to. "Do you mean Anna Anderson?"

"Yes! Yes, that's her! She will never know what pain she caused your Gran-Gran and your great-great-grandma, that opportunistic witch! I mean, really. She looked nothing like Anastasia, she was born in the wrong year, could speak neither French, English nor Russian and had no idea of the customs or etiquette as would any noble lady of that time! Whatever possessed people to, well, she made such a splash all over the papers, everywhere. So much so that people started believing she might well be the real thing, you know. Because of her foot and everything."

"Yes, that's right. Anastasia had something wrong with her foot didn't she? Disfigured, wasn't it?"

"Well, disfigured is perhaps a bit harsh. I mean really, it was hardly noticeable."

Gran paused. "Anyway, when Monsieur Gilliard got involved with the fraudster, Anïs-Katarin became concerned that someone would find her, so she wrote to the Grand Duchess to help arrange a suitable marriage as soon as possible."

"Sorry?" I interrupted, "Arrange a marriage?"

Gran pursed her lips as she said, "Dear, this is very hard for me, would you mind listening for a moment or two and then ask questions?"

I fell into silence.

"At first, Grannie Maria suggested people of noble birth, she was sure she could arrange something without too many questions, but your Gran-Gran wanted nothing to lead back to her real identity and instead pleaded for a commoner who was smart, kind and would be a good provider."

"Your Great-Grandpa Yves was an apprentice to Grannie Maria's jeweller before he set off to work for some of the best jewellers in Europe, returning to start his own business in Paris. He was quite successful and therefore known to the nouveau riche as well as those of rich character and class."

"Gran-Gran was a beautiful woman with a thick mane of hair, perfect complexion, even after all she'd been through, and of course those eyes, those brilliant eyes that captured, captivated and mesmerised all who looked on her. Yves took one look at her and was lost. Within four months they were married."

Arranged marriage was still swirling in my head, and I had to ask, "So what were the terms? Did Gran-Gran love ggYves?"

Gran seemed to consider the question as though I'd asked her to explain nuclear fusion. "I don't rightly know. She cared for him deeply but perhaps because of everything she'd witnessed or because it was common practice for women of her breeding to have arranged marriages, love was not a significant factor in her eyes."

While I was still trying to wrap my head around Gran's indifference to the question, she returned to her story. "Naturally, they moved into her Parisian apartment."

I interrupted again. "Didn't ggYves question where the apartment came from?"

"Well, no? Why would he? He was told that Gran-Gran's mother was handmaid to Princess Maria Feodorovna, later known as the Grand Duchess Maria Feodorovna, and that the Grand Duchess was also Gran-Gran's godmother. My father favoured the royal connection and thought it would benefit his business.

"The Grand Duchess, who'd long since returned to live in peace in her native Denmark, helped arrange and supported the marriage. It was not a huge leap to think that a very loyal and loving servant, so loyal that the servant's child would have the Grand Duchess as godmother, would be rewarded with a lavish apartment, jewels and a regular steady income. He had no desire to question and no reason to assume that Princess Maria Feodorovna was his wife's real grandmother."

Then, as though to cement her point, Gran added, "You must understand the period, dear. There were many people of Russian descent or Russian royal connections living in Paris and Berlin at the time. Even those who were not connected by blood, if they associated with royalty, they had a position in 1920s Paris. Any connection, whether by blood or socially, to royalty, especially the Russian Royal Household, was the equivalent to knowing or being related to a big Hollywood star today. After all, what do you think nouveau riche means?"

"So what happened?"

"Right from the beginning, everything went well. Yves was successful in his business and Anïs-Katarin presented as the perfect hostess-wife. They started mixing in quite avant-garde circles and were very taken with the new Art Deco movement. Your Gran-Gran also became one of Madame Coco Chanel's first clients—"

"Wait, what? Are you saying that my great-grandmother was friends with Coco Chanel?" I stopped for a second before adding, "*The* Coco Chanel?"

"Well yes," replied Gran. "You see, at that time Madame Chanel was living with some lord or duke. Now, what was his name? Let me think, the Duke of Westminster, I think? Or was it Grand Duke Dimitri of Russia? No, no it must have been the English duke, I'm sure of it. Your Gran-Gran would've have worried about the close association with Grand Duke Dimitri. Anyway, as I was saying, Madame Chanel started her own business in the 1920s, firstly as a milliner, and then later she moved into clothing. Gran-Gran was one of Madame Chanel's first clients and they became quite close."

Is there more to this? Another family secret, involving Coco Chanel?

Gran looked at me. "You know of course that Madame Chanel lost her mother at the age of twelve and her father put her in an orphanage and left her with nuns?"

I shook my head no.

"Well, as you can imagine this made Madame Chanel somewhat of a kindred spirit. Though I doubt your Gran-Gran shared much of her own experiences, I know she felt an affinity with Madame Chanel." Gran fell silent for a moment before saying, "She often talked of Madame Chanel, after it was just her and me, when there was a magazine article of the latest fashions, and of course, there was the issue of religion," Gran added matter-of-factly.

"Religion?" I asked.

"You see, Dear, your Gran-Gran lost faith in God, which was understandable, and I must say that I..." Gran stopped herself before starting over. "She lost faith in God and religion and so had Madame Chanel. Raised by a mother who suffered from mental illness and a father who abandoned her to nuns, nuns who loved God more than His children. Madame Chanel felt little affinity with either God or religion."

Gran took another sip of her coffee. "So, as I say they became friends. It was your ggYves' wonderful pieces of jewellery that inspired Madame Chanel to move into jewellery. Anyway, your Gran-Gran had artists and dancers and musicians as friends, many of whom dined with them.

"Six months into the marriage, your Gran-Gran fell pregnant. Yves was over the moon, hoping for a boy but more than happy to have the spitting image of his beautiful wife."

"Wait!"

"You have a brother?" Looking at Gran's face I could have sworn something sucked the oxygen out of the room. I felt guilty and I didn't even know why.

Gran gained her composure and the colour back in her face before she said, "Your Gran-Gran lost the baby. It was a boy. Then, less than a year later she fell pregnant again, and again was blessed with a boy, but, as with his real uncle Alexei, her son had haemophilia. But her son only survived a few months."

So that was the secret of the fear of haemophilia.

Gran got up and took a walk around the kitchen, fetched out what remained of the Easter cakes and, while munching on one of them, offered several to me. As cake crumbs collected in the corner of my mouth and crumbled on the table. I repeated what I'd just learned. "So, Gran-Gran lost two sons? That's, jeez, that's truly tragic."

"Indeed."

I felt a cloud of guilt settle. I'd not considered why Gran-Gran would keep secrets after WWI. I was being selfish, like Mother, selfish, all about what I wanted or needed. Then it struck me. "Is, is that why you didn't want to get married?"

Gran nodded.

"And, and was Mother your only child?"

I saw a slight tremble in Gran's lips. "Yes, thank God. I could not have gone through what your great-grandmother went through."

"So, is that why you waited so long to have a child?

Gran nodded. "Pop Colin wanted children, but I feared to have a son, so avoided getting pregnant. But then, I fell pregnant with your mother. It was unplanned and for the full nine months I prayed every day for a little girl." Gran smirked. "Funny how we all turn to prayer when we need to believe in God."

"So then, you are a carrier?"

Gran's face became stiff. "I don't know. Because I had a little girl, I had no reason to find out and frankly, didn't want to know." Gran cleaned up what remained of the cake crumbs as Ilija tried to call me, but I didn't want to pick up. After the third ring to message-bank Gran said, "Please answer it, Dear.

Just as the phone started ringing for the fourth time I answered. "What?!"

"Wow! Not a good time?"

"I'm not sure. Who else do you need to call to discuss my family secrets?"

"So, feel better?"

"Yes, a little. But I can't talk now."

He laughed. "OK, call me when you can talk."

"OK."

"OK."

"OK, hang up already!" I said and couldn't help the amusement in my voice.

"All well with your boyfriend?"

"Gran, he is not my boyfr... Oh forget it, can we please get back to the story?"

"Yes, yes." She sighed before repeating, "After they lost another child your Gran-Gran became very depressed, convinced she'd been cursed."

"What? How do you know she became depressed?"

"We talked about it when I fell pregnant with your mother."

I was beginning to understand why there were only female children in my family. I think most women expect to have the option of motherhood and I'd always thought I wanted children.

"And your ggYves didn't know how to help his wife. Of course, he had no idea of the death of all her family, but he knew she'd seen atrocities, after all she and her parents, as far as he knew, had fled Russia. I think he believed the deaths of their sons somehow triggered something stagnant inside her. He barely left her side. Their business started suffering as ggYves spent more and more time looking after his wife, but he didn't care. Yet nothing helped."

Gran touched her fingers to her lips as I watched tears well in her cornflower-blues, which suddenly, and for the first time that I could recall, changed to amethyst. This somehow made her look frail, as though her happiness was linked to her eyes. She shook her head free, forced a smile and tried to resume the story.

"It got so bad. Your Gran-Gran started imagining her neighbours were going to poison or assassinate her. She became convinced everyone was a threat. Your ggYves became desperate. He didn't understand why this darkness had entered their lives. He didn't know how to deal with it. Convinced his wife was on the verge of suicide, he wrote to the Duchess, hoping that she would somehow be able to help."

Gran smiled. "You can imagine Yves' surprise when Duchess Maria sent her best physicians. Well, that surprise was topped with a personal letter to him from the Duchess. In it, she said she wished she could visit but was too old to travel long distances. The Duchess also wrote to your Gran-Gran, in Russian, a private letter."

"Didn't ggYves question how she could read Russian?"

"No. Yves simply assumed Gran-Gran had learned Russian from *her* mother, after all, the story was your Gran-Gran was born and spent her first five years in Russia, so why would he?

"The letter and personal physicians did help, however your Gran-Gran's phobia of being found out coupled with her fear she'd never conceive a healthy child haunted her.

"I think it haunted her all her life, as though she believed herself somehow cursed, punished for surviving when her family suffered. I think some of these fears haunted me too. I'm not much for God's influence but I must say I cannot dismiss His existence because there must be a Devil for all this hatred to live. And if I believe in the Devil, I cannot disbelieve in God.

"She began to fear her friends, including Madame Chanel, fearing Chanel's lover was too close to King George V and your Gran-Gran's identity would be discovered.

"Her other former friends, artists, musicians, she imagined were secret spies sent to infiltrate her new existence before kidnapping her. She was convinced that someone would discover her secret and arrange to have both her and her husband murdered.

"Then news came that her grandmother, the Duchess, had passed away. Your Gran-Gran became inconsolable and Yves desperate.

"One day, so my father told me, he was reading the paper and read an article about jewellers based in England, who'd established branches in Sydney and a new branch in Melbourne. He'd heard pleasant things about Melbourne, and it occurred to him that if they left France and Europe, perhaps your Gran-Gran would leave her past pain behind. He arranged for one of his best clients and close friends to contact the London office and introduce him. It seemed things were going very well for the jewellers, Hardy Brothers is their name, and they are still in business, on Collins Street."

"Yes, I know of them, high quality items, very respectable."

"So, after several months of negotiation and letter-writing across the English Channel and globe, your ggYves was offered a position, sight unseen. Once he had the offer, he told his wife. The news was like a magic tonic to her. A few months later they were travelling by boat to Melbourne."

"And that's why Gran-Gran was uncomfortable with closed spaces?"

"She feared people were watching her and thought city apartments made them easier targets."

"But didn't they live in Melbourne city for a year?" I asked.

"Well, not exactly. You are forgetting we are talking about a long time ago. Melbourne was a city but unlike the cities of Europe, it had more of a village feel and so few people knew or cared about Imperial Russia. Your Gran-Gran felt much more at ease, much freer."

"And then you were born?"

"Yes, your Gran-Gran became convinced that moving to Australia saved her life and blessed her with a child. She wanted to become as Australian as possible, so she changed her name again to a much more Anglo-sounding version, though it was never official."

"But the house? The garden? It couldn't be more European?"

This made Gran laugh. "Oh, she loved the freedom Australia gave her but that didn't change the fact that she was European royalty! Besides, it kept the connection alive. I learnt to speak French before I could speak English."

"And the Russian?"

"My Russian isn't particularly good. It's passable but just so. When I was little, your Gran-Gran taught me a few words, literally a few words. It wasn't until ggYves went to war and then went missing that your Gran-Gran started teaching me more, though I've never really learnt to speak it well and I speak it with a strange Australian-French accent and cannot read a word. But I can understand it. That is of course if it's not spoken too quickly, I understand well enough, as I did when your friend Ilija called me."

"Oh?"

"Never learnt the Cyrillic alphabet, which I think was intentional on your Gran-Gran's part. She wanted me to be educated and well-rounded but not too much of the Russian stuff, as she put it. Mind you, she spoke French with a slight Russian accent, though no one questioned it in Paris because she spent her early childhood in Moscow, and no one knew the difference between most accents in Australia at the time. To Australians at that time, a foreign accent was a foreign accent. Australians thought that's how all French women sounded when they spoke English."

"So, so when did you?"

"When did I know? Very little until I was fully grown. Your Gran-Gran told me of a family history of child deaths and haemophilia when I was around eighteen, but I didn't know about my brothers' deaths until I got serious with a particular gentleman straight out of teachers' college."

"Teachers' college?" I had no idea Gran had completed any formal studies.

"Yes, I was quite the student and I know my mother would have preferred me to pursue a medical profession which, I guess she thought, would be a wonderful way to show respect to my aunts who'd worked as nurses during WWI. The trouble is I have always had a fear of hospitals, in fact, all medical places and professions. This is my phobia. Anyone in the medical industry is simply a walking disease carrier in my opinion. I know it's illogical and unfounded but that is how I felt and still do. I went on to become a teacher of music and European history.

"So, when your Gran-Gran told me about the deaths of my brothers, I decided I never wanted to have children. I spent much of my youth and middle youth teaching, never expecting or wanting to marry, turning down several suitors, until your Pop Colin."

Gran tapped her fingers on the table as she finished this part of the story.

"After ggYves' official status changed from missing in action to presumed dead, your Gran-Gran told me the entire story and made me promise never to disclose it."

Poor Gran. She'd carried this hidden truth for much of her adult life with no one to share it with. What a burden.

It was well past lunch, and I could tell Gran was tired and so was I. So many questions remained, but all my resentment of Gran evaporated.

I suggested we go out for a late lunch.

I had a plan. We drove into the city without mentioning Gran-Gran, Russia or the journals. I treated her to one of the best bistros in the city, Vue de Mode on Little Collins Street. And while she went off to the bathroom, I made a call. Though Gran wasn't normally a time-waster, she did have a public bathroom ritual. She never left the house without sanitary wipes. And if she should need to use the ladies' room, everything she came into contact with would be sanitised. The door handles, taps, toilet seats... everything.

Gran was unaware I knew Hardy Brothers Jewellers through Mother. Between, the ages of thirteen and fifteen, not a single trip to the city with Mother didn't include Hardy Brothers and a hot chocolate. Of the few happy moments I had with Mother, all involved food, clothes or jewellery. Sometimes, I guess, I preferred to remember only the bad ones. It was easier to understand her if she was the supreme villainess. On rare occasions, she was the mother who had photos taken of her pregnant and not all sexy-glamorous, and once in a while, she told me I had a good figure and every so often she shared her bower-bird collection of beautiful shiny objects.

Now was my chance to share something positive from my mother, with her mother.

I called Hardy Brothers and quickly explained how ggYves had worked for them, back in the day. As I hoped, Hardy Brothers was able to help. When Gran returned, I paid the bill and suggested we go for a walk around the city. Vue de Mode was less than five minutes' walk from Hardy Brothers at my pace and Gran was not much slower than me. But I needed to give Hardy Brothers more time. So we strolled down Little Collins Street and snuck our heads into Bank Place. "Ilija lives in that building," I said, ignoring Gran's smirk.

We turned into Queen Street and then onto Collins Street, where three of the most beautiful buildings from the late 19th century were located. I shuffled Gran through two of them.

"Let's catch a tram," I suggested. Trams were faster than walking and I didn't want Gran to see Hardy Brothers until I was ready.

Off we got at the Elizabeth Street stop. Across half a street, past one of the many laneways, and we stood in front of Hardy Brothers, the very same building ggYves stood in front of.

"Let's go inside," I nudged.

Gran was hesitant. "What on earth for?"

As we stepped in, we were welcomed with exceptionally fine crystal champagne glasses filled with very fine French champagne. Gran seemed both confused and delighted.

As we admired one of the stunning porcelain merry-go-rounds on display, not dissimilar to the real one we'd seen in Paris, one of the lovely ladies, Sylvia, brought out a copy of the *Letter of Offer* which was sent to ggYves. I didn't know if they'd be able to help but evidently, only a few years earlier, all records were saved electronically. When I gave them the year and approximate month and ggYves' name, it took them minutes to retrieve the PDF of Hardy Brothers copy of the original Letter of Offer and print it.

Gran half shrieked, "How did you manage to do this?"

I shrugged.

She wiped her eyes dry and said, "Did you know that when it came," she pointed to the copy of the letter, "Your ggYves couldn't read it! He needed to find someone who could translate it for him so that he'd know what it said!"

I'd given no thought to ggYves struggling to read his Letter of Offer. Sylvia showed Gran a few of the sketches they had on record which were ggYves' designs and promised to post copies of the designs to us.

During the drive home, Gran talked without pause about ggYves' amazing craftsmanship. I still wanted to know about Mother and about Pop Colin and why Gran married him, but for today I just wanted one more question answered.

As we pulled up in our driveway, I said, "Gran, what is it about 1956?"

"Sorry, Dear?"

"Well, I'd noticed some time ago that whenever you talk about our family history, it kind of always ends in the mid-1950s. Why?"

"Television." Gran said the word as though it was somehow self-explanatory. It wasn't.

"What?"

"It's the year we got our first television," she said. This made sense to her; to me, it was clear as mud.

"What's TV got to do with..."

"November 1956, the date television broadcasting started in Melbourne. We were one of the first houses to own a set, just in time for the 1956 Olympic Games.

"We arranged a big get together, with all our friends to watch the opening ceremony, and for the next two weeks, people dropped in and out to watch athletes around the world compete, in our sitting room, it was quite astonishing!"

I waved one hand in a circle indicating the need for more information.

"Well, once I realised what television could do, watch people all over the world, record things as they happened, I knew from then on, there was no way to tell lies without being caught. So that's when Gran-Gran and I decided to be much more careful with our facts and selective with our memories."

CHAPTER 24

Tree Pruning

By the time we'd returned to the house it was late afternoon, and Gran wanted to just sit in her garden.

I no longer felt the same about Gran. The perception I had just twenty-four hours earlier was gone. Gran-Gran's words may have been coated in sentiment, however that did not make them any less honest.

Maybe it was that look of fragility in Gran's eyes. I was coming to accept her physical body's failing, but I hadn't considered how the truths in these journal entries would impact her emotional state. It sounds stupid, given my reaction to much of what I'd read, but this was Gran, my Gran who could melt a polar icecap with one stare, and she was not the same person today.

As I made us tea, it occurred to me that for the first time I'd admitted, or perhaps accepted, the journals belonged to Gran-Gran, without adding any *what-ifs* or *but maybes*. It was an absolute fact.

As soon as the hot water hit the leaves, an additional aroma mixed with bergamot. I'd placed Lady Grey instead of Earl Grey leaves into the pot. There was a subtle difference. The distinctive fragrance of bergamot was still there, warmed by the steam, but with it something different. I grabbed the tin, looking for the ingredients, and there it was – Lady Grey tea had the addition of cornflowers. Cornflowers! I'd seen the slivers of pale blue among the Lady Grey tea leaves before but hadn't thought much of it. Dismissing them as some exotic ingredient collected by Tibetan Monks on the foothills of the Himalayas and carried down in wicker baskets hanging off cute little donkeys. But nothing so romantic, they were dried cornflower petals!

"Bergamot and cornflowers," I mumbled. Bergamot equalled Gran, and Ilija. And cornflowers featured in Gran's eyes and Nana's blue Wedgwood tea set. I poured the tea.

The soft rattle of clinking cups alerted Gran to my presence and the danger to her precious china. One thing was certain, her hearing was fine! My biting lip indicated my concern as I poured our tea from the correct height as Gran, who'd wandered back in, watched with a critical eye.

I must have passed the tea serving part of my 1-0-1 class on 'Correct Victorian Tea Service Etiquette' because Gran didn't comment. For her that was a compliment. We took our teas and sat on the wooden bench between Dida's roses, and sipped in silence, watching the ring-necked doves coo-coo around us as late afternoon fell to early evening.

Gran went inside first. It was already cooling down and she felt the cold much deeper these days. I followed with the cups, washed everything and joined her in the lounge room. I could see she was exhausted.

I had the second volume in my hands, none of the French or English parts yet read. "Here, you read these first and then we'll read them together, but don't you dare burn this!"

Gran looked at me. "Are you sure?"

She deserved to be the one to read her mother's words, at least the first one. Ilija and I had read what she couldn't, but she deserved to feel her mother's thoughts.

Gran's eyes filled with tears, which were soon running down her

214

face as she reached for the journal. She didn't say anything as she took it from me, got up and retired to her bed. I figured she'd read them that night, or at least as much as she could get through without falling asleep.

After Gran had gone to bed I called Ilija, and after giving him the first of what would be several tongue lashings for warning Gran, I told him what had happened.

"You know it'll take her more than one evening to read the rest of the entries," he said, and he was probably right.

Ilija asked me to call him tomorrow to let him know how things were going. "Just remember I have an English class in the morning and then an afternoon shift at the café, so call me after six."

I agreed and we finished our conversation, thankfully not touching on the subject of the kiss.

A few hours later I went to check on Gran and found her asleep with the journal opened by her side. I placed the journal on her nightstand, covered her with a throw, and went to watch TV in my room.

Even though I was up early when I looked for Gran, I initially couldn't find her until I looked out through the conservatory window. There she was in the rotunda, her reading glasses on and journal stretched out.

As I walked out into another morning blessed with a warm Autumn sun, I noticed how unkempt the fruit trees and rose bushes were. Dida Nik always tended to the Autumn/Winter pruning for Gran. Every year he'd come along and, with snippers, gloves and wheelbarrow, make his way around the acre of shrubbery and trees. He knew the artistry of correct pruning. After his death, even though for a time Gran hired professionals, it wasn't the same. No love, I guessed. I didn't have Dida's skill, but I did have his love and was determined that, as soon as the last of the leaves fell this year, the garden would be embraced with affection again.

I'll have to do the same at Nana's house? I wondered as I approached Gran. Sticking my head through a gap in the rose bushes I startled her with my, "Hello."

"Sorry, I thought you must have seen me."

Gran shut the journal as she said, "Must have been too engrossed in the journal."

"Still reading it?" Stupid question.

"Yes," she said. "I had no idea how sad my mother was inside, none, not even with the things she told me..."

I sat next to her and asked, "Why do you think she didn't tell you about the journals?"

Gran shrugged. "I'm not sure. They stopped just before I was born so perhaps she hid them and then got distracted with me and fixing her garden and what-not, and somehow unintentionally forgot them."

I nodded but didn't agree. "Are you nearly finished? Reading the entries, I mean?"

"Not quite, several pages to go," replied Gran. "You know it's not easy to read, she seemed to change from French to English at the drop of a hat and then, just to confound things, she'd add some Latin here and there."

Jokingly, I said, "As with Nostradamus."

Gran laughed. "Yes, I guess so. He was a Frenchman who was well travelled, knew several languages and suffered his fair share of personal tragedy."

Gran paused. "I can see your Gran-Gran having an affiliation with the great Nostradamus!"

"Breakfast?" to which Gran nodded and said she'd meet me in the conservatory. An hour later we were munching on pancakes smothered in home-made jam and washed down with a decent pot of Irish Breakfast tea, not Earl Grey. I made a huge effort not to bring up the journals, even though I was dying to know the rest of the story, but I held my tongue.

"We should lime-wash those pear and plum trees too, they haven't been done in more than ten, no, oh goodness, more than twelve years," she said to me.

"When Dida last did them?"

Gran nodded.

I pretended not to notice the journal enticing me as it sat on the edge of the table, right through breakfast.

"Funny, I was thinking about pruning and tidying up the fruit trees just this morning," I said after breakfast.

And after I'd washed the dishes and made Gran a fresh pot of tea, I pretended not to notice Gran walk out onto the deck with the journal resting on the silver tray beside the teapot, milk, sugar and cup. I pretended hard, but I *wanted* to know!

Desperate to talk to someone, I called Ilija only to be greeted by his message bank. *That's right, he told me he had English classes this morning.* I thought to myself.

So, I decided to go up to the attic and spend what remained of the morning rearranging the furniture. The only problem was every time I looked out the wonderful new dormer window I could see Gran reading my journal!

I thought it best to escape. I called my real estate agent, the one handling Nana's rental property, and asked if there was any way I could come over to inspect the fruit-trees for pruning. I didn't expect a yes answer, after all, tenants have the right to proper notice, but a few moments later I got a call-back saying I was more than welcome.

My Nana's house was located in West Footscray, over the West Gate Bridge and, in non-peak-hour traffic, was around forty-five minutes from Gran's place.

No. 14 View Street, West Footscray. A double-fronted Californian

Bungalow with a decent veranda, and beautiful, original stained-glass windows overlooking a small front garden, which faced the park. As soon as I stepped onto the veranda, I could feel the ghosts of Dida and Nana.

The family living there had been tenants for the past two years without issue or concern and were happy for me to traipse through their home, even though I could have gone around the back. I guess they wanted to reassure me. The husband introduced himself. His name was Iain and led me through the house to the yard.

As soon as I saw what remained of Dida's fruit trees, I wept inside. It seemed that before this lovely family moved in, the previous tenants, without permission, had kept a dog in the backyard who took great pleasure in using Dida's fruit trees as pee posts while the soil around the trees became pothole-paradise. The husband explained he'd spoken to the agency about calling in a tree-surgeon to try to save the old fruit trees but had never heard back.

"So when the agent said you were coming, we thought you must have changed your mind about saving the trees," he said.

No one had mentioned it to me. A phone call to the agent, and some seriously choice words later, I approved the hiring of a tree-surgeon as a matter of priority. My tenants invited me to stay for afternoon tea, which I was glad to do if only to keep my mind off Gran and the journals. Over store-bought cakes and tea-bag tea I got to know the renters and was pleased the house was in the hands of such a loving and warm family. *They may know nothing about afternoon tea but they love this house.*

That's when they dropped the bombshell. "If ever you should consider selling this place, we would be interested in buying it," said Iain.

As buyers and owners of Nana and Dida's house went, they would be about as good as any I could find, but, I explained the clause in

Nana's will. "I'm not entitled to sell the house until my thirtieth birthday, and that's more than five years away."

I watched the wife's face drop but Iain didn't seem quite as disappointed. He said, "Have you checked the actual conditions of the sale?"

"Yes? I can't sell the house until I'm thirty."

"No. That might be so, but it could also be that you could enter into a contract of sale but just not settle?"

"What?"

As it turned out Iain was a lawyer. Family law mostly but he knew enough about contracts. "Hear me out," he said. "What if we came to an agreement on price but we didn't settle for five years?"

"Wait on," I said, thinking that this was a scam and remembering Gran-Gran's very clever negotiating skills during the Depression. "If we agree on a price today, how on earth is that fair given appreciation increases over another four or five years, that is even if I want to sell?"

Iain suggested we have another tea.

"Though we could set a consumer price index increase based on an average of the past ten years and add that to any valuation and the sale price," he said.

Iain's wife brought the coffees and joined us, taking her husband's hand. I saw instantly they'd been looking at Nana's home as their own. This was much more than some money-making scam. These people wanted to raise their family here.

"So, if we agreed on a price, we could pay you $100,000 deposit and maybe pay you another $100,000 each year until the balance is due."

I sipped and listened.

"That way, we'd not have settled and you will have met your clause restriction and we'd have the opportunity to continue to save our money as we earn more, and you'd get $100,000 for four years plus the balance." They looked at each other. before saying, "At a guess, we think the place is worth around $5-600,000 at the moment, and with most areas having a net increase of around 7%, that would add another fifty-odd thousand to the balloon balance."

"But what do you get out of this?" I asked.

"Well, that's the other part. We'd live here rent-free. Pay the rates and so on but pay you no more rent. That way we can save up a lot and get the loan we need when the times comes."

I finished my coffee as two sets of eyes stared at me. "Hum," I said, but what I meant was, *either these people give me little credit or haven't thought this through.* Given Iain's profession, it seemed more likely the first. "There seems to be a flaw in your plan." I put the coffee mug down. "If I let you live here rent-free for four or five years, and let's say by some miracle the rent doesn't increase at all over the coming five odd years, and, even if we deduct the cost of maintaining this property, rates and so on, I would in effect be giving you some $80-100,000 off the price."

"Yes, but you'd have a certain tenant who you know would look after the place and a guaranteed purchaser," insisted Iain.

"A permanent tenant not paying rent and a secure buyer only if I want to sell," I corrected him.

Iain's wife slumped a little in her seat. I couldn't hold it against them for wanting to take advantage of what they perceived as an opportunity. After all, that's what Gran-Gran did. So I decided to offer them a lifeline. "Perhaps we need to investigate this further and come up with a better plan which could entice me into selling."

I smiled.

"And as I already mentioned, I'm not sure of the exact terms of the will, our family lawyer handles all of that."

Without thinking, I blurted, "If you're a lawyer, why aren't you at work?" As soon as I said it, I wished I could have taken the words back.

"I'm on paternity leave; my wife just had our second baby."

"Oh. Well, congratulations," I said. "To you both, that's wonderful news."

"I could call your solicitors and check?" interrupted Iain. Given I'd been a bit rude in asking about his work situation, I allowed him his abruptness. I gave Iain the name and number of our family law firm saying, "I guess it couldn't hurt to check?"

As I walked out, I said, "Oh, and let me know about the tree-surgeon." Iain shook my hand as though we'd already signed a contract of sale.

Before heading off, I called Gran. "Hi, I'm heading back now, do I need to pick anything up on the way home?" Translation: *have you finished yet?*

"Oh. I think we are low on milk. And what were your plans for dinner?" she asked in turn. Translation: *I'm not ready to talk yet.*

"I'm not overly hungry. What about a warm salmon salad?" I suggested. *Nothing too starchy otherwise you'll fall asleep before 8.00 pm.*

"Oh, that does sound good. It's a lovely evening, perhaps a fruity white wine also?" Translation: *we can talk after dinner but I'm going to need a drink.*

"Great idea, see you soon."

When I got home, Gran had retired to her room. She wanted peace, perhaps to be alone with her thoughts. I cleaned up the kitchen, took lemonade to Gran's room and soon started pin-boning the salmon. As the portions were set to grill, I made a quick mayonnaise with extra lemon. By 6.30pm I was calling Gran to dinner.

CHAPTER 25

A Thimble of Noble Blood

By the time I got through half the meal and almost the full bottle of wine, I blurted out with as much grace as a banshee on steroids, "So, have you finished reading?"

"Yes, mostly. Just before you called, I was re-reading a few of the entries. I know I said I would have burnt the journals if I'd have found them, but I'm so glad we have them."

Then Gran laughed. "Good grief, can you imagine your mother if she'd have known?"

"Mother had no idea of the truth?"

"No. She was treated like a princess by your Gran-Gran, but she just assumed it was because she was a pretty child."

Gran added, "You see, Gran-Gran and your mother have..." I saw Gran crumble a little, it was all too much for her. "Sorry, had, many similar personality traits. The difference is, Gran-Gran was industrious, and your mother was simply spoilt."

I waited for more. "Gran-Gran used her ability to assess and even manipulate people for a bigger picture, though she never did it to intentionally hurt or destroy others, whereas your mother!"

She shook her head. "One of the few things she did right was marrying your father, and of course have you."

"Hold on!" I demanded, "But you? I thought you weren't fond of Dad?"

Gran chuckled. "Oh, Marica, that daughter of mine, goodness gracious if I said white, she'd say black! So, even though I had concerns about her marrying, it was not because of your father. I just kept that lie going in the hope she would not leave your father as soon as she became bored."

Gran's smile disappeared. "Sadly, it didn't matter. When your father died, if it had not been for you, I think your Dida Nik would have died also. Perhaps he did a little."

Gran indicated more wine. "But I imagine you are more interested in what I read within the journals? Well, I think you should read them first, but I'd like you to consider something before you decide what to do with them."

"OK."

"Your Gran-Gran hid them for a reason. What that reason was we'll never know for certain, however, I can only imagine it was to one day have the truth told."

"Well, that's what I'm thinking; otherwise, why keep writing after her family's death?"

"Yes, that is the very point, who was it aimed at? Was it intended for her family, her great-granddaughter or for the world? As I read her words, and perhaps because I knew her voice, I could hear her speaking to me as though her ghost was whispering in my ear."

She gulped what remained in her glass. "When you read these pages, you'll come across an entry where it begs not to let the world know who she was and who we are. Even beyond her grave, she feared for our futures."

I'd always planned on letting Gran in on the journals and then, at some point, sharing them with the world, but now I felt a duty to Gran-Gran, who had lived through so much tragedy just so I could sit here, in this lovely house, in this lovely affluent suburb, safe. I considered how much I longed for stability and a safe place to call home and realised that's what Gran-Gran wanted also.

"But don't you think the world deserves to know the truth? And don't you think the Russian people would want to know that Anastasia lived, that her great-granddaughter lives?"

Gran huffed at me. "Oh please! Since the fall of Communist Russia there are more supposed Romanov family members and descendants currently living in New York than there ever were at the height of the royal Russian dynasty."

I started laughing.

"No! Think about it. Almost every other month some this-and-that who was married to the second cousin of the sister-of-such-and-such, whose great-grandmother was someone-or-other in the Russian royal dynasty, pops up to claim an obscure and likely fabricated title."

I'd never heard her speak like this, and I liked it!

"Understand, Marica, few things are easier than fabricating a lineage from the rubble of murder, war and misinformation, and few things are more appealing than claiming royal pedigree. It was true of the Middle Ages and 1920s Paris and it's even more so now."

She smirked. "For all I know, some of these 'Romanovs' might even have a thimble-full of genuine noble blood running through their veins. Miracles and wonders do happen."

Gran dropped her voice. "Marica, you need to read these entries and if you still want to share them with the world, well?"

"Well what, you'll agree to have the journals published?"

"I'll agree to discuss it further." She passed Volume-two back to me.

I noticed some of the pages marked with bits of white paper. I flipped to the first marker. "Why did you mark these ones?"

"Because I wanted us to read them together."
I started reading the first market entry, in French.

28th August 1918

From the vantage point of a stunning apartment with an even more impressive view of the Eiffel Tower, I sit, looking out the window – ashamed. My family is dead and yet I live; or perhaps I should say I am alive, I am yet unsure if I live.

It's a perfect August morn, warm, still and promising a bright future. The world promises the war is almost over. God promises a sunny day. But promises are often broken, are they not, England?

There's a squirrel in the wild chestnut tree opposite my window, eagerly testing the still unripe fruit. Too early little one, you will not eat today. He must have heard my thoughts as I see him look up, his round chocolate eyes frozen on mine. Perhaps he can sense my sadness? God, dear God, why is it I am not dead?

Life is so simple for the dead.

We stare at each other, my squirrel friend and I, motionless for what must be a minute or more before he shudders, his fur ruffling as though my thoughts of death frighten him. One last look and off he scurries into the thick of heavy leaf canopy.

Even though the closed window I can smell Paris.

Not just the gasoline of the odd car, the scent of horses or the aroma of delicious pastries, but Paris herself. She is once again living.

Part of me admires her resilience and the other part wonders how she can seem so alive when so many of her children are dead.

3rd Nov 1918

Today should have been Olga's birthday. 23 – She would have been 23 today and somewhere she is buried without cross or wreath.

I should be wrapping her gift and laughing at Alexei's silly jokes or jealously admiring Maria's needlepoint or perhaps singing to Tatiana's piano playing, yet here I sit, alone, not even me, not even 17 but again 14 years old; not even again but in-place-of a sister I never knew.

The first flushes of Autumn's splendour have long since passed and many trees are more than half-bare. I felt Winter's whisper in a breeze yesterday or perhaps I am just sensing the cold ghosts of secrets past.

30th Nov 1918

Desperate for any reminder of Russia I strolled around the city longing for a bookstore – any bookstore – yet I fear to head into the Russian Quarter. What if someone should recognise me?

So few book stores remain.

Parisians burnt many books for warmth during the war; some even used the pages as toilet paper. Has war no limit on its blasphemy? By chance I found one still living, a nook of a bookstore, hidden down a narrow laneway, its entrance little more than the doorway as though still hiding from war. Yet inside I found a myriad of shelves stacked and stuffed haphazardly among a labyrinth of aisles and corridors.

Among hardbacks with no front covers and paperbacks with missing pages, I found a hardcover copy of Alice in Wonderland, surprisingly in good condition. The edges frayed and its spine cracked but intact for the most part.

Alice in Wonderland in French.

I approached who I believe to be the owner of the bookstore but sometimes it's hard to tell and asked why this one seems in such good condition and was told that some people could not burn the classics, even for heat, and gave them away in hope of better days when stories and fairy tales would again dominate children's minds.

I pray, wondering when such a day will come.

On the way home I overheard someone talking of Monsieur Gilliard. It seems he is safely returned to Switzerland. I wonder if ghosts haunt him also.

15th December 1918

Christmas is almost here – a Catholic Christmas.

All of Paris is decorated from The Champs-Élysées to the Place de la Concorde, the square where Marie-Antoinette and Louis XVI were executed. How bizarre that a place of such brutality and hate would be a place for people to meet, celebrate and even laugh. I wonder if one day Russian's will place Christmas decorations on my family's graves.

The sky is grey and threatens us with snow flurries. What other monsters lurk in its darkness?

Christmas Eve 1918

My adopted parents are to hold a small party before midnight Mass and therefore I must dye my hair today for some of the guests knew Anya as a child. Although we are similar as all sisters are, she was much slimmer. This though can be explained easily. Not so easily how my hair is now so dark. For the secret to remain, my natural hair cannot.

Christmas Day 1918

Anastasia is now truly dead, and Anya must live again – I must be reborn.

Many of my adoptive parents' guests commented on how much healthier I looked but I think all believed me to be Anya. War changes people physically and mentally. Men, who go to war can return changed so why not women? One friend asked why I seemed so sad, I smiled, saying only I am not yet able to believe the war is over. No one questioned my answer.

Winter has come and all which was is now either dormant or dead – I am no longer certain which category I fall into.

2nd January 1919

It is the New Year, Anya's New Year and now I must learn to accept I am Anya.

Last night Paris was covered in a blanket of snow, soft at first, individual flakes, transparent and drifting, disappearing even before landing on the ground. Then more and more until individual flakes became masses of white powder. As the powder landed and settled it formed into a doona of white.

Everything touched by white.

Grey buildings dusted with white, grey streets edged with mounds of white, grey trees burdened with clumps of white and grey skies releasing the miracle of white into the sky.

Watching the snow I saw my little squirrel friend again, now dressed in his finest Winter fur. This time though he paid no attention to me. It seems even squirrels don't care who I am any longer.

You know when you are reading a really good novel and before you know it, you're up to the bit where it all kind of comes together, which is wonderful, but it also means the novel is almost over? Well, that's where I was, only this was my life, and Mother's, Grandmother's, Great-Grandmother's and most of all the life of a great aunt called Anya who was always fated to die young. I felt the yolk of responsibility hanging on my shoulders and I was struggling with its weight. With the journal still resting in my lap, Gran turned to the last marked page, took the book from me, and read this entry out loud.

25th February 1919

I know I must renew this Spring. I must shed what remains of Anastasia and become the new me. My adoptive parents have mentioned my sombre state and I think perhaps they fear I will not be able to break this cycle

229

though I think also they are focused on me so that they do not have to think of their loss – the loss of the real Anya. Sometimes I forget they raised and loved her as their own from her birth. I hope Spring will give us all a new life.

Surely the scare of war must one day heal? But can all scars heal or just the ones on the surface?

I have decided, I think once and for all I have decided that Anastasia is dead and must remain so. I hear talk of White Russian forces in the north and discussions of the Treaty of Versailles and echoes of the horrors still in Russia, Lenin's Russia, no longer my Russia, her Russia...

Good night, Russia, Anastasia is now dead with you and I think it is best for all if she remains so; I think perhaps forever. If not for me then for those I now call ma mère et mon père for they too carry wounds and scars and deserve to have an end to their pain.

I hadn't given Anya's adoptive parents much thought, what they must have suffered. I was beginning to understand why and how Gran-Gran maintained her hatred for all things Russian. Irrational though it was, it came from a place of loss and love.

Yet even this was a lie. She longed to find Russian novels and mentioned her homeland, but the Revolution, Lenin and especially Stalin, killed all she knew; that's what she hated, what Russia had become. No Cossack dancers or riders, no songs, no food, no safety, no shelter, no honour or pride.

"There are many pages for you to read, Marica, why she changed her name again, her relationship with her friends, her fears of the Socialism movement in Paris in the 1920s and so much more. This, I believe, you must read alone."

230

I nodded but remained silent.

"Marica." Gran interrupted my reflections. "Go call him."

"Who?"

"Ilija. I think you need to talk to someone other than me."

I shrugged.

"Dear, be grateful that you've got someone in your life that you have not had to lie to. Think about how it was for your Gran-Gran and me and even, in her way, your mother. I don't think she loved anyone completely enough to be truly honest. But you have someone who knows the real you, the greatest of secrets are already shared. Do not devalue that, Dear."

"We're just friends, Gran," I protested.

"Maybe so, but there's a kind of love which exists between friends and is as valuable and as fragile. I think, and I could be wrong, but I think you trust him. Why don't you go call him?"

I took Gran's advice and called Ilija. We talked for several hours about the day, and what I was feeling, about what Gran had said to me and those pages we'd just shared.

In the end, Ilija said, "You have to decide for yourself, but I'll leave you with two thoughts. The first is you need to read the last entries; this will help you know what to do. Secondly, if I were in your place, I guess I'd consider that perhaps the journals and Anya's photo belong to your Gran. After all, they were her mother's possessions."

By the time I got off the phone with Ilija, Gran was in bed. I took Volume-two and a glass of red wine to my room, switched on my bedside table night-light, and started reading.

CHAPTER 26

Ms. Wallace

The next day it was almost lunchtime before I woke, and only then because of Gran's incessant knocking.

"Dear, are you awake? Marica? It's just, oh, some snooty woman on the phone for you."

"Huh?"

"The phone, the phone, Dear. She said she tried to call you on your mobile, but it's been switched off so she's now waiting on the phone in the kitchen."

"Oh?' I was still half asleep. "Who is she?"

"I don't know, Dear, someone called Ms. Wallace from that law firm which handles your Nana's estate. Is everything OK?"

I was conscious enough to know who Gran was talking about, and Gran was right. Ms. Wallace, who never disclosed her first name, not even on emails, MS G J WALLACE Executive Assistant to Mr. Albert F. Rosen –Partner, was indeed snooty.

"Hang on, I'll be right out," I said as I grabbed for my dressing gown.

"Yes," I replied. "Yes, that's my tenant's name. Yes, we talked yesterday, and he put forward a proposition but as I told him I didn't think it would be possi...

"Oh? Really? Are you sure?" I asked.

"Yes, of course, I've every confidence the firm knows how to read an agreement they wrote up. However, you were not employed at the practice when the contract was first drawn up and..."

"...And you might remind Miss Snooty-Face that she works for you," whisper-hissed Gran.

"No, no I'm not implying nor inferi..."

Gran saw me roll my eyes and did the same.

"Yes, thank-you, will do, bye."

I gave Gran a brief overview of Iain's proposal. "And by the sounds of things you could agree before your thirtieth as long as you don't settle?"

"Looks that way."

"And do you want to sell?"

"I'm not sure. I mean, part of me would love to see the house go to someone who will appreciate and care for it as much as Nana and Dida did."

"And you don't feel as though you want to keep their house, for yourself?" asked Gran.

"It's funny, if you'd have asked me that a few months back, I would never sell the house. But now things are different. I love Dida and Nana's house but it's not the same as this one, is it? They made it, but they didn't build it."

I looked around. "This house was the heart of our family. Dida helping with the garden, you and Nana and your cakes, family parties, the only birthdays worth remembering, special occasions like my communion and confirmation, for example. The parties were here because everyone loved the house and the garden."

As I filled my bowl with rice bubbles I said, "This is really the family home, isn't it?"

"You're going to sell then?" asked Gran.

I shook my head. "No, not on those terms, they have all the advantage and I all the risk. I'm happy to come to some sort of agreement but it'll be on my terms."

"Did you get to finish it last night?"

I stopped crunching my rice bubbles. "Some of it was hard to read, Gran, especially those dark pages after she lost her second baby, it was so painful. Even her handwriting became scrawl."

I caught my emotions. "I think I cried more last night than I did at, oh jeez, this is going to sound so bad, but I cried more about those pages than I did at even Dida Nik's funeral." I bit my lip, the pain usually worked to stop tears.

"Sweetheart, it's not wrong. You cried plenty for your grandparents and your mother. You don't measure love by tears. When your grandparents died, you were prepared. Those pages, nothing could prepare you for them."

I watched Gran pour the tea. "I knew she was in pain, we shared so much when I was carrying your mother. But the pain was beyond her ability to vocalise. In a way, I think her journals may have saved her life."

After our impromptu brunch of cereal and tea, Gran said, "Come with me. I've something to show you." For the next three hours, we sat in her bedroom as she shared family photos and little trinkets, items which only had a value to us. I knew of the fine jewels and expensive porcelain figurines, but most of these photos, faded sections of ribbon and whatnots I'd never seen. Then Gran said, "Here." She pointed to a blank corner of one page. "Here's where I'd like to put the photo of Anya."

For the first time, I realised how alone Gran must have been when Mother sent for me in France. I don't know why it hadn't occurred to me, but she was truly alone for the best part of eight years! I felt a little ashamed not to have realised until that moment how excited she was every Sunday evening when I'd call her or how much she treasured the few photos I occasionally sent. Yet, here they were, every single photo I'd sent her, dated and with a little footnote. Marica: music recital, Marica: graduation and so on. She'd missed all those important moments, and even worse she'd lived in this house all alone but for these photos and family ghosts.

"Have you thought about what you want to do with the journals?" asked Gran.

"I spoke to Ilija and he thinks that they aren't mine. He thinks they belong to you."

"There is something about that young man, Marica!" Gran proclaimed.

"Only because he agrees with you."

"Speaking of Ilija, when will you see him again?"

"I was thinking of seeing him this evening, after his shift, do you mind?"

"Not at all, I'm quite fond of him, as you know," she said.

"I know! And you have no idea how much that has surprised me!"

"He reminds me of your father and Dida, his mannerisms and the way he conducts himself."

CHAPTER 27

Ilija & Me

We agreed to meet at Koko Black, a café located at the Paris End of Collins Street, *where else,* with an excellent assortment of handmade chocolates, as good as any in Paris. Well, almost as good. By the time Ilija joined me I'd indulged in one too many dark and white chocolate treats. I'm not a fan of milk chocolate, I don't get the point, dark, milk, pick a side for God's sake.

Ilija suggested he was in the mood for a thick steak, chips and a beer. If he added an AFL football match, he'd be honorary Aussie of the year. We headed straight down Collins Street toward his apartment and the steakhouse in Bank Place. Once we sat down, Ilija wasted no time in ordering his beer and chips but I was still stuffed from overindulging on chocolate, so I settled on just a bowl of chips without the beer. I don't drink beer. Given a stomach full of chocolate never goes well with wine, I decided to settle on plain, flat tap water.

As we waited for Ilija's steak, I began filling him in. He listened almost without interruption. Even when his steak came, he chewed and gulped without pausing, only occasionally nodding his head.

As the plates were taken away, Ilija said, "So are you sure? Are you sure you don't want the world to know who you are and what happened to Anastasia?"

"I'm not sure of anything," I said, "I think I should just let it rest."

"And I had no idea what Gran had gone through. I get the feeling she would be disappointed in me if I disclosed to the world her mother's secrets, given how much effort Gran-Gran took to hide everything," I said.

"I'll know for sure what to do when I know in my heart why Gran-Gran kept the journals. Why didn't she either destroy them or let the family know? There must be a reason for them to remain in limbo. Until I can reconcile where her head was when she hid them, I can't be certain of what to do next."

Ilija invited me back to his place for coffee, which I happily accepted even if his coffee-making skills were not great; it was no coincidence he worked as a waiter and not a barista. Still, it's not like he made dishwater for coffee or something, he just could never get the coffee to milk ratio right.

Although I'd thought about our kiss, and despite the many conversations we'd had, neither of us brought it up. My guess was he either thought I had enough going on or too much was going on for him. Or maybe the kiss just sucked.

Night had long fallen by the time we walked into his place. Ilija turned on the kitchen light and the small side-table lamp. It was all the light the place needed. I don't know if he instinctively knew I didn't like harsh light or if he also preferred subtle lighting but either way, I was happy with this half-light.

He leaned into me just close enough for the sandalwood to make me twitchy. As I sipped my coffee, he asked me, "So what now? I mean, you've kind of put your life on hold to work on these journals and now that they're finished, at least for the most part, what are your plans?"

Funny, it hadn't occurred to me that my life was on hold, as he put it. Shrugging, I said, "Not sure, maybe go back to my original plan of painting?"

"What about you?" I asked. "How's the English study going?"

"I wanted to talk to you about that," he said.

"OK?"

"I always planned on spending about twelve months studying English, six months or so here and the rest in the United Kingdom. That way I could have two Summers and also gain a really good handle on accents."

"OK?" I repeated. Nothing new in what he was telling me.

"The thing is, I never expected to meet someone like you or to go on such a crazy journey. I mean it's been incredible in so many ways. But Winter is coming, and I need to start making plans, that is if I don't stay."

I thought I'd managed to avoid that kiss, but I could feel a kind of panic overcoming me. It was the strangest of sensations. Part of me was excited that he would care enough to want to stay but the other part was wishing he'd leave before I stuffed everything up.

He mumbled something. "... So, it's like this." He sat down next to me. "If you were going to announce to the world who you are, then I think it's pretty obvious there's no place for me in your life. I mean..." He smirked before finishing, "... Seriously, how do I tell people I'm dating a princess? Hi, Dad, I met this girl and she's great, but guess what? She's the real great-granddaughter of Anastasia of Russia. No, Dad, I'm not drunk. No, Dad, she's not crazy. No, Dad, I'm not taking drugs."

Dating?

"I'd have to take a back step, which is fine, except not forever, it's not; I've never been one for major attention, but now, now that it's just two people, you and I, maybe there's room for us?"

238

He grinned. "You know, you must know, I have room for you in my life?"

I blushed.

"Marica, I'm not one for playing games, not with feelings, so I'll just come out and say it—"

No, no, don't say it – my head was screaming.

Yes, yes say it, say it – my body was wishing.

"There's something between us, we both know it, and it's real. I know it's real because, well if it was just physical then," he grinned again, "I would have made some cheap I-don't-care-what-happens move on you and if I was shot down, no loss. I would have tried something that night you stayed over and again that day you kissed me."

Wait on, who kissed who?

"Hell, did you kiss me! Thought you were going to bite my lip at one point, and, if something had happened, I would've been up for it. Shit, look at you. You're as hot as hell and you don't even know it."

I should say something, right?

"But I didn't push, because it wasn't about sex, OK, maybe it was or is, but it's not just about sex, it's about the way you tasted, the way I feel when you look up at me or scrunch your nose when you don't agree. It's about how you've done and seen so much. How you've lived so much and yet you're still sweet and warm under all that heavy armour."

He's going to stop talking any second now, think, Marica, think!

"I wanted to grab you that night and throw you on the bed and I knew you would have been up for it. But I didn't, because I want more than just one night. We have something, Marica."

He's staring at me, is this it? The point at which I fall?

"So I was thinking?"

Oh good, he's still talking, time to think. No, no wait, not good, the more he says the more there's to answer. Stop talking!

"Maybe I should stay for the Winter?"

Pause. Wait, no, I think that's a stop, is it my turn now? Why the hell does this feel like a modern scene from Emma? *Jane Austen, you have so much to answer for.*

"You can get on with your painting and we can get to know each other without one hundred years of your family history interrupting us. And this would give you time to decide what to do with your Nana's house, too?"

Then there was silence. He'd stopped. It was my turn. His mouth attempted a sad excuse for a smile and suddenly he didn't know what to do with his hands, crossing one second and dropping them to his side the next. But I couldn't speak. I was afraid to say the wrong thing and I knew, whatever I said, was going to be wrong. I didn't want him to go, but I didn't want him to stay. I didn't want a boyfriend, but I wanted more than just one night with him. More than his velvet mouth and long lean legs, which I wanted to be wrapped around me more than I'd ever wanted a man's legs before. I tried to imagine, was he a quiet or loud kind of guy? I did all this without saying a word.

"Umm, Marica, I need you to say something, anything. I'm putting myself out there and you're just staring at me."

I was focused on the shape of his mouth and his awkward grin. "Ilija." *Sound, OK, good, it's a start.*

"Ilija, I would be blind not to notice how wonderful a person you are. Almost from the first time I looked up at you back in that café, I sensed you were more than the sum of very fortunate genetics, though that certainly helped." I couldn't conceal my grin, unconsciously squirming up next to him, on his already snug little sofa. So close I could feel the warmth of his body, and it made words difficult.

"So that's a good thing, right?"

"Yes, yes it's a very good thing but it's also not in some ways.

"You said it yourself, you felt it too, there was something between us, more than simply a one-night-stand, which, let's face it, makes things more serious." I crossed one leg over the other and took a sip of the coffee.

Before I could open my mouth to speak, his hand was on my thigh and his face close to mine, so close the warmth of his breath tingled my cheek. I could have removed his hand, or squirmed away, but I didn't.

"As I was saying, you are a great guy and a great kisser, boy are you great!"

He whispered, "Funny, the way I remember it, you were the one doing the kissing."

My hips turned in to face him. Voluntary, involuntary, I wasn't sure. What I was sure of, was that it felt wonderful even as I tried to reason why we should just be friends. "Arh, uhm, what I'm trying to say is, I don't have many friends. We moved around a lot and I'd hate to—"

"—Oh God!"

His hand was moving up between my thighs as he turned and bit and nibbled my ear. I didn't want to speak, and I didn't want him to stop, but most of all I didn't want to think. If I thought this through, I'd stop, *us*.

His lips moved from my ear and before I could think, his mouth was on mine. This was no delicate innocent peck but a full kiss, passionate, probing and delicious. I could taste coffee mixed with chilli-sauce from his steak. I could smell the sandalwood from his cologne mixed with peach from his shampoo.

He freed the coffee cup from my hand as his tongue grazed my teeth. I bit it gently. This made him groan, a primitive and dirty groan. His body moved into mine.

Our breath became heavy as our bodies rubbed and clung together. His chest pushed against me, nudging me down, his arm reached down and scooped my legs, lifting them onto the sofa and spreading my legs just enough for his body to slide over me, cover me, still kissing, wet and soft, and hard and wild all at the same time.

He pulled away just a little and I clawed to have him back. I didn't care about logic or friendship or anything other than him and me, and he knew it.

He grinned as he pulled his jumper over his head, showing his chest. That chest, which I wanted to lick and taste so badly last time, was now mine to devour. The first taste, sweet and slightly salty.

I tickled my fingers down his chest to his jeans, unbuckled his belt and listened as the zipper freed his red boxers. He let out another soft groan and rubbed his bare chest into mine. My mouth found the tip of his nipple. My tongue now licking and flicking and sucking flesh and nipple while my hand reached further into his pants.

I gasped for air as I whispered, "You taste like warm, salty caramel," and then watched as his eyes pressed me to keep going.

I felt twitchy and trembled as I freed his jeans more and put my hand down his boxers, finding him hard, firm, and thick.

He lowered himself down onto me, my hand still in his boxers, as he pulled up my shirt and started kissing and licking my belly button while his fingers unbuttoned the remaining buttons. He rose a little and, with one hand freed the top button of my trousers, while his index finger on his other hand drew little circles on my flesh, teasing me into happy submission. Then, slowly, his face came down, his lips just tickling my lower belly. He let the zipper of my trousers slide, as his warm breath prickled the top of my panties. My hand slipped from his boxers as I arched and groaned. I wanted him.

I squirmed and shimmied down, reaching back into his boxers and rubbing harder and harder, wanting him to go down on me and me on him. He rose a little again, pulling my hand free from his boxers as he whispered, "Not yet, you first. I want to watch you."

He blew hot breath into my ear, before saying, "I'll have my turn."

The words made me tremble. I did as I was told, happily. His tongue and lips were kissing and nibbling my exposed breasts. He could tell I liked it so he went harder, rubbing, and kneading and biting until I let out a pleasure-pain squeal. He whispered my name, over and over. Between breaths and kisses, I hummed and purred, and arched and wriggled, to his will, and I loved every second of it.

He pulled me up, throwing my shirt to the floor, along with my bra. I watched his face, a flush of crimson, his eyes stormy-grey, bewitching, and his mouth gentle and arousing. Then he came back down on me, attacking all of me, my neck, my breasts, my mouth, my ears.

He lifted me up and somehow in one movement, lowered my trousers down past my hips, all the while still kissing and biting. I could hardly breathe, and I could hardly wait. He kept kissing as he nudged my panties down. He ran his finger so gently along my slit. It tickled and tingled. I squirmed and groaned, trying to force it deeper.

He rolled me onto my side, with him now behind me. I was wrapped in him like a cocoon, my pants and panties down to my knees, his one leg over me, the other I don't even know where. Attacking my neck and ears while his free hand cupped my breast from beneath like it was a trophy.

Then I felt it, I felt as his fingers and penis tip tickled between my legs, making me throb. I spread my legs more as I gasped for fresh air. He pushed my back out and my butt harder into him. I rubbed him, harder and harder as I reached down to help him get inside me. I wanted him inside me.

I groaned, "Fuck me now." Just as I was about to climax, he stopped.

I whispered, a little worried and a little desperate, "Don't stop."

He twisted me up and then onto my stomach and I got excited at the prospect of being trapped by his body weight. But instead, he got up off the sofa. I felt heat and disappointment, had I done something wrong?

But then he offered his hand and said, "Now, now you're ready." Everything was perfect.

How did I get so lucky to have such perfection?

He was perfect.

The night was perfect.

The room was perfect – natural, nothing stupid and cheesy like rose petals and candles, just lust – as sex should be. *Lust.*

He looked good, smelled good and tasted good, and I was looking forward to discovering all of him.

I watched him fall to the bed and remove his jeans. I knew I wanted to ride him, so I could watch him too. I started kicking free what remained of my clothing, but he shook his head no. He wanted to finish undressing me and I was more than happy to comply. I fell on the bed beside him and wrapped my legs around his.

He pushed me down and just stared at me for a second. I loved that stare. It was dirty and wild and full of promise. He wriggled free to reach over to turn off the lamp, but I whispered, "No, leave it, I want to see you."

His smile said it all as he discarded his red boxers.

"Close your eyes," he said.

I did as I was told.

I felt his touch, sometimes gentle, barely-there, and other times fierce and devouring. I moaned and squirmed until I couldn't take it any longer. Opening my eyes, I asked, "Do you have protection?"

I turned on my side as I watched him retrieve a row of condoms from the bedside table drawer. I smiled as I said, "I hope that's enough."

He groaned at the dirty huskiness in my voice and threw himself on top of me. He wasn't asking or considering. I felt him sliding inside, gently at first but I didn't want gentle, I wanted rough and hard.

"More," I demanded.

He pushed harder and deeper.

"Harder," I ordered.

He groaned as he thrust into me.

I wrapped my legs around him as I gasped for air.

Groaning, panting, rocking, "Arrh, arrh, harder, harder, God, yes God," I shouted, not caring if the apartment walls were thin, lost with him inside me.

I could feel the breathlessness and the heat, as I moaned, "Fuck me, Ilija, fuck me harder."

I gasped for cool air as the spasms decreased and I focused back on him, into his eyes, tingles and sensations still rippling in my pelvis, Ilija still inside me, rocking gently with me. I'd orgasmed but he hadn't yet and—

OH, FUCK NO, HOW DID HE DO THAT!

I let out an uncontrollable "Oh God – yes!" as the spasms came one after the other. I felt the wet and the hot, as everything tingled and ached and I had no idea where I was or who I was with, and my back arched and my pelvis swayed and pricked with electricity, and my breathing almost failed me. I twisted to have him grind even harder and he grunted in understanding. I pushed and rocked, sounding primal until my body started to settle.

Another orgasm even before the first was finished, that was a new one for me. I smiled as my spasms slowed, my breathing steadied.

I don't know how he could have known, but instinctively he did. Before I'd even caught my breath, Ilija twisted us over, me on top, him beneath me, watching me wriggle and sway over him. I leaned back, my arms braced around his legs as I started grinding and rocking, squeezing and relaxing my pelvic muscles as they tightened around his penis, still deep inside me.

I rocked slowly, then fast, sometimes in a jiggle and sometimes in a sway. I watched his face start to contort in pleasure. I increased the motion, watching him and feeling him get harder and harder inside me.

He groaned. "Oh Jesus."

He grabbed me, pulling me down to him, my breasts jumping up and down in his face as our bodies began to spasm together. I was losing control. We were about to lose control together. I turned slightly to the side, knowing the angle would increase his pleasure, and then started grinding slowly.

"God, Marica!" He huffed between breaths. "You're a fucking animal!" His final thrust pushed so hard inside me it almost hurt. We both groaned together, as he pushed up into me and I pushed back at him, rolling over to our sides, finishing each other off, we writhed in the erotic deliciousness, of panting for fresh air.

After we caught our breath, Ilija wriggled free of me, got up, kissed me on the forehead and went to the bathroom. He came out a few seconds later, condom discarded, robe on but open, nothing to hide between us now. I was still lying on his bed, naked and uncovered, unable to take my eyes off him and enjoying his admiration.

Filling a glass of water for us to share, he sat up next to me. I turned to my side and rested my head in the middle of his damp and sticky chest. He smelled of musk and me.

Ilija ran his hand along my body and down to my butt, blowing air over my damp skin. He patted it gently as he asked, "Will you stay the night?"

I nodded yes without even lifting my head. He moved down so that my head was now higher up and wrapped one side of his robe over me.

I reached for the now half-empty glass and snuggled further into him as I drank my thirst away.

"Are you hungry?"

"A little."

"Do you want to go out and get something to eat?

He grinned. "I'll order a pizza."

After he ordered the pizza, I realised that his place was so small that, if I didn't put some clothes on, the pizza delivery guy would get quite a tip.

"Could I borrow a shirt and a pair of your boxers?" I asked. Ilija got me a shirt but no boxers.

My puzzled expression made him chuckle. "You only need the shirt to keep the pizza guy from seeing anything and you are not going to need pants tonight, babe."

I buttoned up his shirt, happy to hear he planned repeat performances. Everything was perfect. We spent that night in bed, eating pizza, drinking vodka, watching TV. I imagined every night might be like this, every night with him.

CHAPTER 28

The trouble with Perfection

The next morning Ilija got up and left the apartment without saying a word.

I woke to the sound of the door closing, and to a strange feeling. Five minutes later, he was back with two coffees. How did I get so lucky to have such perfection?

He was wonderful.

The night was magical.

I heard a voice in my head, but I dismissed it or ignored it, or something. We drank our coffees –me once again nestled into his chest, him occasionally kissing my head, hardly a word spoken. His silence was obvious, he was genuinely happy. Mine stemmed from contentment and something else. A nagging feeling I'd forgotten something.

After he'd finished his coffee he said, "I'm going to have a shower." A smirk crept over his face. "Wanna join me?"

He was perfect.

My forced smile said no. I've no idea why I didn't want to jump in the shower with him. He was still hot, still wonderful, he was still Ilija. Hell, now that I knew what he could do with his body and mine, it was perfect, yet I resisted.

A look of slight disappointment touched his face, but he brushed it away as he wandered into the bathroom. I felt bad and considered just walking in and surprising him. But I couldn't get up.

I looked around the room.

Nothing had changed.

Last night was amazing yet, I felt... uneasy.

I heard the water in the shower.

My unease grew.

Something he said last night.

You know, you must know, I have room in my life?

What was so wrong with saying that anyway? I kept repeating it to myself. This wasn't some one-night stand, he said that last night. If there was any doubt, his face confirmed it this morning. He wanted me, all of me. He was the kind of man Pop Colin wanted for Mother, and if my father had lived, would have wanted for me. My very own Mr. Darcy. Yet, I suddenly felt more like Lydia than Elizabeth Bennet.

Part of me was saying, *enjoy this you idiot*, and the other part was screaming *run! Run now before you break his heart before he is the next to suffer the foolishness of loving you.* I was back in Nice and Monaco. Back to the last time, I felt love with lust and like, and back to breaking a promise to myself.

Women like Mother, and me, didn't deserve men like Dad and Maurice and Ilija, and eventually Ilija would come to discover the truth about me. Good people who love women like us are left alone and broken-hearted, or dead.

I searched the room for my clothes, dropped and dumped like a trail of sex-crumbs. Everything was perfect. God! *What is wrong with me! Some women spend their entire lives looking for someone like him.* He was even a fantastic lover.

The wobble in my legs settled. I jumped out of bed. The shower was still running.

Guilt, from somewhere deep in my soul, rose and then overcame me. In the seconds between drinking coffee and him having a shower, something happened. Jane Austen would have called it sensibility. I think she might have got it wrong. It was more like susceptibility. I listened as the man I might have loved showered. Anxiety groped at me as I hurriedly dressed, praying he liked long showers.

"There's cereal in the cupboard," I heard him shout through the door. "Or, if you want, we could go out, you know, make a morning of it."

"Thanks." I found my scarf and jacket. "I'm not much for breakfast," I said as I searched the room for my other belongings – it all had to be taken away – everything, no sign of me. No sign of us.

He was remarkable, and not just the sex, but everything.

"Turn the kettle on!" he shouted.

I needed to escape, to free myself from his eyes and to free him from me. "This is wrong," I mumbled. "It'll never work." I knew I had to get out. I unlatched the door just as I heard the shower stop running, and slammed it behind me, suppressing my desire to go back inside, back to him, suppressing it into my black pit of hidden emotions. I was *not* my mother and I could prove it, by walking away.

I'd never intended to hurt him or to even lead him on. I might have wanted him, but I never imagined feeling so much.

I failed. I failed both of us. He'd never understand, but I was doing this for him as much as for me. He was perfect, and perfect had no place in my life. The perfect and the good died, one way or another, in my family.

"That," I said aloud, "Was the real family legacy." I rushed at the lift-door as though I was fleeing a crime scene.

My phone rang. I refused to look. I knew it was him.

Coward! I thought to myself as I started my car. I wasn't a coward for leaving; I was a coward for starting something.

I hated myself.

I hated him for – I didn't even know why.

I hated myself.

I hated, hated, hated, being such a coward.

When I got home, Gran was up and about and seemed not at all surprised to find I'd been out all night.

"How was dinner?" Her real question, *are you happy?*

"Great, fine, good, um, he had a steak I wasn't all that hungry. Gran, I might go lay down for a bit."

"But it's," she looked at her grandfather clock, "It's 8am. Are you feeling all right?"

"A bit of a headache, nothing serious that a Panadol or two can't fix."

Gran went to say something, but I shut the door on her questions. In my bedroom I sat, for hours, thinking, regretting, wishing things were different, that I was different. Yes, I'd had lovers. Some even lasted beyond a weekend, but nothing serious, no one serious. I was not built for serious, or for decent and good. I promised myself, after my first time, I'd not break someone's heart. I knew I'd just gone back on that promise. Yet, I could still save him from me, if I kept him away. I was weak last night. Now, now I had to remain strong.

I kept my phone switched off. I didn't want to hear from him or have to answer his questions. I kept the phone off all day and did the same the next day and the day after. When the tree surgeon couldn't reach me, he called Gran. I fabricated a lie saying my phone must be playing up.

The days turned into a week. Seven days of doing little more than watching the Winter come to greet us. When Gran asked about Ilija, I avoided the questions or lied. But she persisted. "I know a grandmother shouldn't ask such questions," she started, saying. "But did he hurt you?"

I stared at her blankly. She must have read the stare as confirmation. I saw her mouth droop and her eyes glisten. "Dear, we must call the police if he—"

"No!" I shouted, "No, nothing like that, Gran. He's leaving for the UK soon and I think it would be better if we didn't see each other. He's leaving and I'm staying, that's all."

Gran was unconvinced. Now, I had the added guilt of making Gran upset.

One week became two and I ignored every single one of Ilija's calls. He started emailing me. I didn't open them. At the start of week three, Ilija turned up at our door. Well, at our gates. Much to Gran's amazement, I'd taken to locking the gates. Ilija couldn't get in and I had no intention of going out. Trouble was, Gran was of a different mindset. She invited him into the conservatory and, after a few minutes of chatting with Ilija, asked me to join them. I refused.

Gran made a pot of tea and, in Russian, they had a private conversation, with me just in the other room. I became the stranger, the outsider in that house.

Less than an hour later, Ilija left.

Gran called. "What are you doing, child?" she demanded. "That boy is very fond of you and I think you feel the same way, but the poor boy's a confused mess!"

I kept silent.

"Marica, tell me honestly, do you have feelings for him?"

"Yes."

Gran huffed. "Then what is it?"

I shrugged my shoulders.

"Well, was it... is it that the sex was bad?"

"Gran!" I was shocked to hear the word *SEX* brought up in context to me.

"I thought that perhaps he'd hurt or forced you, like..."

I didn't let her finish. "I already told you no, please, Gran, let it rest." But even as I said the words, I knew they were pointless. Gran rarely let anything rest.

"Then I thought perhaps you realised, after spending the night together, that you wanted him only as a friend, but you just said you have feelings for him?"

Silence infested the room. For the longest moment, nothing was said.

I turned to retreat to my room as Gran said, "So will you at least promise to call him?"

"Yes." I lied.

"And will you listen to what he has to say?"

"Yes." I lied again.

A month passed and I'd not called Ilija. I didn't send him an email in reply to his one with the subject matter LEAVING FOR THE UK PLEASE CALL ME. I didn't text him to wish him a safe trip. I did nothing to stop him. The only thing for days and weeks I managed to accomplish was the tree pruning.

Gran's garden, or perhaps I should say Gran-Gran's garden, was so overgrown and a little abandoned. It was a personification of three generations before me. Beauty, hidden in the overgrown bushes and the dead knotted branches, hidden. Hidden, among the shrubs and the crevasses, secrets and whispered half-truths, hushed with generations of time.

I didn't talk much in those weeks and rarely slept more than a few hours a night. Each day was spent in the garden, clearing and burning the deadwood, the tangled and twisted branches of forgotten fruit trees and the knotted borer-infested limbs of the silver birches and the bare, half-dead twigs and lanky stems of long-overlooked roses. I cut and clipped and gnawed away at the garden. I plucked and pulled at the weeds and stabbed at the hard earth without a day's break, even when it rained. With Dida's tools and the same old coat I wore when Uncle Steve tried to rape me, I kept going. I needed to be outside, uprooting weeds that clung to the past, and clipping off dead flower heads. In Gran-Gran's garden, in Gran's garden with Dida's tools.

My hands developed blisters and welts and my nails, split, and constantly stained with dirt and tree-sap; it made me more determined. My shoulders ached and lips cracked from the sharpness of cruel Winter winds, but the garden wanted her freedom. Gran kept her thoughts and let me work out mine in the solitude of the garden. As I burned the last of the Autumn leaves and too many years of buried lies, I felt relief in the plumes of dove-grey smoke. For weeks I clawed and scratched and tore and burned and scorched until I felt the possibility of freedom.

CHAPTER 29

Forgiveness

One day, when all that remained was charcoal and oxygen, when the screaming in my head became silent, I was ready to ask Gran. "Why did you tell me the truth about Dad?"

"Because I knew you deserved the truth. I'd always intended to tell you. I wanted to tell you even when we were in Paris but thought it too soon after your mother's death."

Gran looked over the rejuvenated garden before saying, "You deserved to know even if you blamed me, even if you never forgave me, for the deceit."

"But why did Dida and Nana forgive her? After Mother practically killed Dad, I mean?"

"Because of you, they wanted to protect you. We knew your mother would never live with me and would never listen to me, but if we remained close, between the three of us, Dida, Nana and me, we wanted to protect you. We hoped she'd be a little more respectful, perhaps even become the mother you deserved."

"And was she?"

Gran's face turned grey. "Not really. She paraded man after man before us. For the most part, your Nana, Dida and I raised you and then she married that awful Mike fellow. When that marriage ended, we three were relieved. We could not have imagined the next one would be even worse."

Gran paused before adding, "Though after Steve she seemed to settle down a bit. Perhaps she, at last, felt some shame."

It took me many more days, or perhaps weeks – time had no relevance – to take it all in. Somehow, everything was now about Ilija and me, what happened or didn't happen. What should have happened and why I couldn't let it.

I needed to try and place everything in some sort of order. Or was it logic I was looking for? Just to make sense of it, and, eventually, it kind of did.

It was all about love, no, not just love, unconditional love. Love conquering regret. Love conquering anger, and hate. I guess what surprised me most was how much fear and hate mixed in with that much love. Gran-Gran loved her family yet hated her countrymen. Pop Colin hated wars yet loved his brother more than his values, and ggYves loved his wife too much to ask the real questions.

And then there was Gran, dear, sweet, stubborn, lonely Gran. To have carried so many memories she could not share, and to be forced to overlook Mother for my sake, how could I judge her without condemning her absolute love for me?

Even though I'd had Gran-Gran's journals for months I'd not reopened them since Ilija left. Ilija. I now measured time by when Ilija was here last. I was ready to absorb those painful pages, the ones where Gran-Gran lost her children. I poured myself a glass of merlot and braced myself for a new flood of emotion.

22 September 1924

We buried him today, my little Martin, our little boy. I wept inside but there were no more tears at the funeral. I am dried of tears; somehow this made it worse.

Yves tells me that it is God's wish to have our babies with Him but I find it difficult to believe in the kindness of God, I have seen His indifference. He seems to need so many babies these days.

Or, perhaps He is punishing me for living when the others are all dead.

I cannot think how I shall wake tomorrow; it is so dark everywhere I walk.

But strangely it was Gran's birth which had her fear everything the most.

3rd March 1930

She lives, my, no, our little Ana – Yves is so happy, and I am happy for him and us!

Such a beautiful child, but will she to be taken from me also?

And then this.

3rd June 1930

Today our little Ana is twelve months old! Oh, can it be?

Bless this country for not taking my child; perhaps I am truly no longer damned for the sins of all Russians.

I decided never to talk about Mother again, not even to Ilija, though, given he was living in London there was little chance of that. Ilija again. Perhaps when I could put the journals away once-and-for-all, I would be able to do the same with Ilija.

CHAPTER 30

What's in the Boxes?

Another month passed and, even though I felt a kind of peace, I found no desire to think of the future. Tom had done a wonderful job of transforming the attic into a studio, but the room had become a kind of tomb, empty and devoid of a soul. It was as though Winter had crept into the attic and laced the studio with emotional frost.

Outside was no better. Everything was so cold, wet and dead – still. I was beginning to understand how Gran-Gran felt about the ghosts of Winters past.

Late Winter in Melbourne. One cloudy late August day, when the wind was howling through Gran's garden as though determined to frighten the Spring bulbs, Gran called me to the little snug which we hardly ever used. She'd managed to get a fire going. She'd pulled out some boxes I'd never seen before from God knows where.

"Marica, when Nana was falling ill she gave these boxes to me. They hold the precious memories of your Dida and your Nana."

Three boxes. The first was a dark-wood box, probably oak, with brass or perhaps copper hinges and reinforced edges. An older style key poked out of its keyhole. Gran turned the key and opened the box as she said, "In here are Dida Nik's medals and awards while in the Legion."

Gran took out the medals for me to better admire them. I touched the cold medals and their soft fabric. Some had their jewellery-like boxes, aubergine-coloured velvet and inside, resting on untouched silk, untouched medals. Symbols and shapes foreign to me, each so distinguished. I wondered why Dida never wore any of them.

Gran reached deeper into the box and pulled out several envelopes and what appeared to be awards, in foreign languages. At a guess, I thought they might be in Spanish or similar. Another world lived in these boxes. A quiet world of a past never really hidden yet never discussed. It wasn't the same as Gran's past because Dida never denied his time in France, yet I felt a bit embarrassed I'd not wanted to know more.

I put the envelopes and medals back as Gran opened a little lilac-coloured papier-mâché box. She said, "And love letters your Nana wrote to Dida Nik before they were married."

My fingers ran over the slightly yellowed letters, neatly tied together with a faded purple ribbon. The handwriting, with the perfectly looped characters, the swoop of an extra-large N for Nikola as though it mattered beyond words to emphasize the N. I tugged at the ribbon, releasing the letters free. I flicked through the pile, as though about to shuffle a deck of cards. I wasn't ready to read them, not yet.

As I secured the letters again with their ribbon, Gran opened the next box. A large Arnott's Biscuits tin box from the 1970s I guessed. The tin itself was now a collector's item but inside was what money could not buy.

Gran waited for me to look inside before she said, "This one's got memories of your Nana as a young woman. She was quite a talented pianist as you know but were you aware that she also studied ballet?"

I shrugged.

"And she was an acquaintance of Jacqueline Rogue."

260

"Who?"

Gran, stone-faced as though I'd just denied the existence of Monet, repeated, "Jacqueline Rogue, model to artists and Picasso's lover."

"Wait, what?"

"Picasso, Dear, the artist, you know."

"Are you saying Nana knew them both?"

"Yes, of course, Dear. Your Nana moved in those circles, that's what artists and musicians and dancers did in Paris," said Gran.

"Here's a photo of her and a few of her dancer girlfriends with Picasso at a restaurant in Paris. And here's another one in his studio."

I grabbed the photos and then the box. I rummaged through and found a postcard addressed to my grandparents and signed PP with a very Picasso-like doodle under their name and address.

Before I could grasp I might be holding a Picasso original, Gran said, "But, it's your Dida Nik who has the more interesting history. If only you knew his adventures."

I think time might have stopped again. Nana knew Picasso, and Dida was the interesting one?

Gran turned back to the wooden box and retrieved the awards in foreign languages. "Well, he never talked about it too much, however, on one of those drinking sessions with Pop Colin, Dida Nik mentioned a few of his escapades. Pop Colin and I always thought Dida led a kind of secret-agent life which started when he escaped former communist Yugoslavia."

I set the sketch aside and started thumbing through the box again, looking for a clue to this secret life. "You're kidding right?"

Gran started telling me about his time in Egypt and Africa, and evidently, he'd also worked as a private bodyguard to some very famous European officials in the time between leaving the Legion and moving to Australia.

Then she added, "That's why he was determined to move as soon as the 1972 uprising in Croatia failed. It seems your Dida was very heavily involved in it and Europe was no longer a safe place for him."

I'd read something about 1972, but to my shame, I couldn't recall a single detail and was never interested enough to ask.

"Maybe it's time you knew about your father's side of the family?"

As usual Gran's seed planting bore fruit instantly. I took the boxes and went through them piece by piece. Then I tried Ancestry.com to fill in missing pieces but it didn't help much. It seems if your father's family comes from a former communist country, you're on your own.

A few days turned into a week and then two. Without realising it, I was eating again. I was alive again, just like the garden. With fresh determination, the first of the daffodils and jonquils forced their way through the earth and toward the sun in June and July. Now, perfumed paths and golden blooms kissed each new day.

Some of Dida's awards were easier to decipher, with words like *bravery, courage, valour* screaming out at me. Others were more secretive, more questions, more links to a family I'd neglected or, perhaps more accurately, dismissed to the realms of fishing trips and Easter sweets.

Gran placed the first of Spring into vases around the house, saying to me, "Perhaps the answers are not here but in Paris?"

"What?" I asked.

"I think maybe you are starting your Dida's search at the wrong end. Just as with the journals you need to start at the beginning."

I shrugged. Paris was far away, and I wasn't going to leave Gran, never again.

Another week passed before Gran scented our home with her idea. "I have never experienced what it's like to have Easter in the Spring," she said. "Marica, tell me what it's like in Paris in the Spring?"

I was happy to share April showers and street stalls filled with window boxes of geraniums and daffodils and pansies, and chocolate rabbits and eggs, looking like works of art shop displays, the change in dress from heavy Winter coats to knitted cardigans and sweaters.

Gran smiled. "It must be lovely."

Out of the blue, Gran asked me, "Have you heard from Ilija?"

How odd she should mention his name. Although hearing his name vocalised made my stomach feel warm, I forced myself to ignore it and replied with a silent shrug.

"Oh?" she added. "It's just that I got a postcard from him today and I thought maybe..."

"What?" I was shocked and angry and, and... glad he hadn't forgotten Gran at least. I attempted to conceal my combined disappointment and excitement by saying, "Oh? And what does he have to say for himself?"

"Here." Gran handed me the postcard. "Read it," she said but I knew she was fishing for signs. It was short and polite and quite to the point, talking about the weather and the difference in the accent and that he missed Melbourne, but no mention of me, not even to say hi to me. He missed *Melbourne*.

"I was going to reply to him and was wondering if you wanted to add anything?"

"Oh, just say hi and that I hope things are going well for him."

"Dear, could you please re-write the address for me? It's just that his handwriting is not too clear to me. I'm not very good with people's handwriting."

Two days later, while in the garden inspecting the rose bushes, Gran approached. "Could you do me a favour, Marica, and post this for me?" It was a reply to Ilija. I had to grin; the post box was not five houses down the road.

"Sure," I replied, "And you can put the kettle on, it might come to the boil before I get back if you don't overfill it."

By October's first warmth, the garden and I were both feeling happier. It looked like life outside and I felt less death in my soul.

263

One evening, the first evening warm enough for dinner on the terrace, Gran asked, "So have you discovered anything wonderful yet about Dida?"

Between crunches of crisp salad, I managed to say, "Some, but a lot is hidden behind terminology I don't quite understand."

"I don't think the answers are here in Melbourne. Perhaps you'd have better luck if you approached the Legionnaire societies in Paris or Algiers? Or, isn't there a military museum in Paris, what's it called?"

"The Musée de l'Armée," I said.

"That must be the one," she insisted. "Isn't that the place with an entire wall dedicated to Croatian soldiers who helped the French, or something of that nature?"

"Yes," I said. "But how do you—"

"Your Dida once told Pop Colin and me."

"It's not like Paris is a few hours away."

"Oh good grief, Marica, you make it sound like it's Mars!"

I still didn't quite get it. Was Gran suggesting I leave her?

"But I don't have anywhere to go?"

"Not true, Dear." Gran was up to something. "Please don't be upset with me but I called Maurice and explained we were looking into Dida's history—"

"Why would you ever think he'd—?"

"He was most helpful when we left and he *is* a distant relative of Nana's."

Gran persisted. "Your Nana's father had a cousin who is Maurice's grandmother. When I explained what we were doing he was very willing to help. And it seems he even knows a few facts on Dida Nik."

The word 'we' was not missed by me. "Just how long have you been discussing this with Maurice?" I wasn't even aware Gran had his contact details.

"Well, Dear, with all the time you'd spent in the garden, saying little

264

more than nothing, I was worried about you. And, well, quite honestly, I didn't know who else to talk to about it. Ilija was gone and I'd not had that postcard from him yet."

A grin formed across my face. My Gran, the sly old fox with the steel-ice eyes and Victorian manners, the woman who made me crumble with love and sometimes still tremble like a child, was at her best when manipulating my life. Only now I held no resentment. Unconditional love comes at a cost, and the cost is interference.

"What are you smirking at?"

"It's a great idea but I'm more than happy to stay here. I want to stay here."

She looked at me over her brewing pot of tea. "And exactly how many sketches, drawings or paintings have you done since coming back with me?"

"Well, I didn't know I would be competing with Picasso," I said, though she was right.

CHAPTER 31

Where's the Ring?

Gran's little bit of mischief aside, I was still struggling with some of my past and I still had not let Ilija rest.

Mother's behaviour.

My grandparents, on both sides, and their sacrifices.

Dad. He should still be here, with me. If he'd lived, there would've been no Uncle Mike, oh God, and no Uncle Steve, and no vagabond life. Safety.

And Gran-Gran. The last of the Romanovs. The secrets she kept. The pain she carried. The lies she lived. It was too much. Everything swirled and twisted.

Facts and fiction.

Real and make-believe.

Regret.

Remorse.

Ilija.

Love.

Lust.

Sorrow.

I needed to focus on one thing, just one thing. I returned to the journals. I'd read them so quickly, barely absorbing everything. Now... now perhaps I could make more sense of it.

I flicked to several pages I'd barely skimmed the first time, and started re-reading them, reading the words of my great-grandmother. My great-grandmother. Mine!

30th July 1919

Mid-Summer.

The war is over, so the Politicians say. Politicians lie. They're only concerned themselves with how to manipulate numbers.

Silly men arguing over the terms of the Treaty of Versailles while Russians continue to starve – tell them the war is over.

Today is Anya's birthday – Alexei's birthday – my birthday; now.

I heard ma mère crying this morning – alone –soft whimpers which echoed through my soul.

She cannot comfort me, and I cannot comfort her.

She has aged so much–the woman I must call ma mère, the woman who must call me ma fille.

Only eight months ago we were all different people with different names and different parents and children. Yet she has aged so much – perhaps we all have.

Yet it is mon père I worry for. He seems almost to have given up on life completely and now, so the doctors tell us, he is suffering from tuberculosis.

Soon I think he will be free.

There will be no birthday party today.

14th October 1919

We all wore black today matching the dark clouds. Even the heavens are dark now.

Black dresses.

Black suits.

Black sky.

Mon père was buried today.

20th Feb 1920

ma mère is unwell. The doctors can't say exactly why, but I know why, sorrow is killing her.

15th March 1920

Beware the ides of March.

The Grand Duchess Maria is now officially my legal guardian. I will need one should ma mère leave me also before I am legally old enough for the law says I am not yet even 16 years old, 16, 16, 16 years old.

I do not even expect ma mère to see next Christmas.

1st November 1920

Ma mère rarely rises from her bed now.

Today we talked, for the first time about Anya, the real Anya, the dead Anya, her daughter.

She loved her as any mother would. She must hate me at least a little, for I hate me a lot.

The Grand Duchess sent her personal physicians last week to try and help but even they, with all their studies and practice and knowledge and money, they say they can do nothing for her but make her comfortable.

24th December 1920

A funeral instead of Mass.

Ma mère is at last free to return to her daughter.

4th September 1925

The Grand Duchess has found me a good match.

He is strong, respectable, diligent in his work and handsome. With a shock of black hair and eyes as green as the sea, tall and reed-thin, the presence of a duke, the moustache of a Prussian baron, the pride of a Cossack and the heart of a peasant.

I read the last bit again. It was such a wonderful description... pride of a Cossack and heart of a peasant... so poetic. She must have loved him, perhaps in her own way. Perhaps as much as someone who'd been shadowed by death could ever love.

Yves, I think, will make a good husband. He has not been poisoned by the stigma of the curse of noble blood.

He thinks me too young for him, just 21.

21 going on 24, Dear Husband, yet even that I cannot share with you, not even that. A lifetime of lies has begun.

The wedding is next week.

The Grand Duchess' gift to us, a diamond as big as my husband-to-be's thumbnail, as pure as a snowflake and as brilliant as the lies I continue to tell.

Yves promises he will make me a wonderful ring for our wedding and I have no doubt. He is so talented with gold and gems.

A good man.

Tomorrow I go to Gabrielle's for my final dress fitting.

How did I miss all of this? I wondered. How had I not seen this entry the last time? Did I flick over the page by accident? Or did fate play a part in my life again, ensuring I read this when I was ready?

For a moment I thought about it, all of it, then something struck me.

The Grand Duchess' gift to us, a diamond as big as my husband-to-be's thumbnail, as pure as a snowflake and as brilliant as the lies I continue to tell.

Gran read the entire journal, over several days and said nothing; could it be lost, or worse?! Could it have been given to Mother?

Gran was sitting quietly reading the paper as I burst in, page open.

"Gran!" I shouted.

Startled, she looked up and stood up all in one action, the paper floating to the floor. "Good grief, Marica, what is it?"

"This."

"What?"

"This entry in the diary, about Gran-Gran's wedding dress and ring and ggYves?"

"Yes?"

She seemed not to have any idea of what I was getting at.

"What happened to the dress and the ring?" I demanded.

"Ah!" she said, "I was wondering why you hadn't asked me about that."

I shook my head as I grasped for words.

"I don't know how, but I missed it."

Gran was about to open her mouth but I beat her to it. "Please tell me Mother didn't sell them, please!"

Gran motioned for me to sit down as she took the journal from me. "Well, the dress, after your Gran-Gran decided to move to Australia, Madame Chanel asked if she could have it, for her display, her business was just beginning..."

"No, sorry? What. No, someone called Gabrielle made the dress."

Gran smiled. "Yes, Dear, Gabrielle, Gabrielle Chanel was Coco Chanel's real name. And, as your Gran-Gran knew her before she took on the persona of Coco, she remained Gabrielle to her."

I thought this through, but something still didn't add up. Gran-Gran forgot her friends, refused to see them. Why would she give her wedding dress back? "Didn't you say Gran-Gran thought everyone was against her and refused to see her friends?"

"Yes, but after she and ggYves arranged passage, she felt settled enough to try and make amends to some of her once good friends. For Madame Chanel, it was the wedding dress."

I thought for a moment. "And the ring?"

"Oh yes, the ring."

By this stage I was standing at the edge of Gran's room watching her retrieve her jewellery box, full of wonderful treasures and magnificent jewels. I watched her do something with the side of the box and then heard a 'click' which opened a small secret panel hidden in the design of the wooden box with its parquetry, the herringbone design of numerous shades of wood. I'd never seen this little magical hidden compartment.

"When your ggYves was given the stone for this ring, he didn't know the woman passing it to his future wife was not his future wife's godmother, but her grandmother." she said.

Gran turned. "Or perhaps he did? After reading the journals and thinking on the conversations I had with my mother, I now wonder if ggYves knew all along he was married to a Russian princess."

She smiled. "Maybe that's what true love is, even when you know your love is lying to you, you choose to believe the lie because that is what they want, and you'll do anything to make the other person happy."

She sighed. "Including live a lie."

Even in the half-light of the bedside lamp, I could see its brilliance and its massive size. Almost too big to be real, more like a cheap cubic zirconia replica, but it was real. Gran walked up to me and handed me the ring, almost one hundred years old, designed by ggYves, it's stone, God knows where it came from originally.

"Now it's yours."

I stood, thumb holding the gold band, its crown, this stunning, magnificent, extraordinary stone cradled by six golden claws. It was beautiful, but that wasn't what made it valuable. It was like Dida's banjo or Pop Colin's paintings or Nana's wedding dress. What made it valuable was where it came from, and who made it into a ring, and who wore it and who hid it, protected it, for a lifetime. It was a link to my great-great-great-grandmother and down four generations to me.

"Look inside."

I moved closer to the light to read the inscription. It was in French. *The only thing more beautiful than this ring is you.*

I heard Gran saying something about the diamond being in the family for hundreds of years, but I wasn't listening, not really. All I could think of was its beauty, like the eyes Mother, Gran and Gran-Gran shared. Its secrets, its battles to get here, in this lovely suburban home in Melbourne, Australia. The world seemed huge and small at the same time.

I remember hugging Gran but I cannot recall if the hug came with any words. All I remember was going into my room, sitting on my bed and trying it on.

She had thinner fingers than me, my Gran-Gran. I was barely able to get it on my ring finger. It didn't matter, I'd never wear it, or perhaps I would. I wasn't sure if I should wear it. Was I at that point in my life at last where I had earned the right? For now, I was just glad I had it.

This ring bound all of us. Together and separately, we'd each played our part in getting to this point in time, and this ring followed the generations, waiting to be freed again, like the garden.

"Ilija would love to know the story of this ring," I caught myself mumbling.

That night I went to sleep with images of ggYves, with his 'baron's moustache and Cossack pride and peasant's heart,' returning the stone to Gran-Gran, set in rose-gold, cradled by little delicate claws, no embellishments, no fussy swirls of twisted metal, just a simple gold band and a perfect diamond. It was the last puzzle, perhaps the last secret Gran was forced to keep.

CHAPTER 32

Calling London

"Marica!" Gran was yelling for me to come inside. Damn! The garden looked so lovely right now. Why couldn't I just sit out here and enjoy its tranquillity?

The ring-neck doves were back, cooing in the apple tree, heads bobbing with each coo-coo. And among the twisted shoots of the wisteria, a blue wren, in his best florescent-blue Summer plumes, performing a flurry of excited manoeuvres for his lady-friends. I was blissfully lost in their happiness.

"Marica! Dear, are you out there?" She'd found me, though I must admit since trimming the life out of the roses they hadn't quite recovered enough to hide me in the rotunda.

"Yes!" I shouted back, frightening the wrens and silencing the doves. "What is it?"

"Look," she half barked at me as she shuffled as fast as her legs would take her. For a moment I panicked it was a letter from Ilija.

"Dear, take a look at this," she huffed as she slumped next to me, envelope in one hand and a selection of photos in the other.

I reached out for the photos as I said, "What's this?" But the answer was self-evident: these were photos of an apartment, in Paris.

I sat with eyes glued to the first photo, my legs cemented to the ground, and butt to the seat. What was she up to?

"And the letter," she said. "It's from Maurice. The last time we spoke he told me of a place; oh I don't understand how to use your Interweb thingy so he sent me these for you. Take a look, Dear, two bedrooms and, well I don't know Paris but Maurice say's it's a good area, but then you'll know, so?"

"Are you saying *we* should?"

"Go live in Paris and do some research? Yes, that's exactly what I'm suggesting. And Maurice has found us this lovely two-bedroom apartment not far from your Gran-Gran's old apartment block, which if we combine my pension and your income from Nana's house and if we also add in the rental of this house, then we'll have more than enough to live and to discover a new family secret, if you're willing?"

I was still catching up on the 'we' part.

"Here, read the letter. He said something about using your Interweb goggles to see more pictures?"

I chuckled. "Do you mean Google?"

Gran huffed. Then she scanned over the letter finding the word GOOGLE.

"I thought it was a mistake, English not being his first language."

Gran wore an expression of frustration and confusion.

"It's Google, Gran."

"What in God's name is a *google*?" She looked at the letter again before saying, "It's not even a real word!"

Ignoring the last comment, I quickly read Maurice's letter.

"Sorry? Did you say rent out this house?" I questioned. "Who to?"

"We can work that out, always people in need of lovely homes, and we could include a permanent gardener to ensure all the gardens are looked after."

Pausing to quickly look out over the flourishing garden, she added, "You've done such a lovely job, Dida would be proud."

Her smile of approval warmed me.

"And with a gardener popping in every other week, we could also make sure the place is looked after."

Gran had given this quite some thought and evidently had a co-conspirator. I quickly read Maurice's letter once more. It was in French, and I had to familiarize myself with his handwriting. By the time I was shuffling through the photos, I knew Gran was already set on the idea.

"Are you sure you are up to this, Gran?"

"Marica, let's not pretend. Yes, I am getting somewhat mature, but I missed out on so much with you and you also missed too many family moments."

3pm Melbourne, which made it the early hours of the morning in Brittany.

"I'm just a bit overwhelmed."

"Of course," she replied. "Why not call Maurice this evening, have a chat, you know, about the apartment and everything?"

After dinner, I called Maurice and was pleased to learn just how willing he was to help.

By the end of October, Gran had arranged for our belongings to go into storage, and we found a lovely family to rent Gran's house. And although my tenants in Nana's house were disappointed there'd be no sale, I promised we'd discuss it again at some point in the future, which seemed to lessen their discontent.

Gran's prospective tenants were friends of Tom's, a lovely Italian couple with one child and a mother-in-law to boot, parents working, mother-in-law as an unofficial babysitter and quite the gardening enthusiast. The family intended to use our cute and seriously sweet snug as a nursery and the attic-room as a home office.

Just before we were due to leave, fate sent me the ghost of opportunities missed. Gran got another postcard from Ilija. It seemed he was almost ready to return to Croatia and, in his words, *wanted to stay in touch*, saying his parents offered an open invitation to Gran and *anyone* from the family. Gran couldn't help herself. "What a lovely young man, so few around these days.

"Oh look, he's added his phone number in London and said he'll remain in the UK until the 5th of November. We'll have arrived in Paris by then." Gran smirked as she dropped the postcard on the coffee table beside me.

With little left to take care of, Gran suggested it would be nice to go out to dinner in the city, as a treat. "No point in dirtying too many dishes before we go."

I took her to meet Michel. We enjoyed a lovely hot chocolate and Gran got to do a trial run with her French. Just before we were ready to head off to the Docklands for dinner, Michel joined us for a quick chat. The conversation moved from Paris to Brittany to Lyon, where he was from, and back to Melbourne.

Then he asked, "What happened to your boyfriend, the tall one?"

Gran huffed and I blushed. "Oh, Ilija? Well, he's in London at the moment."

"Oh lovely, London to Paris on the Eurostar!"

Gran chuckled, "I don't think my granddaughter realised how fond she was of him until he was gone."

I shuffled in my seat.

"The Eurostar, you say?" asked Gran. "That's a wonderful idea, isn't it, Marica?"

"You know it travels under the sea?"

"Well, it was built by the French, so I have to think it was done well?"

"And the English," I protested.

"Still, one must own, those English find a way to put their stamp everywhere."

Defeated, I found refuge in the dregs of my hot chocolate.

Michel wished us a safe trip and then, to add salt to the wound, finished off with, "Say hi to him, your Ilija."

The old Wharfs were renamed the Docklands, even before I'd left the first time. I guessed politicians thought it sounded move expensive, or perhaps less like the rat-infested boggy swamp it had previously been. Although I'd been back for almost a year, I really hadn't been to the Docklands. Nothing to draw me, I guess. But, given I was unlikely to return soon, curiosity overcame old impressions. Besides, the review for this place was great!

When we passed Southern Cross Station, I felt I'd somehow *Star-Trek*ed to another dimension. All new buildings had sprung up where once weeds grew.

We parked and, as I stepped out of the car, I took in the city from this entirely new angle. Melbourne had changed so much, yet much of it stayed the same. It was Melbourne, my Melbourne.

Gran and I were seated by a window with a view of the bay and the city skyline. I took it all in and regretted I hadn't explored this new Melbourne sooner. Before I left, the Docklands was little more than cold slabs of concrete and glass, with scaffolding wrapped around unfinished buildings like metal ivy. Those half-completed high-rises promising potential had become a bustling extension of the Central Business District. Almost without exception, the shiny new dwellings had views of the bay. And freshly cut blocks of bluestone-paved walkways in an attempt to suggest age. Yet even with the fakery, it worked.

Dinner consisted of aged Wagyu beef with crispy sweet potato chips for me and Asian-style pork belly with steamed bok-choy for Gran, which surprised me. I'd never have guessed her choice of something so *not* French.

As the excellent wine and a shared chocolate panna cotta with toasted pumpkin seeds arrived, I said to her, "Ilija wants something serious."

"What's wrong with that?"

"Well, what if I have it?"

"Haemophilia?"

I nodded.

"Firstly, the chances you have it, are extremely low. Secondly, this is the 21st not the 19th century, I'm sure there are answers now that never existed before. And lastly, if Ilija was genuinely concerned, he would not have come to see me. Dear, he knows your truth."

"What did you two talk about for almost an hour that day?"

"While you were lurking around the corner?"

I didn't realise she knew I was there. "Yes."

"You."

"What about me?"

"How you're this wonderful combination of stubborn and sweet and if only you'd trust your instincts you might actually start to enjoy your life?"

I grunted.

The waiter took away our plates and we ordered coffees.

"Well, that's not all I'm worried about," I said.

"Then what is it?"

"Our family's track record with love and death."

"What are you talking about, Marica?"

"Look at our record."

"Yes, let's do," she replied. "The two of us can, without much effort, go back four or five generations on either side and among all those marriages only one, your mother's, has been questionable. And even that, I hazard a guess, had it not ended so tragically, would likely have lasted for quite a long while."

As I sipped the coffee, I considered her words. Was she really so blind to the truth?

"Marica, every family has heartache, and every family has trials, and yes, ours has a few more secrets and a few less happy family dinners than most, but, Dear, you must admit, there has been a lot of good also."

On the ride home we didn't talk much, mostly because I realised Gran had a point. But there was something else nagging at me.

When we got inside, Gran suggested a glass of sherry in the conservatory. I wasn't fond of sherry, but I also wasn't ready for bed and our TVs were already in storage.

We sat in silence for a while.

"What's really the issue, Marica, with this young man? Has he tried something or done something to offend you?"

"No!" I exclaimed. "He's been the perfect gentleman." I took a sip.

"Then? Has he been too much of a gentleman?" she asked.

"What?"

"Is it that the two of you have a fondness but perhaps not a passion?"

I played with my sherry glass as I said, "We've already covered that, Gran." I looked up at her as I said, "And talking about my sex life with my grandmother isn't something I'm really keen on doing."

"Oh tisk! Good heavens, Marica, I was born during the Great Depression, lived through the Second World War, buried my father, mother and husband, lived through the wildest of your mother's days and buried her too. I think it fair to assume I know a little of life and love, and passion and sex."

"While all that is true, I'd rather not talk about Ilija in terms of sex with you."

I saw a small frown add to Gran's crinkled forehead. She wanted to ask something but, unusually for Gran, she hesitated.

"What?"

"Is it," she bit her lip. "Is it because of what happened with that awful Steve fellow? When I try to talk to you about it, you refuse, but I just wonder?"

I didn't like to talk about him and tried not to. And I didn't appreciate Gran putting Ilija and Uncle Steve in the same group of sentences. My silence didn't stop her. "It's just that, in all the time you were living in France, I'd read your letters and you'd talk about this friend or that, but it never seemed as though there was anyone special?"

"So, now, with this lovely young man, Ilija, I wonder if, perhaps the memory of that dreadful man has bruised you more than you've ever admitted, even to yourself?"

I wanted to shout at her, *mind your own business* but the price of a family was intrusion. I forced a soft smile before saying, "Uncle Steve wounded me and I guess if I were honest, I am more reserved than I might have been."

I saw Gran's head slump a little. It was regret, I guess, from not being able to protect me.

"Gran, he wounded me, and the scar will never fully heal, but he didn't destroy me. It wasn't fatal. Believe me, I'm OK when it comes to that."

I saw her smile return as those eyes lit up again. "You have no idea how happy I am to hear you say that Marica. It has haunted me ever since it happened. And when you were taken away to France I worried so, thinking who would protect you, who would you run to if, if, if ever you needed a safe place."

"As I said, I'm fine." I patted her hand.

"Well then, it must be something? Is it?"

"What?"

"Are you, gosh, how do you young people put it, a lipstick lesbian?"

I almost choked on my sherry. "Where did you hear that?"

"Oh, I think I read it in a magazine once, did I say it right?"

"What sort of magazine were you reading?"

"Well alright, it wasn't a magazine. There was some program on television, and I noticed a woman, she looked like she might be in her 60s, and I thought they said *'lipstick lesson'* so I started watching."

Gran paused before adding, "The truth is, even once I realised what they were talking about, I couldn't turn it off! It was so interesting! My goodness, what an eye-opener!"

I couldn't help being amused at my octogenarian grandmother talking to me about lesbians. "Do you even know what that means?" I asked.

"Well." Gran's voice had an uneasy shrill, which made her seem cute for the first time ever. "Aren't the lipstick kind the ones that look like, well, you?" She gave me a side glance. before adding, "And the other kind are the ones that wear their hair really short and can pull apart and put back together an engine." Cliché stereotypes aside, which coming from anyone else I would have found unacceptable, my Gran was awesome!

I wasn't going to talk to Gran about my experimental phase, which included a flirtation with a very stylish Hélène. I said her name. I hadn't said her name in years, not even in my head. Hélène was worthy of a name. Unlike too many men, none of whom even warranted a mention. However, the thought of my Gran reading about lesbians was beyond amusing. "No, Gran, I'm not a lesbian."

"Marica?"

"Yes?" I couldn't wait to hear what came out of her mouth next.

"You're not one of those, oh goodness... do you like dark, milk and white chocolate or do you..."

"...I'm not bisexual either, Gran, I like men."

"Well," she said, "That's just fine, just fine indeed, not that, you know, Marica, if you were, you could talk to me, I mean, even if you like milk chocolate. I will always love you."

"Gran!"

"Then, you really are not interested, or have lost interest in Ilija?"

I shrugged.

"So that would be a yes or no?"

"I mean?"

"Ah, so, that's a definite to being interested."

I shrugged again. This dance went on for several minutes until the combination of wine for dinner and sherry allowed me the courage to say it. "What if I'm like Mother?"

Gran looked gob smacked.

"Like you said, we are both stubborn and, aside from the eyes, and, well, the fact I'm a little shorter, we even look alike, and I've always had people take care of things for me, and well she is my mother."

"AND?"

"And I don't want to be as indifferent and removed as she was, but I'll never know until I'm in a relationship and, well, if I am like her, I wouldn't want to find out with such a great person as Ilija. I mean that would just be wrong!"

"Listen to yourself, Marica," Gran demanded. "Just in what you said, that one cluster of words, you have already shown you are nothing like your mother."

Gran's voice softened. "Marica, look at me."

I put the glass down and turned to her.

"Your Gran-Gran and your mother shared more similar traits than she and I did, and yet they were two entirely different people.

"And you and your mother, yes, you have similar personalities, but you have approached life from an entirely different direction and will continue to do so.

"I tried with that daughter of mine, when she was younger but, even with all her gifts and talents, she valued her beauty and vanity over and above all else, over family, over morals, over her husband and daughter. Even her marriage to Maurice, a good man in the end, but really? Who goes after a man at their mother-in-law's funeral? WHO?"

Gran stood up. "Sorry, my darling, I love you, but to put it bluntly, you are finding reasons and excuses not see this young man. If those reasons and excuses come from a place where he doesn't interest you, and perhaps you cannot pinpoint why, fine. But should that not be the case and you are even half interested in him, then frankly, Dear, you are being a coward.

"And, Dear, I, your Dida and your Nana expect more of you."

Damn, she was good, another direct hit.

"Now, you can find excuses not to live or find reasons to take life on, that is your choice. Given what you know of your Gran-Gran and what I dare say we are about to learn of your Dida's life, it seems to me that if these people could embrace life, so can you."

She paused, before adding, "You have been blessed with the blood of heroes and survivors, the least you could do is accept happiness when it's thrust at you."

And with that, Tornado Gran said, "I'm off to bed."

Halfway out the room, she turned. "Oh, and Marica, I've always thought your eyes to be stunning, almond-shaped, green like a Winter valley with flecks of gold. You have beautiful eyes which reflect the beautiful soul behind them."

A smile formed as she said, "You know, Marica, you have the best of all of us. I see within you your Gran-Gran's instinct for survival, your father's and Dida's sense of duty to family, your Nana's warm smile, Pop Colin's talent with a brush, my stubbornness, your mother's ability to draw everyone in. I even see you've inherited something from ggYves. How did she put it? The pride of a Cossack and the heart of a peasant; it's all there in those beautiful green eyes with their gold flecks and cobalt blue rims. Each one of us, reflected back at you every time you look in the mirror. You really are the best of us all."

As she turned, I heard her add, "And unlike your mother, you've kept the best of us all."

"Gran?"

"What is it?"

"Dida Nik, did he know?"

"You mean who your great-grandma really was? Why would you ask that?"

"The song he'd sing to me when I was little, the Mari-ca, Mari-ca, song. I remembered it my first night back when we got home, and I was at the kitchen window. Gran, he'd sing I was his Tsar-ica, why else if he didn't know?"

"You know, I knew nothing of that song, not until your Dida passed and your Nana told me about how he'd sing that to you when your mother would go off on one of her extended breaks with whatever new man she'd snared."

"It seems too much of a coincidence, don't you think? Especially singing about me being a Russian princess, I mean him, an old-guard-Croat-and-all?"

"I was surprised when our Nana told me about it. I honestly can't tell you if he suspected or if he knew, and if so, how he could have known. I suppose it's possible, your Dida had resources and skills that none of us knew of. I guess he could have worked it out himself. Honestly, child, I haven't a clue."

Gran smiled, turned, and headed to bed.

I finished what remained of the sherry before retrieving Gran-Gran's journals and my cigarette stash. I grabbed a thicker jumper, switched the patio lights on and nestled into one of the lounge-chairs to re-read many of the pages while smoking four or five cigarettes. I would have stayed inside but we couldn't leave the house smelling of stale cigarette smoke for the new tenants.

Between swatting mosquitoes and batting away moths, it wasn't exactly a blissful relaxing spot, but it did its magic. There, among the crickets and the sizzle sound of bugs crackling to a singe in the blue-light bug-zapper, the world started to make some sense. Many months ago, when I thought I knew everything, I thought of myself as fraudster, a pretender, but I was wrong. I now knew I'd been a coward, in the truest sense of the word. I'd been afraid of living. I blamed everyone rather than sucking in the oxygen that is life. Admitting this to myself, like someone with an addiction, freed me from the weight of distrust.

It was after midnight before I was tired enough to go to sleep. The next morning, everything was in place. I'd been on a journey, not knowing where it might lead me, not even knowing why it mattered so much, and at the end of it I'd uncovered extraordinary things about my family and about world history, but I'd almost missed the point. All my life I desired stability, somewhere to call home. Looking at everything in the clear light of an unconfused mind, I think I was focusing on the wrong things. After all, whose life is stable?

Gran-Gran. There was so much unstable with almost every aspect of her life I felt had no need to even summarise.

ggYves. Moving from country to country, learning his trade, a marriage which resulted in the death of two children and then moving to Australia. He didn't even know what his letter of offer said. Gran. To carry the burden of fear of discovery of her mother's secret was hardly easy. Add to that her fears about having children.

Pop Colin. Scotland to Australia. Loss of a brother, missing in action. That wasn't ringing true of someone who had the world handed to him on a platter.

Dida. Life was far from stable. Fleeing his home country, working as a Legionnaire and moving again, across the globe.

Nana. A dancer who lived a life of artists and writers and musicians, and then moved to Australia and to an unknown future in a foreign land.

Dad. He was a toddler who came to a land where he started school not knowing the language and then married a woman who was less than ordinary.

And lastly, Ilija. He'd been moved from pillar to post by his own father's work and then thrust into the chaos which apparently was my life.

It came to me. Then. Stability is a state of mind, not the state of one's house. I knew what I needed to do. Just before Gran went to bed for the last time in her home of a lifetime, she threw one more idea at me. "Dear?"

"Hum?"

"I was thinking, while we are in Europe, I would very much like to travel to Russia, and lay a wreath at their graves. Do you think that might be possible?"

"I think I'd like that too."

"I just hope my Russian is good enough, it would be so much better if we knew someone who could read and speak it fluently." Good old Gran, never giving up.

I re-read one part of the journals.

When I began this journey with you I was so young and naïve. I knew nothing of love and hate or even of life and death, yet it seems we both have lingered too long in death. I feel it is time to let life breathe in complete freedom.

It took me two reads to find the courage. To make *that* call.

Deep breath. Deep breath.

I took a third deep breath, looked up as though Gran-Gran would be listening, and with the ring resting on the table beside me, started dialling. With each *blrurp blrurp* I gulped away the instinct to hang up. I formed words in my head and cleared my throat while trying to remember what to say. I listened to more *blrurp blrurps*. Perhaps there was no one home or perhaps this was fate playing its part. Perhaps?

You are no longer a coward, Marica!

Another set of *blrurp blrurps*,

Oh God, what if I was interrupting something, or someone? What if? My stomach butterflies had transformed into buzzards.

Blrurp blrurp I took Gran-Gran's ring and placed it on the middle finger of my right hand.

I remembered the last line of the journal.

I felt it was time to let life breathe in complete freedom.

Blurp blurp. The ring shone and sparkled at me, telling me to keep the faith.

Blurp Blurp I felt the echoes of all the family secrets past. Of fate and God, of the dead and the living, willing me to maintain my resolve.

I started mumbling to myself. "What if he doesn't live alone? What if someone else answers? What if that someone else is a woman?"

Blurp... "Hell-o?"

Connection. *Voice, don't betray me now.* I had so much to tell him but I had no voice.

"Hell-o?'

Silence. *I can't find my voice!*

"Hell-o? Is dat enyvone?" That accent, his accent.

"Hi, stranger," I said, as though no time had passed, and I hadn't acted like an idiot, a child, like a coward.

A gasp, his gasp. *Is that a gasp of relief or shock or, or? Oh God!*

I bit my lip to keep the tremble at bay. "It's me, Marica." I held my breath to see if he'd want to talk to me or hang up.

Silence. Another gulp of courage.

"Marica?" He spoke!

"Yes, it's me. I know I've been—"

"—From Australia? My Marica?"

I spoke at the speed of light, fearing he might still hang-up. "So-it's-

been-a-while-so-how's-London-treating-you-so-what's-the-weather-like?"
The frigging weather? Christ, Marica!

I gulped for air and, without giving Ilija a chance to reply, I asked, "Hey, what do you know about the French Foreign Legion?" That's when his laugh filled my head. Between his bouts of laughter, he managed to ask, "What are you on about?"

"The French Foreign Legion," I said. "I was going through some of Dida Nik's stuff and, I, I guess he was some sort of covert spy, Green Beret or something, so anyway."

I feared if I stopped talking, I'd hang up. "So anyway, Gran and I, we decided to rent out her house here in Melbourne and go off for a visit to Russia, you know to see where they were buried and—"

"—Marica, Christ! Slow down! I haven't heard from you in months and now you're like on speed on something."

I sucked in a deep breath and fidgeted with the ring.

After several seconds, Ilija said, "Now what's this about the French Foreign Legion and your Dida?"

"Well, after Gran and I have gone to Russia we wanted to look into Dida's history and maybe stay in Paris for a bit, and Gran was thinking it'd be great if we knew someone who spoke Russian, so I was wondering?"

The phone, the room, the universe became still until he said, "Marica?"

"Oh God, Ilija, I'm so sorry for being such a bitch! I wasn't trying to be a bitch, I thought I was doing the right thing, but I fucked up royally."

"When are you leaving for Russia?"

"We're going to Paris first, to settle in and then we'll kind of play it by ear."

"And when's that happening?"

"Oh God, um yeah, we're catching the plane tomorrow and we'll be in Par—"

"—Text me once you're in Paris, it's only a Eurostar ride away."

I wanted to yelp. "Oh, OK, I'll buy you a croissant and hot chocolate at this place along the Seine."

"No, babe, I'll buy you one."

"Listen, don't get all Marica-weird on me but I have to go, I've got a tutor gig in the East End, OK?"

Babe, he called me babe.

"Marica, you still there?"

"Oh! Yes, yes, I'm here. Yes, great, you go do your thing in the East End and, and I'll text you."

He laughed loudly. "Marica, everything's fine, just let me know when you get to Paris, but I've really got to go, I was already out the door when the phone rang. Marica, I've missed you."

I sent him a text message with our flight details and finished with "xoxo." It took all of one minute before he replied. *I've missed U2, & FYI, next time I have a shower, I'm tying U 2 the bed...get used 2 it, xoxo*

I put my phone in my handbag, next to my passport, my tickets and the two journals, and looked around the room. My bedroom, from when I was eight, or nine, or fourteen. Same porcelain bear playing the flute Dida Nik bought me, there on the bookshelf. I turned slowly anti-clockwise. The same embroidery cushions on my bed, hand-stitched by Nana, same painting on the wall by Pop Colin. And now, over the bureau, the same stoic smile Gran and Mother shared, reflected in the mirror, the only difference was the eyes, my Dad's eyes.

I knew there was one last thing I needed, and it was in the attic. I almost picked it that first time but chose *Pride & Prejudice* instead. I wanted to re-read *Doctor Zhivago* and there was a hard cover copy in the attic. With Tom's handiwork complete, all the attic books were now stacked along the back shelf. I knew exactly where it was. "The perfect book for plane-travel-reading."

Doctor Zhivago. A direct translation would be Doctor of Life.

www.ingramcontent.com/pod-product-compliance
Lightning Source LLC
Chambersburg PA
CBHW051527260626
47170CB00003B/827